Legacy of Evil

by

Sharon Buchbinder

The Hotel LaBelle Series, Book 2

Legacy of Evil

Cover Art by *Rae Monet, Inc. Design*

The Wild Rose Press, Inc.
PO Box 708
Adams Basin, NY 14410-0708
Visit us at www.thewildrosepress.com

Publishing History
First Fantasy Rose Edition, 2017
Print ISBN 978-1-5092-1722-9
Digital ISBN 978-1-5092-1723-6

The Hotel LaBelle Series, Book 2
Published in the United States of America

Dedications

This book is dedicated with love
to my first reader and husband, Dale.

~*~

To our son, Joshua,
our daughter-in-law, Elyse,
and our grandson, Dexter.
They remind me every day
that family ties bind with love
and priceless memories.

~*~

It is also dedicated
to my tireless and supportive editor,
Amanda Barnett.
She is my book midwife,
helping to bring my book babies into the world.

~*~

And to Sharon Saracino,
my funny and fun critique partner and friend.
She helps me see the humor in all things
in the writing life
and other parts of my sometimes-crazy world.

Author's Note

Anyone who has read my previous novels knows that before I begin to write, I conduct extensive research and steep myself in the materials. This approach enables me to speak through the characters and narrative with rich and correct content. I also rely on subject matter experts and readers from diverse disciplines and cultural backgrounds who provide corrections and feedback to me before I submit a story for consideration for publication. I would be remiss if I did not thank my readers here, starting with my ever patient husband, Dale Buchbinder, who read every single draft of the story.

My deep gratitude goes to the following people for their expertise and feedback: Cheryl Bosse, Toni Chiazza Diblasi, Sherri Denora, Hal Dorin, Karen and Ken Giek, Ernest and Toni Goetling, Nancy Greenwald, Sharon Saracino, Fred and Robin Vandenbroeck, Sonia Vitale-Richardson, Beth White Werrell, and Susan Willis. Big hugs to my brilliant editor and book mid-wife, Amanda Barnett, who assists with the birth of my book babies.

Thanks to the hard work of Frank B. Linderman in the late 1920s, the world has a written history of the Absaalooke, or Crow Nation, a traditionally oral culture. If you have not read his work and are interested in Native American stories, biographies, and autobiographies. I recommend beginning with *Pretty Shield: Medicine Woman of the Crows* and *Plenty-Coups: Chief of the Crows.* Pretty Shield's granddaughter, Alma Hogan Snell, offers us more contemporary perspectives with her books,

Grandmother's Grandchild: My Crow Indian Life and *A Taste of Heritage: Crow Indian Recipes and Herbal Medicines.* A fictionalized account of one of the most interesting Native American Warrior Women, Pine Leaf, can be found in *Woman Chief* by Benjamin Capps.

Undercover agents for all our government agencies are unsung heroes and heroines. The assignments are dangerous, the agents must be consummate performers, and the lifestyle of the world the agents infiltrate can be enticing. If they remain undercover for a long time, some agents have difficulty removing the persona they assume. If you are interested in the ATFE's undercover operations in motorcycle clubs, and the personal odyssey of one agent, I highly recommend *No Angel* by Jay Dobyns.

The Central Intelligence Agency's work with psychic spies, remote viewing, and the infamous MK ULTRA behavioral modification program is well documented. Disbanded for ethical reasons, the full text of the *Project MKULTRA, the CIA's Program on Research in Behavioral Modification 1977 Joint Hearing Before the Select Committee on Intelligence and the Subcommittee on Health and Scientific Research of the Committee on Human Resources* United States Senate, Ninety-Fifth Congress, First Session, August 3, 1977 is available online and as a reprint from the collection of the University of Michigan Library. If you are interested in learning more about this unusual chapter in our intelligence agency's history, I recommend the following: "Paranormal Activity: CIA Dimension" by Jim Popkin, in the November 11, 2015 issue of *Newsweek*; *The Men Who*

Stare at Goats by Jon Ronson (also adapted to film), and *The Search for the Manchurian Candidate: The CIA and Mind Control, The Secret History of the Behavioral Sciences* by John Marks. There are some who believe the CIA's more unusually talented people have moved to the Homeland Security Agency. Who knows? Maybe the Anomaly Defense Division I created in 2015 is alive and well under another name!

I hope you enjoy the story. If you are interested in additional sources I used to research this novel, I would be happy to send you a list. Just email me at:

sharonbellbuchbinder@gmail.com

Happy reading!

Sharon Buchbinder

Prologue

Wild Mustang Ranch, Montana/Wyoming Border

Emma Horserider pressed the gas pedal of her battered pick-up truck like a NASCAR driver in a dead heat with the devil. She hoped no mountain goats decided to go for a walk in the middle of the road winding around the side of the rocky cliff. She didn't have time to stop and wait for the stubborn beasts to decide if they would charge her truck or get out of the way. She was on a mission to protect the horses she loved and help to keep them unfettered by human saddles and reins.

The call from Margie Hunter, the long-time director of the Wild Mustang Ranch, had been frantic, almost incoherent, "Terrible. Slaughtered. Horses panicked. Get here fast!"

A lump rose in her throat, and tears threatened at the recollection of Margie's grief-strangled message. She shook her head.

"None of that nonsense, Horserider. Marines don't cry. *Semper Fi*!" As she shouted out the last words with a defiant whoop, she rounded the last bend in the road. Stunned at seeing the gates closed, she skidded to a halt in front of the white truck with the ranch logo parked dead center in the way. A string bean of a man in a worn Stetson, boots, and shearling vest leaned against the hood of the vehicle, a shotgun cradled in his arms.

"Holy crap." She'd never seen anyone bearing arms out here, much less standing guard. Things must be even worse than she thought. Grateful she'd brought her trusty Mossberg, Emma rolled down her window.

"Thank God you're here, Miss Emma." Ralph, the director's aged right hand man removed his hat and dragged the sleeve of his red plaid shirt across his pleated brow. "This is the worst thing I've ever seen in my life." The creases on his sun-weathered face deepened. "We have no idea how it happened. No one's been up here except the employees." He pointed at the video camera mounted on the gatepost. "Nobody came through this gate last night. *No one.*"

"Let me get in, see what's going on."

Shoulders sagging, he nodded and opened the gate. "Talk to them, Miss Emma," he called as she drove through. "They trust you."

Much as she kept her gift under wraps from the outside world, here in this equine sanctuary, everyone knew of her special bond with the animals. Her ancestor, Beautiful Blackfeather, would have called it horse medicine. Her brother Bert called it telepathy, in keeping with his work as Director of Homeland Security's Anomaly Defense Division. No matter what other people called this ability, Emma had been born with an unbreakable sacred bond with horses, one handed down through generations of the Crow or Absaalooke people. When old age, sickness, or injury carried a mustang away, it was hard on the entire herd. But...

Death by violence?

She shivered. Every member would be

traumatized. She had to get in there and communicate with the alpha mare, her best link to find out what happened and calm them.

The rutted road came to an end, and Emma stopped the truck next to Margie's four-wheel drive. Pulling on a denim jacket and slinging the tactical shotgun scabbard over her shoulder, she glanced inside the SUV for signs of Margie's whereabouts. A backpack and walkie-talkie lay on the seat. She reached in and keyed the radio.

"Margie, you out there? It's Emma."

Static, then muffled noises that sounded like sobbing.

"C'mon back?"

A sorrow clogged voice responded. "Oh, Emma, I'm so glad you're here. I'm over the rise, with him..." Her voice faded.

Emma climbed a boulder strewn hillside and scanned the lush green valley below. A speckled horse lay on its side, and a woman knelt by its head, stroking its muzzle. A geyser of curses in English and Crow erupted from Emma's lips.

Powderkeg. The stallion had battled with every other male in the herd and had passed his distinctive gray spots on a white background to each of his offspring in varying patterns, so they knew exactly which youngsters were his.

Emma took deep gulps of crisp, cold air scented with the hardy prairie grasses and began the hike down the hillside to Margie and the victim. Horses huddled together in clusters away from the stallion's body—like mourners at a funeral—standing a discreet distance from the dearly departed. Mares encircled their foals, nickering, whinnying, and nipping at little ones when they attempted to exit the protective barrier. Halfway to Margie, she locked gazes with the alpha mare, a blue roan named Indigo. The horse cantered over, and Emma threw her arms around Indigo's big neck, locking her fingers in her mane. Foreheads touching, she whispered, "I'm so sorry for your loss."

Indigo shook her head and chuffed.

"What happened?" Emma closed her eyes, and the image of a large silver bird came into her mind. It dove down, buzzed the herd, and flashes of fire shot out. The horses reared up on their legs, wheeled away from the thing and bolted, but the mechanical monster pressed down on them and followed Powderkeg. One shot hit the mustang, then another, then a burst of gunfire slammed into him until the big stallion crumpled to his knees and fell. Full scale panic ensued—and the machine disappeared into the clouds.

Overwhelmed with grief, Emma broke the connection. Unbidden, tears poured down her cheeks onto Indigo's forelocks and muzzle. Just as she began to regain control of herself, something whined in the distance. Indigo's ears flattened, and she jerked out of Emma's hands. The herd, which had just begun to settle down, neighed and shuddered into action. The adults bolted with their youngsters, leaving Margie and Emma exposed and vulnerable.

Emma screamed, "Lie down next to Powderkeg and stay there!"

The unmanned aerial vehicle—a drone—dropped out of the sky. Sun reflected a blinding flash on glass, telling Emma the thing had a camera aimed straight at her—and was coming closer. The outcropping of rock was her best bet for cover. She turned and sprinted across the valley, but tripped and fell head first into a hummock of grass, pumping up her heart rate and kicking her military training into higher gear. As she leaped to her feet, a staccato burst of bullets tore into the grass ahead of her, throwing dirt into Emma's face. The sound of the drone receded, as she raced for the boulders, and seemed to be moving away from her. Then the buzz grew louder. The machine circled back and came right at her like an angry raptor.

"It's my turn, you bastard." Emma drew the pre-loaded Mossberg out of the holder, pumped, aimed, and fired six times at the dancing metal dragonfly. She nicked it—but that only seemed to make it more intent on aiming back at her. She dropped to her knees and covered her head. If only she could get a message to Bert—

A thunder of hooves shook the ground, and a shadow fell over her. She looked up.

"Indigo! No! Save yourself—take care of the herd!"

The big blue mare snorted, shook her head—and screamed.

"No, no, no, no, no!"

The unmanned drone unleashed its load with cold-blooded efficiency.

The mare staggered and sank to her knees. Great brown eyes fixed on the sky, she flashed Emma one last message before dropping to her side.

"Save my foal. Save the herd."

Chapter One

Crow Reservation, Montana

Brandon Winchester, aka Bronco, rapped at the door of the address his boss, Bert Blackfeather, had texted him that morning with instructions to get there pronto. Pushing the big bike as hard as he dared, it had taken him most of the day to get from Colorado to the Crow Reservation in Montana. Once there, he had to navigate his way through the maze of streets, pick-up trucks, SUVs, horseback riders, kids kicking a soccer ball, clusters of adults, and a yappy little dog determined to pursue him for the last mile. Saddle sore, tired, and hungry, he thought about his breakfast back in Denver, and his stomach growled.

Much earlier that day, he'd been sitting in a restaurant, the kind he preferred with three glass sides and the kitchen at his back. On a much needed break between cases, Bronco had been inhaling a mountain of sausages and pancakes dripping with syrup, occasionally slipping a link to his whining friend in his mesh-topped leather backpack. When his phone buzzed and Bert's number popped up, he knew it was urgent. Sticky fingers smearing prints on the screen, he had finally gotten the phone up to his ear.

Bert's voice boomed. "We've got a situation, and you're the closest guy I've got in the region."

"What's the assignment?"

His boss barked, "When you get there you'll find out."

Bert *never* snapped at his agents. Calm and cool under pressure, the big man's voice held a note of panic.

Something was wrong. Dreadfully wrong.

"Hey, man." Bronco waved at the server for the check. "I'm not trying to give you a hard time. Just trying to figure out what you need me to take care of."

"I'm texting you the address. Drop whatever you're doing and get out there. Call me on my secure line when you arrive."

Bronco licked his fingers and sighed. He'd been hoping to break the long dry spell created by his last two assignments. So much for asking that cute little blonde in the next booth who'd been flirting with him for the last thirty minutes if she wanted to go for a ride.

"Okay, boss, I'm on it."

"Good. And by the way, don't take no for an answer."

He stared at the silent phone. *Don't take no for an answer?* What was that supposed to mean? Mounting his bike and kicking it into high gear, he guessed he'd find out soon enough.

Bronco now stood squinting in the late afternoon sun, knocking at a door with no bell, and waiting for a response. Dogs barked and a window curtain twitched. *Good. Someone was home.* He adjusted his pack, leaned his head back, closed his eyes, and said, "Any time now." As the words slid out of his mouth, he heard the unmistakable sound of a shotgun being pumped.

Uh. Oh.

He raised his hands. "Don't shoot. I'm unarmed." Turning slowly to face his fate, his jaw fell open, and his heart rate kicked up a notch from being on the wrong end of a shotgun or from the weapon holder's looks, he wasn't sure. A raven haired Amazon in a tank top, jeans, and metal tipped cowboy boots held the Mossberg 500 in a perfect military stance. Long strands of hair blew across her face in the hot breeze. A large purple bruise bloomed on her left cheek. She squinted her dark brown eyes and gave him a laser-beam once over from his dusty black boots to his sweat soaked do-rag.

"Who are you, and what do you want?"

If he hadn't been so intent on not getting killed, he would have spent more time staring at those full, luscious, kissable lips and thinking about how she would taste. As it was, he guessed he had less than a minute to respond before getting blasted into the next county.

"Bronco Winchester. Bert Blackfeather sent me."

Shaking her head, she lowered her weapon, a grimace pulling those pretty lips downward. "Tell him I said no."

"We have a problem. My boss specifically ordered me *not* to take no for an answer."

She scowled, and he could have sworn sparks flew from her eyes. "Asshat."

"Pardon me?"

She pointed at the door. "Go ahead. It's not locked. I don't need a security system."

Bronco stepped aside. "Ladies first." Just as the woman passed him to enter the house, his backpack shifted and wiggled. *Not a good time.* The weight bounced up and down and paws thumped his back in response.

She stood in the doorway and waved him inside. Three large, mixed-breed dogs greeted them with howls and wagging tails.

He chuckled. "These are your watch dogs?" His laugh caught in his throat when she gestured and the pack stood and began to growl and raise their hackles. "Just kidding. Good doggies."

Another hand signal and the snarling Cujo wannabes sat and wagged their tails. He could have sworn they were smirking at him. "I stand corrected."

"Yes, you do. And yes, you will be." After retrieving the chambered shells, she placed the weapon in a rack at the side of the door. "We're going to call my darling brother and get this little misunderstanding straightened out."

Bronco's tongue untangled, "Your what?"

She snorted, "Let me guess. He didn't tell you I'm his sister."

He shook his head, and the backpack quaked and emitted a low growl.

The dogs took note, three heads swiveling in a choreographed move that would have broken the Internet, had he gotten it on video. The largest dog, a German shepherd mix, stood on his hind legs like a human and stared at the now dancing rucksack.

"Whatever you've got in your pack, you'd better let it out before my dogs knock you down."

"Probably not a great idea." The beast on his back yowled. *Bad timing, my friend.*

Hand on her hip, Amazon woman stared at him and waited in silence.

Bronco sighed. "Okay. Don't say I didn't warn you. You can come out now, Gaucho." He set the pack on a chair and unzipped the mesh top. An enormous harness-wearing spotted cat with long tufts at the tips of his black ears launched himself out of the bag, landed on his shoulder, teetered for a nanosecond, and then wrapped himself around Bronco's neck. The end of a long leash rested in Bronco's hand. Loud purring commenced—and the dogs erupted in howling.

"Well, I'll be damned." His boss' sister turned to the dogs and gave them a hand signal. Slowly, each dog sat, gazes glued on the feline. The woman walked around Bronco. "A bobcat. He's a beauty. Did you get him from the folks out west near Missoula? What's he weigh? Twenty, thirty pounds? Looks kinda small, compared to others I've seen up close. How old is he? How do you keep him locked up in that backpack for that long ride? I don't see any space for a litter pan."

He'd expected her to be alarmed when the big cat leaped out of the bag, literally. She'd shown him, hadn't she? She hadn't blinked an eye or missed a beat.

"He prefers to use a toilet." He chuckled at her look of amazement. "But, there were lots of open spaces between Denver and here. No issues finding relief areas for either of us." He winked. "It's a long story about how Gaucho came into my life."

She began to lift her hand, then stopped. "Okay if I pet him?"

Bronco turned and nuzzled the cat's cheek. "What do you think, Gaucho?"

The cat leaped down to the floor and rubbed against her legs. The dogs circled her, tails wagging so hard they beat against Bronco's legs with the force of a police baton. As he knew the cat would, Gaucho took it all in stride, head butting each dog in turn. Standing on his hind legs, the bobcat raised his front paws to the woman, who immediately picked him up. Giggling with each butt of her head, she rubbed her nose against his fur. At last she lifted her shining face to Bronco.

"Thank you. This guy has made me happy, something I didn't think possible after yesterday's events."

"Feline therapy," he said with a grin. "Cheaper than psychiatrists, safer than medications. I can tell you lots of stories about this guy." Ones he'd love to share with her over drinks and dinner, under way different circumstances. Right now, he was on assignment. And his orders were to call his boss as soon as he got to the address. "I never got your name."

"I didn't give it to you."

Cradling the cat, she extended her hand and he took it, expecting a firm, but feminine grasp. Iron bands wrapped around his larger hand and squeezed. Hard. He tried not to wince without success. Amazon, indeed. He bet she liked to be in charge in bed, too. Heat danced along his skin from head to toes and all points in between, causing his neglected body part to spring to eager attention. Shifting the backpack to a strategic location with his left hand, he worked to turn down his body's thermostat.

No way, no how, was he *ever* going to bed the boss's sister.

****

She hadn't been in the house ten minutes after returning from the mustang sanctuary before the phone began ringing. Her brother had known as he always did

11

when she was in trouble. Just as she'd known when her brother stepped on an IED in Iraq, feeling the shock of the explosion and the pain in her legs. Injured and near death, her brother's pain had traveled along their special connection at the time of the event and let her know he was alive, but weak. Her heart rate in sync with her brother's, she didn't sleep until her pulse went from thin and thready, to strong and steady. Likewise, when Emma was in trouble and attacked by the unmanned drone, Bert told her he felt her fear—and anguish over the loss of the horse that came between her and certain death. Now, instead of letting her work the Indian telegraph to determine who the perpetrator was, big brother had stepped in saying it was terrorism, a matter for Homeland Security.

So he sent this, this—drop dead gorgeous biker in his denim jacket with the sleeves ripped off—commonly referred to as a cut by motorcycle clubs—with his club colors and this loving, spotted beauty of a bobcat. The man's road name should have been *Easy* as in "easy on the eyes." While she reluctantly returned the cat to his owner, and he readjusted him on his shoulders, she gave Bronco another once over. The first time she'd been looking for weapons. This scan was a different kind of threat assessment. She guessed he was about six foot-two inches, and a little over two-hundred pounds. No visible fat. Arms roped with sinewy muscles and decorated with biker tattoos, the man clearly worked out. With long dark hair pulled back into a pony tail under an orange bandana and a scar on his left cheek, he looked like a bad boy you would cross the street to avoid. Except he worked for her brother in the Anomaly Defense Division, which put him in the good guy category. And in the irresistible-to-Emma category. Yup. The next time she saw her brother she was going to kill him.

"I'm here." Bronco—even his name was targeted to hook her—spoke into his cell phone. "Yes, she said no. Standing right here." He handed the mobile over to her. "Sorry, it's sticky. I came here straight from my favorite pancake place in Denver."

"Have you heard of this new thing called soap?" She put it on speaker and kept the phone away from her face. "Yo, bro', what are you doing to me? I can take care of this myself."

"Yes, yes, I know you can. *Semper Fi* and all that," Bert's voice emerged from the speaker. "This isn't just about you, little sister. We have no idea where that drone came from, who made it, or who's controlling it. Just to be sure I wasn't jumping to conclusions, I spoke with the FBI profilers at Quantico. They told me violence against animals is one way a beginning serial killer starts."

Emma's stomach roiled at the thought of animal cruelty, and she shook her head. "Do they have any other incidents like these in their files?"

"No. They've never seen one involving the use of drones. They said psychopaths who become serial killers enjoy the act of killing. This long distance attack using drones is not typical of a serial killer or even a spree killer. They want to be up close and personal, get their hands dirty, and witness the terror and mayhem in person not via a camera. They thought the video surveillance had the hallmarks of an enemy combatant. Since we aren't at war on our soil, we have to operate on the assumption that this could be a domestic or international terrorist."

She white knuckled the phone. "I'm the only good witness you have. The horses can't testify, and Margie took cover when the second attack occurred. I need to be in on this investigation."

"No. Neither you, nor are the local law enforcement officers in charge. No matter how much I trust the LEOs out there, this supersedes their authority—and your meddling, Emma."

"Meddling? Are you kidding me? You better not expect me to sit on the sidelines and make fry bread," she needled. "These are my friends, humans *and* horses."

Her chest tightened at the memory of the horses, too big to be lifted to the pick-up bed without larger equipment, being examined in the pasture. Not surprisingly, the state police vet's autopsy showed the bullets to be the cause of death. *Dr. Obvious, at your service.*

"I know, but if that mare hadn't protected you, we wouldn't be having this conversation."

"I have the shell casings. Can we work with the locals to get those examined? It's no secret. The attacks are all over the local news. My guess is Ralph told a couple hundred of his closest friends when he went to the Hanging Tree to calm down with a few beers."

"He's lucky I don't take him to a real hanging tree and not that drinking hole for broken down cowpokes." Then her brother let out a stream of curses in Crow, most of which involved Ralph, his tongue, and what Bert would do with him if he had the old man's throat in his grip.

Emma glanced at Bronco's profile. A smile played

on his lips as he stroked the bobcat's head. Had the cat given him that long scar on his cheek? He caught her staring and quirked a brow. His sky blue eyes seemed to see into her thoughts—and given the kinds of agents who worked for her brother, that was a distinct possibility. Heat rose in her neck, and she glanced away.

"Bert, just tell me where you want us to go, and what you want us to do."

"You're not *doing* anything," he snapped. "Your job is to tell my agent everything that happened. You are also to take him to Hotel LaBelle and introduce him to Lucius and Tallulah Stewart. Tallulah's pregnancy hormones have her spirit sightings and remote viewings messed up. Now she only sees nurseries and babies."

Last year, hotel inspector and granddaughter of a Choctaw medicine woman, Tallulah Thompson, had been invited to Billings, Montana to assist a hapless proprietor in getting the historic Hotel LaBelle back on her feet. On the first night in the hotel, she had met the original owner, "Love 'Em and Leave 'Em" Lucius Stewart, a man cursed by Beautiful Blackfeather, a powerful Crow medicine woman and Emma and Bert's ancestor. Trapped between the living and the dead, no human had seen Lucius for over a century—until Tallulah and her pug, Franny, appeared. After a series of visions, a visit from Beautiful Blackfeather, and a fire in the historic hotel, Tallulah had been able to use Beautiful's medicine stick to free the dapper innkeeper from his century in limbo.

Her brother continued, "Bronco's a remote viewer."

Emma gave Bronco a hard look and spoke to her

brother. "Is he a mind reader, too?"

Bronco shook his head. "Only with Gaucho." At that the big cat lifted his head and stared at her with glowing golden eyes. "We're a team."

Her brother cleared his throat. "Ahem. If you'll let me finish, I'd appreciate it. Lucius, with his ability to use Beautiful's medicine stick to disappear and reappear, will be an invaluable team member as well."

"Boss, I don't even know where to start, much less how to utilize this guy Lucius and his *stick*? Do you have some other intel you'd like to share with me? Like what exactly you want *me* to do?"

"Emma, would you please tell Bronco what happened?"

Keeping emotions in check, her voice low and even, Emma recapped the drone attack at the Wyoming and Montana border. Gazing at the agent assigned to the case, she noticed his pained response to her recitation when she described how the mare saved her life.

He rubbed the cat's head and looked thoughtful. "Can you tell me what this thing looked like?"

"Smaller than a Predator, bigger than a Raven." At his quizzical look, she motioned to the nearby computer and in a few mouse clicks pulled up an aviation channel focused on every variation of drones from toys to professional ones. "I went through a bunch of online videos. There's a zillion on unmanned aerial vehicles, more commonly called unmanned drones, or just drones. The closest thing I found to what I saw is a cross between a Blackjack and an Eagle, only about twice the size, equipped with a camera and an automatic weapon."

Setting the cat back on the floor, he stared at the screen and clicked on the stills. "So the gun would have been mounted underneath, camera right on top of it. Any ideas on the weapon?"

She smiled and said in a loud voice, "I may have." She pulled a brass casing out of her pocket and dropped it on the computer desk. "The ammo is .308 ballistic, one that has the power to take down a big stallion—and a mare. The weapon has to be ultra light, otherwise, the drone wouldn't be able to move that fast. Which leads me to believe the gun was manufactured with a 3D printer."

"You better have kept some of those casings without your fingerprints," Bert chided.

"Duh. I know not to mess up the evidence. They can even have this one. My fingerprints are in the FBI's military files. They can rule me out, if they want."

Bronco lifted the brass with a pen and examined it more closely. "Winchester. There must be only a hundred thousand sporting goods retailers selling these. Like looking for a needle in a haystack to backtrack who sold these to whom." He let out a low whistle. "Wait a minute. Bert, what are the odds our terrorist stole some time from a satellite to direct this drone?"

"I ran the queries as soon as I got off the phone with Emma. None of our military or commercial satellites have any evidence of unauthorized use."

"So that leaves either a very long range for a remote controller—"

"Or a foreign power has infiltrated the U.S., set up shop in our backyard, and is using their satellites to control the drone. The horses were perfect tests for them. They were in a remote area, with no surveillance on them—and they're icons of the American West. You know how much these jerks love symbolism. That's why they went after the Twin Towers, the Pentagon, and the White House on 9-11."

The color drained out of Bronco's sunburned face. "Shit."

A moment of silence filled the room. Even the dogs and Gaucho were quiet.

Bert's voice boomed, "Which is why, my gifted and talented agent, you need a team."

"And that team is going to include me, bro', or I'm going to make your life a living hell."

"And what makes you think you haven't done that already?" Bert yelled. "Fine. You're on the team—as a *consultant.* And if you get hurt, I'm pulling you off and having my friend the Yellowstone County Sheriff lock you up until this case is cleared. You got it?"

"Got it. We'll keep you informed. Talk to you later." She pressed the end button and returned the phone to Bronco, pointing with her chin. "Bathroom is to the right, kitchen sink is over there. Did you know cell phones are dirtier than toilets? You are welcome to use hand sanitizer or the window cleaner under the sink on this Petri dish."

Gaucho still mounted on his shoulders, Bronco followed her directions and emerged shortly after holding up the phone. "All better. Thanks. Gaucho appreciated the rest room. Much better than the highway ones—or the desert."

Pulling her olive drab jacket on she guffawed. "Come on. Did the cat *really* use the toilet?"

"Of course he did. He even left the seat down."

"A gentleman. Next you'll tell me he's a scholar,"

Emma smirked. "Time to get out to Hotel LaBelle, before it gets too late. It's an hour ride."

"Can we take your truck? I've been on the bike for almost ten hours—"

"And you've got monkey butt?" She chortled as his face turned bright red, maybe matching that cute little bottom of his which must be horribly chafed right now. Oh, he was going to be so much fun to tease.

"I was going to say I was saddle sore, but since you put it that way, yeah."

"Come on then, bring your cat, and let's go meet the rest of the family."

Chapter Two

Riding through the verdant rolling countryside toward Billings, Bronco eyed his new team member—no, *consultant*—and couldn't help but wonder about a lot of things. Like what she'd done while in the Marines, was she ever deployed to a combat zone, and how she looked when she dressed up for a dinner date. Without even picking his head up from Bronco's lap, Gaucho sent him a sharp mental nudge, as if to say, *"Just ask her."*

He cleared his throat and rubbed Gaucho's white spotted ears. "How long were you in the Marines?"

"Four years. All in San Diego at Camp Pendleton. I trained dogs to find bombs, and I worked in the base animal shelter. Then I came home to run the horse ranch after my brother—your boss—got his first job with Homeland."

Bronco opened his mouth to follow up with another question, but she stopped him with an upraised waggling index finger.

"*Quid pro quo,* Mr. Winchester. My turn."

Emma favored him with a sideways glance and flashed a sizzling grin so hot, he was pretty sure his bones were melting—while other parts of his body hardened. *Good thing Gaucho's on my lap.*

"Why are you called Bronco?"

Instead of saying, "Let me *show* you why," his

usual response when trying to pick up a woman, he said, "Would you believe me if I said it was my given name?"

"Given by whom? You or your motorcycle club?"

"It's the road name I picked before I began to work undercover for Alcohol, Tobacco, Firearms and Explosives." He shifted in his seat, and the cat grunted. "My real name is Brandon. At first, it was easier for me to remember my road name because it began with the same letters as my real name. Now—" he shrugged—"I barely respond to my real name. I've *become* Bronco. Occupational risk in undercover work. Glad your brother pulled me out of the ATFE. I was pretty close to—" *She doesn't need to know what happened on that last assignment.* He pointed his index finger at her. "Now you have to answer my question."

"No problem. We can play this game all the way to the hotel."

He gently traced the outline of an eagle holding a banner that said *Semper Fidelis* sitting on a globe against the backdrop of an American flag on her upper right arm. The three inch by three inch design must have taken hours of painstaking attention to detail. "Nice ink. The person who did this is an artist."

She glanced down at his index finger, and he pulled his hand away—but not before he noticed the goose bumps that erupted under his scrutiny.

"One of the local guys," she said. "We have a lot of tattoo parlors, but he's the best. If you want your ink touched up, or something new, I'd be happy to recommend you to him. He's pretty picky about who he takes. No teenagers, no drunks, and no assholes."

"I got my first tattoo when I was nineteen and

stinking drunk," he paused. "I may have been an asshole, too, come to think of it."

She laughed. "Have you grown out of that stage, or have you become a *certified* asshole?"

Smiling, Bronco pretended to consider the question. "Hmmm. Some say I have a chronic disease that arises when I become annoyed. I guess you'll have to let me know."

Quirking an eyebrow, she retorted, "That, Mr. Winchester, is a promise."

He smiled and glanced at the rearview mirror and swallowed hard. A stupidly quick, underdressed, imminently dead motorcycle rider, or SQUID, was rapidly gaining on them in the breakdown lane. Straight black hair trailed out from under his red do-rag. The shirtless, helmetless teen-ager looked barely old enough to have a license to drive, much less be a hooligan driving at high speed. Hanging on high handlebars—an ape-hanger in biker parlance—the kid drew alongside the rusty old truck and glared at Bronco.

Keeping his voice even Bronco asked, "Should we be concerned about this dude?"

She glanced at his window and did a double take. "Oh for the love of—roll your window down," she ordered.

Bronco complied and leaned back, right hand resting on the cat's spine, the other behind his back, ready to yank out his Glock.

"Jimmy Two Toes, you're gonna have no toes and no head if you keep riding like that," she yelled.

The kid grinned, revved his engine, popped a wheelie and cut in front of them, forcing her to hit the brakes. Bronco clutched Gaucho. Fortunately, no one was behind them or they would have been rear-ended.

"Good thing I had my seatbelt on." Bronco rolled up the window. "I take it you know him?"

Pressing on the gas, Emma nodded. "Idiot. Thinks he's riding in the Indian relay races. Unless his grandmother takes that thing away from him, he's gonna kill himself one of these days."

"He keeps driving around without a helmet, he's gonna be an organ donor. How do you know him?"

"He's a teasing cousin—one of my father's clan members in the same generation as me. His mother had him very late in life, and he's an only child, so he's spoiled rotten by his grandmother."

Looking sideways at her, he asked, "Would it be rude of me to ask how he got that name?"

"If you saw his bare feet, you'd know." She chuckled.

He raised a questioning eyebrow.

"He has an extra pinky toe on both feet, hence two toes."

"Guess I should have figured that out."

"Not necessarily." She shrugged. "Things and people aren't always what they seem, are they? Like you, for instance. Who would ever guess that you have a special talent, one that makes you good enough to be a Special Agent with Homeland?"

Gaucho stood, stretched, turned around, and put his paws on the dashboard. The weight of the cat on his groin made him wince. The twenty-pound beast tossed a look over his shoulder, as if to say, "Serves you right. You had me *neutered*, remember?"

She tilted her head in the cat's direction. "Not to mention having a four-legged partner."

"Okay, next question. Aside from being a very ballsy lady, going after attack drones armed only with a shotgun, what's your 'special' talent?" He put air quotes around the word special.

She smirked and waved her hand as if brushing away a fly. "Nothing to see here, Mr. Bronco, just move along."

"I find that hard to believe. That mare—what was her name? Indigo? She didn't throw herself in front of you out of love for humans. If I were a betting man, I'd say you were a telepath. With horses. A horse whisperer times a thousand. And dogs, too, if I'm not mistaken."

She gripped the steering wheel so hard, her knuckles turned white. "Sure you're not a mind reader?"

"I'm a people reader. So is Gaucho. He's already extremely comfortable with you." The bobcat's instant approval of Emma was more than a little unusual. In fact, it had never happened in the five years since he'd rescued him. While the majority of pet bobcats loved dogs, domestic cats, and people, Gaucho's history had instilled caution when it came to humans.

"I have to confess, I'm not much of a cat person. Horses and dogs are more my thing."

Bronco nodded. "He trusts you, which tells me I can trust you, too."

"What does he do if he doesn't trust someone?"

"He stays in his safe space, my backpack—unless they're dangerous," he paused. "He was a kitten when I rescued him. I was hanging around a dive and one of the miscreants brought in this tiny kitten, saying he'd shot the mother in the parking lot—just for fun. Then he spotted the baby she'd been carrying in her mouth and picked him up. His drinking buddy thought it would be entertaining to see how long it would take for the kitten to drown."

A little gasp escaped Emma's lips. "That's horrible."

He nodded. "Fortunately, the thug was stinking drunk and had trouble finding just the right bucket for this live show he wanted to put on. I told him I'd hold the kitten for him so he could look in the back room. I slipped the little guy into my pack and took off like a bat out of hell."

Gaucho growled. "I know, buddy, it was a terrible night." He stroked his head. "He has returned the favor many times over and saved my sorry butt."

Bronco relayed how the vet he'd taken the cat to in Nevada shortly after he rescued him from the bar told him the little guy was probably around four weeks old, not weaned, and in need of constant care. Bottle feeding the kitten at the start, Bronco had transitioned to canned cat food mixed with lactose treated milk. At first the kitten had only eaten, slept, and eliminated. Over time, he began to explore the world outside Bronco's backpack—and to grow by leaps and bounds.

A year later, he knew the cat was unusual—but had no idea how special he was until a burglar broke into his undercover apartment in a crappy part of town. Sleeping on Bronco's chest, the cat heard the burglar enter the bedroom before he did. An ear-splitting series of screams woke him from a deep sleep just in time to see the crook turn tail and try to run. Bounding into the air, Gaucho had scaled the shrieking man's back like a tree, bit his scalp, and clutched at his face with his needle sharp claws. By the time Bronco put the lights on, the man was on his knees sobbing and begging for help. When he peeled the cat off, he realized it was the man who had brought the kitten into the dive that night after bragging about shooting a large female bobcat.

"I told him," Bronco finished, "for some karma is a bitch, but for you, karma is an angry bobcat on four legs."

The raven-haired beauty thumped her chest with her fist and pointed at the bobcat. "Respect, man."

Gaucho tipped his head and chirped.

Chirping? So soon? Bronco shot his sidekick a mental jab. *Oh man, you are a goner.*

Emma put her turn signal on to go left under a sign that said Yellowstone River. "You want to hear one of my worst stories?"

"Only if you lived to tell the tale."

She burst out laughing. "Yes, of course I lived."

"Something worse than the one you told me earlier today?" Awe for this woman grew—no, professional respect, that was it. *Nothing more.* "I wasn't sure that was possible."

"Well, you can be the judge of that. So, here I am back in Montana, after four years of going nowhere and fighting nobody in the Marines. Which is a bit annoying, given that I'm a descendant of a powerful Medicine Woman *and* a Woman Warrior, and I wanted to kick some ass. Doesn't happen while I'm in the good old U.S.M.C. Nope, one unremarkable, completely boring day four years ago, I pull into a little gas and go convenience store, out near the rez. It's closed now. Anyhow. I'm gassing up the truck, this same lovely beater you are riding in, pulling a horse trailer, on my way to pick up a mare an owner asked me to break in."

"So you not only train them, but also pick up and deliver horses? Like take out?" Gaucho lifted his head and glared at Bronco, as if to say, *that* was a terrible joke.

"Right. So, while I'm in the rest room, a meth addict walks in with a pistol and points it at the old woman behind the counter, demanding cash. When she doesn't move fast enough, he hits her with the butt of the gun and knocks her out. I come out of the bathroom, see the bloodied elder and the scumbag tweaker reaching over the counter to grab the cash."

"Holy crap. What happened?"

She shrugged. "I go a little crazy. I jumped on his back, put my hunting knife at his throat—yes, it's always on me—and this cranked up creep throws me off. He turns his gun on me and shoots just as I'm throwing my knife at his chest. I take a bullet in my upper chest, missing my vital organs. He takes a blade in his heart."

"My god, woman." Bronco released a long breath he didn't realize he'd been holding. "A *little* crazy? When I met you, I thought you were an Amazon. I was wrong. You are a bad ass Amazon. A Super. Bad. Ass. Amazon."

A carved wooden sign accented with blue and white denoted the entrance to Hotel LaBelle, and Emma turned the truck onto a long, blacktopped driveway. "So, can you top that?"

The phrase took him off guard, hurtling him back to dark times, his childhood. His father, a loser with a capital L, would end all his verbally and physically abusive tantrums with, "So you little shit. Can you top that?" No one could ever top *that*. Not his mother, nor his brother, or any of the dogs that ran away as soon as they could get loose. When there was no reply, the SOB would take a swig of beer, wipe his mouth with the back of his hand, and say, "I didn't think so."

Gaucho jerked his head up and moaned, his golden eyes fixed on Bronco's face. Looking down, he scratched behind the big cat's ear, cleared his throat, and said with a forced guffaw, "Well, if I told you, I'd have to kill you."

Chapter Three

Emma didn't need to be a telepath to recognize the false laughter and the wild cat's throaty worry. What had she said to change Bronco's mood? She turned to search his expression for some clue, but his formerly easy-to-read face had undergone a transformation. Flat and cold, his eyes belonged to a killer, not to the gentle man she'd bantered with for the last hour. A chill slithered down her spine. When he appeared at her house, all tattoos and testosterone, she'd taken him for just another arrogant jerk—and she'd had her fill of them in the service.

When the bobcat jumped out of his backpack and wrapped himself around his neck like a domestic feline, she'd been forced to adjust her opinion. Against her better judgment, she'd been warming up to this ink-illustrated man, enjoying the banter—not to mention the primal pleasure of his male presence triggering the alarm on her biological clock. *Oh, my aching ovaries.* This man was a pheromone weapon of mass distraction, a natural hazard to any woman between the age of eighteen and eighty-five.

Over the course of the ride to the hotel, she had begun to know a gentle, kind man capable of risking his life to protect a helpless, vulnerable creature—or so she thought. This shift into a dead-eyed robot disoriented her and made her touch her hunting knife to reassure her it was still there—just to be safe. *Is this how he looks when he's undercover?* He was good, *scary* good at wearing the mask of evil. She wondered if the strain of pretending to be one thing, while actually being another had forced him into his new line of work with Homeland. He'd been about to tell her something, then abruptly switched topics.

The clandestine division Bronco worked in was full of odd people with talents and skills that didn't fit neatly into any other agency's boxes. Was this an evil twin of the man Emma thought she was getting to know or was it the *real* Bronco?

Purring loudly, Gaucho stood, put his front paws around Bronco's neck and head-butted him until the man laughed. "Okay, okay, big fella." As if waking from a trance, the Bronco she had begun to know and like returned from wherever he'd gone.

"How close are we? This guy needs a relief area and some food."

"Right around the next bend," Emma said blowing out a long breath she hadn't realized she'd been holding. He—the good-natured hunk with the mischievous smile—was back, and she hoped that other guy, the creepy one, never returned.

As she spoke, the Victorian mansion came into view at the end of the long driveway, and the modern world fell away. She could picture fine carriages at the entryway and horses tied to the railing, cowboys and gentlewomen flirting in the afternoon sun. Even today, the green rolling plains provided a jewel-box setting for the spectacular two-story manor. Light reflected off the Yellowstone River in the distance, inviting fly fishermen to cast their lines and try their luck catching trout. As they nosed the truck up to the grassy verge of the partially filled parking area and parked, several mule deer lifted their heads away from the grasses, twitched their ears, and then went back to grazing.

At the sight of the small herd, Gaucho's eyes widened, and a low growl rumbled in his throat. Holding the lead to the cat's harness, Bronco opened the door and allowed his four-legged partner to hop down and search for the right spot. The bobcat ducked behind a bush, and Bronco whistled a song about sitting on some dock on a bay while he waited for the cat to finish.

The damn man could even carry a tune—what *couldn't* he do?

Emma called, "If he's so smart, why isn't he using the toilet?"

Dirt flew into the air from behind the shrub, and Gaucho reappeared, trotting ahead of his owner's long fluid steps. "He can. Just likes to mark his territory, let other predators know there's a new boss in town."

"Who needs a watchdog when you can have a watch cat?" Or a watch man. *Oh, stop, you are not going there, Emma.* The guy was here on an assignment, not a booty call. "So he keeps everyone in line, is that what you're saying?"

"Exactly." Bronco grabbed his backpack out of the truck, slung it over his shoulder, and closed the door. "This place is beautiful. What can you tell me about it?"

Heading up the path, Emma began to provide a brief history of the majestic hotel. "This place has always been in my family. It was built in the early 1900s by Lucius Stewart, the man my brother said would be an asset to your team. He's my great-great-great—well too many greats to count—grandfather."

Sputtering in protest, Bronco reminded her of a cartoon character she'd enjoyed as a child. She chuckled and held her hand up. "Hold on there, Rooster McFusspot."

Mouth agape, he stared at her with an expression of disbelief. "Rooster McFusspot?"

"Yeah, I'm looking at you, mister. When I told you I was descended from a great Medicine Woman, I wasn't kidding." She pointed at the mustachioed man standing on the verandah. "That's Lucius Stewart. My ancestor, Beautiful Blackfeather, cursed him to limbo when her daughter—his wife—died in childbirth. Trapped in the LaBelle for over a century, he wandered the halls and watched his beloved hotel disintegrate around him, unable to do a damn thing about it."

Lucius waved at her and grinned. She waved back and called, "Be with you in a minute." She turned back to Bronco, continuing her story.

"That is, until Tallulah showed up. His wife, who must be inside, is Tallulah Thompson. Also a descendant of a powerful Medicine Woman, only Choctaw, not Crow. She was called in by the current owner to inspect the hotel and help him reboot his renovations efforts. She saw and heard Lucius after no one had seen him or heard him speak in over a hundred years. With help from our Crow ancestors and her visions of Beings without Bodies that we couldn't see, Tallulah was able to lift the curse and bring him out of limbo."

The sputtering sounds of disbelief coming from Bronco stopped, and he pursed his lips, almost as if he was puckering up for a kiss. She stepped closer and poked him on his extremely hard, exceptionally muscular chest, just above a patch on his denim cut that read, "*It Is What It Is.*"

"If you believe what this flash says, then hold your judgment in check. Just as few would ever believe in your ability as a remote viewer, the same is true for what I just told you. To the rest of the world, Lucius is a distant cousin come home from long travels. But to our family, and now to you, because you need to understand his gifts to do your job, he is truly a man from another time."

"If you weren't Bert's sister and if I didn't work for the Anomaly Defense Division, I wouldn't believe a word you said." He shook his head. "Wow. Just wow. You're right. Things and people aren't always what they seem."

"One more thing—" For an instant, the present, here and now disappeared and an image flashed into her mind of the two of them in a darkened barn, her back against a wall, her legs wrapped around his waist. She blinked, stumbled backward, and took a deep shuddering breath. Nipples hard as erasers, her nether regions in a tizzy, she stared at the man in front of her in the here and now. Had he sent her that vision? Discerning not even a hint of a smirk, she gulped and continued in a raspy breath, "—they have a dog. I hope Gaucho and she get along."

He grinned and waggled his eyebrows. "Let's go find out."

She grabbed his arm. "If that cat hurts Franny, you are going to be in a world of pain."

As the words left her mouth a shrieking beige and

black sphere streaked toward them.

Bronco burst out laughing, gasping, "What. The. Hell?"

"*That's* Franny. You didn't know pugs could sound like banshees?"

She glanced at the wide-eyed Gaucho who, for his part, appeared to be equally astonished at the noises coming out of the meteoric approach of the fur bowling ball. The cat stood its ground, not backing down, but not going after the dog, either. Franny skidded to a halt, stood on her hind legs and danced in front of the cat, her shrieks subsiding to yips. Gaucho plopped down at Bronco's feet, occasionally glancing up at his partner, as if to say, "What is this thing?"

"It's a dog, Gaucho," Bronco explained. "She's just—different."

The pug dropped to her feet, rolled on her back, and offered her belly. With her ears flopped back on the ground, the dog resembled an overweight, grinning bat. To Emma's astonishment, the bobcat flopped over onto his back next to Franny on the brick walkway at the foot of the steps and rubbed his angular head against the dog's flat nosed one.

Lucius's voice boomed from the porch. "Well, I'll be doggoned."

"Looks like Franny has a new friend."

"I see you do, too," Lucius said and winked. "Bout time you got yourself a beau."

"Lucius!" Heat flooded her face and filled her chest where her heart jack hammered on her ribs. "He's *not* my boyfriend. He's here on business."

"I bet he is." Lucius rolled his eyes. "Monkey business."

Frowning and shaking her head, she tried to lower her heart rate, which was racing in annoyance at her persistent relative, not in response to the hot wild man on a bike. She lowered her voice, "*Government* business."

"Oh. In that case, let's talk inside." He waved them up the stairs, toward the door. "The guests are out fishing."

Emma held the door for the pug. Once in the foyer, Lucius embraced her in a bear hug, lifting her off the ground, her words of introduction muffled in his chest. "Lucius this is Bronco, Bronco this is Lucius."

Lucius extended his hand to Bronco. "Nice to meet you and your cat. What's his name?"

"Most times—" he grinned and shook hands—"he answers to Gaucho." Rubbing her enormous belly, a smiling Tallulah made her way into the foyer. "He kicked me—*again.* I think we have a soccer player in the making."

Panting, the pug sat in front of Gaucho and tilted her head back and forth.

Tallulah stared at the cat and extended her hand slowly. "Is he—"

"This is Gaucho," Bronco said. "He's my partner and won't hurt anyone—unless they're coming after me."

"Duly noted." Tallulah gasped, snatched up her husband's hand and placed his palm on her abdomen. "Did you feel that?"

"You mean the attempted jail break?" He grinned. "I sure did. He wants out."

"Only a few more weeks, or so the doctor says." She shook her head. "I don't know how much longer I can take the kicking, punching, and dancing baby visions. He'd better not try to overstay his check out time."

Emma's stomach growled, and they all turned toward her, including the animals.

Shrugging, she jerked her thumb at Bronco. "Had to calm down a dozen neighbors who saw him ride onto the rez."

Bronco frowned. "Neighborhood watch?"

"Something *much* more powerful: Indian telegraph." At the puzzled expression on his face, she said, "The kids playing ball in the street you passed? They told the adults talking on the sidewalk you looked like a bad man. The adults watched you pull onto my street and the grandmothers saw you, too. See something, say something, is a way of life with my people. We watch out for each other. All eyes were on you, my scary looking friend."

"Welcome to our world, Bronco." Tallulah smiled. "Bison burgers okay?"

As they headed to the kitchen, Emma pointed out the long, smooth registration desk made of highly polished mahogany, and the intricately carved walls and ceiling of the same wood to Bronco. "Ask Lucius to tell you about the artist he hired to create the carvings of the deer, fish, and waterways—he wanted to be another Frederic Remington. Anyway, the elevator was one of the first in Montana," she said, feeling like a tour guide. She loved the gleaming wooden stairs and the metal lattice work surrounding the wooden box that comprised the elaborate cage elevator. "I personally polished all that blackened brass and made it shine again."

Turning in a slow circle, Bronco let out a long low whistle. "This place is amazing. It's like I stepped back in time."

"It took a lot of elbow grease, hard work, and love to bring the place back to her original glory." Hard to believe only a year had passed since Tallulah and Lucius had become wife and husband. Even harder to believe how their love had transformed the two-story building from a half-assed restoration from the previous profligate owner, Will Wellington. The historic Hotel LaBelle had experienced a complete rebirth to her original glory and grandeur, albeit updated and modernized in tastefully understated ways.

Emma noticed a new display of intricate beadwork, along with the hefty price tags next to them, courtesy of a Crow interior decorator, a laughing cousin named Stephanie. A sign noted the names of the Crow artists who had created them, along with a suggestion to take home a lovely memento of a wonderful vacation in Big Sky Country. Leave it to Steph to come up with a great marketing strategy to benefit the tribe. Emma would have to tease her and ask if they were made in China.

"You haven't even seen my saloon yet," Lucius called over his shoulder. "Now, *that's* a beauty."

Emma snorted at Bronco's slack-jawed expression at the sight of the bar. "You want to move in?'

"Yes! With the player piano in the corner, the brass rail and the animal trophies on the wall, it feels like we're in another century." He pointed at the stuffed jackalope, a mythical creature created topping the taxidermied body of a jackrabbit with antelope antlers. "Even I know that thing isn't real."

Lucius guffawed. "We keep it here for fun,

alongside the deer, bear, and bison."

"Let's eat in the kitchen," Tallulah broke in. "It's easier for me to talk and cook."

"Shouldn't you be letting Lucius wait on you hand and foot?" Emma teased.

"Nah. If I sit too long, the baby gets restless. He dances and uses my belly as a drum." The blonde pointed to a large wooden table in the kitchen. "Emma, could you set the table, please? Lucius, would you get the water?"

"What would you like me to do?" Bronco stood in the doorway glancing around the large sunny space. "Other than read your sticky notes that appear to be on every surface of this beautiful kitchen."

Lucius smothered a laugh and hid his face behind a cabinet door with a yellow sticky note that read "Water glasses."

Tallulah flushed. "I've always had a thing for sticky notes, but with the baby, well, I've been forgetting a lot. Like I open the refrigerator door and wonder what I was getting out. Wait. What was your question?"

"What would you like me to do?" Bronco repeated with a smile.

"Well, for one thing, you can have a seat and for another, you can keep that big cat off the table. Princess Franny would be miffed if a visiting pet was able to get closer to the food than she could."

The pug in question settled the matter by coming to Bronco's feet and dancing on her hind legs. Gaucho touched noses with the bug-eyed creature. Franny's curlicue tail wagged faster, until her whole body shook, and she licked the cat's face.

"Okaaaaay." Tallulah, blue eyes wide, glanced between the animals and Bronco. "We know Emma's a horse and dog whisperer. Are you a cat whisperer?"

Bronco laughed and rubbed Gaucho's back. "Not all cats. Just this one. He's pretty special."

"I want to see him use the toilet," Emma threw over her shoulder as she filled water glasses. "And flush it."

"Please," Bronco said covering the cat's tufted ears. "You're embarrassing him. He likes his privacy in the bathroom."

A short time later, over mouthfuls of bison burger dripping with caramelized onions, tomatoes, lettuce, and pickles, Bronco relayed the tale of the biker bar and the orphaned kitten, probably the runt of the litter, because of Gaucho's relatively small size for a male at twenty pounds. The cat and he had bonded, and over time, he realized he could send images to the cat and Gaucho, in return could do the same with him.

"He's like a feline remote viewer," Bronco said.

"Good thing the CIA didn't know about animals having that ability." Emma shuddered, thinking about her bond with horses and dogs. "God only knows what kind of experiments they might have cooked up."

In the seventies, the CIA had a program to see if certain paranormal methods would have intelligence applications. One of these activities was remote viewing. Researchers would ask someone to envision a place or object that a sender would be looking at. In other experiments, they would put a photograph into an envelope and ask the person to describe the picture. The program continued for about twenty years. A large evaluation study of the program found the results were positive. However, while the statistics were good, the intelligence wasn't detailed enough for practical uses in the field. They discontinued the program, but Bert Blackfeather, Director of the Anomaly Defense Division of Homeland Security's Science and Technology Directorate found a way to bring these talented people into his domain to fight terrorism.

Tallulah sighed, "I know. Not much oversight nor interest in animal welfare in those days." She dropped a piece of meat on the floor, and the pug vacuumed it up.

Emma rubbed Franny's head with her free hand. "You ready for a little brother or sister?" Franny chuffed and snorted. "Think of all the dropped food you can get from a baby. You'll be in hog heaven."

"Don't encourage her. She's five pounds overweight now," Tallulah said and sighed again. "Pugs live to eat. What about Gaucho? Will he eat bison?"

Bronco nodded. "He will. But he only eats what I give him—or what he catches outside."

Tallulah slid her plate across the table. "Please. I can't eat large portions anymore."

Lucius patted her belly. "You've got no room, darlin', what with L.J. taking up space."

"L.J.? You have a name?" Emma asked around a mouthful of meat. "So you do know the sex!"

"Ha! Not really." Lucius chuckled. "I need a name to call the little one. Can't just keep sayin' 'the baby this' or 'the baby that.' L.J. is for Lucius Junior." He smirked and rolled his eyes. "After all, we can't call him 'Love 'Em and 'Leave 'Em,' it wouldn't be right."

Tallulah jabbed his arm, and he winced in mock pain.

Pushing his plate aside, Bronco wiped his mouth

with a napkin and tapped the table with his index fingertip. "I hate to have to talk business, but the boss sent me here on an assignment. He'll have my hide if we don't get started."

Lucius stretched and said, "We're all ears."

"Emma's on my team as a 'consultant' since she doesn't officially work for Homeland. However, you two"—he pointed at the couple—"work for Bert and have an idea of what to do."

"I'm in the room, sitting right next to you," Emma objected. "I was the one who nearly got killed, so despite my dear brother's discounting me, I'm invested in finding out who did this and why—even more than you are, Mr. Biker Man."

"Point taken." He patted her hand, and she snatched it away.

"How dare you patronize me!" A rush of anger made the scar on her chest throb. What made her think he might be different from the rest of the testosterone drenched jerks she had to deal with all her life? It was the military all over again. Well, she paid her dues, served her hitch, and now she was in charge. She didn't have to take his crap. "I can kick your ass and mop up the floor with you."

Bronco threw his hands up. "Hold on. I wasn't trying to downplay your role. If you'll let me continue—"

"Whoa, Nelly!" Lucius chortled. "What's all the ruckus? Do I need to get you two a pair of boxing gloves so you can duke it out?"

41

Chapter Four

"No!" Bronco and Emma shouted in unison.

Lucius sipped his coffee. "If you're gonna work together, you can't be picking fights like a couple of trigger happy gun slingers."

Emma glared at her relative, and Tallulah poked his arm. "You're not one to give advice."

The kitchen became so quiet, Bronco swore the others could hear his heart thrumming in his chest—in time with Gaucho's paw slapping at his thigh. He took deep cleansing breaths and sent the cat a message. *"I'm okay, buddy, everything's fine."*

Instead of responding with their all clear sign—an image of a curled up and sleeping Gaucho—the cat shot him a smoking hot mental image of Emma and Bronco locked in a passionate embrace. Where the hell did Gaucho get that from? In all the years they'd been partners, the feline had not once intruded into his love life. Why now?

"You're not helping." He shot back his thought at the cat.

The bobcat gave a short snort and a bark. The four-legged pain in the butt was *laughing* at him, as if to say, *What flew up your nose?*

He needed a human partner, not a lover. This was not the time for a romantic entanglement. It was one thing to take a risk with his life, another to take a risk with hers, the boss's sister. Bert would kill him if anything happened to Emma.

"So," he breathed and steepled his fingers to keep them away from Emma's slapping hands. *Lesson learned.* "We have a situation that needs to be addressed ASAP. I'll let Emma tell you about it, then fill in my role."

She gave him a short nod and described the drone attack and horse killings. As she spoke, Tallulah covered her mouth and gave a muffled sob.

"We need to find out who is doing this and why. There's no evidence of external terrorist involvement which really leaves only two choices. A foreign operative embedded in U.S. territory orchestrating the attacks or—"

"Home grown domestic terrorists," Bronco finished. "Hate groups are spiraling out of control, and armed militia claiming sovereign rights have expanded their base over the last five years. A watchdog group estimates there are over eight-hundred active hate groups in the U.S., one of which is right in our back yard, the Neo-Nazi American Schutzstaffel."

"Honey, I can tell you all about those sons of bitches."

A woman stepped into the kitchen, and the room erupted into a chorus of greetings, hugs, and air kisses. Sweeping Emma onto her feet, the six foot tall, dressed-to-the-nines in the middle of the day female, showered her with kisses.

"Bronco," Emma gasped between smooches, "this is one of my cousins, Stephanie."

"You can call me Steph," she said and gave Bronco's hand an iron fisted shake, along with a lingering once over. "Emma, you sure got a cute one."

"He's not my boyfriend," Emma ground out between clenched teeth. "We're working together."

"Mmmm, m-mm, mmm. Sure you are, darlin'." Steph shook her head.

As Steph spoke Bronco realized the tall woman before him was—or had been—a man. Steph's Adam's apple plus the bone crushing grip pretty much sealed it for him. "Do you have a last name, Steph?"

"No, darlin'." She waved a hand in the air. "I'm like a movie star, ya know, one name is more than enough for me."

"So what can you tell us about the American S.S.?"

Steph grimaced, slid into a chair, and waved her hand at Lucius, "Honey, can you get me a double espresso, please?"

To Bronco's surprise, Lucius jumped up and fussed with the gleaming Italian machine parked on the kitchen counter. Knobs turned, water hissed, and the aroma of the freshly ground beans filled the air.

Twirling her long black hair, Steph sighed. "They are the worst. They have a major hate on for LGBT folk and go out of their way to harass us at every turn."

Lucius handed Steph the demitasse cup, and she sipped before breathing out, "Delish."

"What did they do to you?"

"Not to me, specifically, but to our LGBT community. Those Neo-Nazi's hate Two-Spirit people like me *and* the fact that we've been accepted in Crow society for-evah. Did you know that, back in the day, we were very much in demand as wives because we could work as hard as a man and be nurturing. We also served in sacred roles in our society, because we were considered to be prophets. We were consulted before major decisions for the tribe." Steph sipped her espresso and sighed again. "Last year, one of those vile brown shirts lured a friend of mine away from a gay bar, promised her a night of wild sex. Put her in the hospital. She still has to walk with a cane."

Bronco's gut twisted. He recalled all too well the brutal ways of the Neo-Nazis. "Your friend recall seeing any tattoos on the guy—or his associates?"

"Tattoos? The thug who picked her up was clean-shaven, handsome—like you would look, minus the tats. She said he looked like the boy next door, only grown up. Not a tat on him. But his friends? They wore masks on their faces, and their arms were covered in tattoos. All ugly, but mostly of the numbers eighty-eight and eighteen eighty-eight."

Bronco nodded. "Those numbers stand for the position of the letters in the English alphabet. A is the first letter and H is the eighth letter, so eighty-eight means "Heil Hitler", and eighteen eighty-eight means. "Adolf Hitler, Heil Hitler."

Steph shuddered. "Disgusting and frightening."

"You got that right," Bronco agreed. "What else can you tell me about them?"

She waved her hand for a refill, and her bracelets jangled. "Well, they are no fan of our government, I can tell you that. My friend said the whole time they were beating her, they kept calling her a lackey and a tool of liberals, the Elders of Zion, and the international banking cabal. Crazy talk."

The wheels began turning in Bronco's head. Catching his drift, Gaucho growled his disapproval. "Where did they pick her up?"

"The Garret. It's a dance hall, karaoke bar, terribly safe. Which is why it was so shocking. Nothing bad ever happened at the Garret." Steph shook her head. "Until that night."

"Do they have security tapes?"

"Yes, of course," Steph said with a quivering voice. "The Neo-Nazi wore a hoodie, kept his face covered. The creeps dumped my friend in the Saint Vic's parking lot, naked, with a pink triangle tattooed on her chest."

Emma cleared her throat. "Are you okay, Steph?"

"Yes, it's just—so shocking. That's not us. Billings isn't like that. It's the largest city in Montana, and it's always been LGBT friendly. An attack of this nature—well, it's disturbing. It's like having a serial killer next door. It could be our neighbor."

Bronco nodded. "The clean cut, fine upstanding citizen. Evil rarely wears a label that says 'Caution: filled with molten lava of hate'."

"I can't talk about this anymore." Steph slapped the table. "Enough doom and gloom. Do you like the décor? Have you sold any beadwork? When is that baby coming out so I can hold him?"

While Tallulah and Lucius filled Steph in all things LaBelle, Bronco leaned over and whispered to Emma. "Can we call a truce? I need to ask you a few questions—outside."

She stood, stretched, and put her coffee cup and plate in the sink. "Come on, Franny. I bet you could use a walk by the river."

Engrossed in their conversation, the other three merely nodded when Bronco and Emma stepped out the back door with both four-legged critters in tow.

They walked in silence to the river's edge where the sun lapped at the water and trout teased Gaucho and Franny. Off his leash, the cat pounced at fish while the pug ran back and forth along the sand barking and yipping. Emma looked off into the distance, her gaze fixed on the other side of the river.

Bronco put his hands in his pockets and leaned back on his heels. "I'm sorry. I didn't mean to talk down to you. I really need your help."

She gave him the side eye, as if waiting for the other boot to drop.

"This assignment worries me. Bert will hand me my ass if you get hurt. Tallulah is too far along and way too hormonally challenged to be of assistance. I still haven't heard what special ability Lucius has, but with that baby due in less than a month, it doesn't seem fair to drag him into this investigation."

"So what do you suggest?"

"We need to get eyes on this drone and find out where it came from. If we can figure that out, we can jam the radio signals between the person controlling it and the bird. My remote viewing can help us lay eyes on the source, but I'd feel better if we had hard data to back us up. I'm going to call your brother and tell him we need satellite images of the state, with a focus on the area around the Mustang Ranch."

"Okay." She quirked a brow at him. "What's this have to do with me?"

Struggling to come up with the right words, he dragged the toe of his boot in the sand. "We need to find out if the Neo-Nazis are behind this. I want to get into Billings and scope out the gay scene."

Emma began to laugh, and he put his hand up like

a traffic cop. "I was hoping you and Steph would go with me, be my guides. I'd be a new guy in town, looking for a good time. If I can lure one of those cretins, get him to take the bait, we'd have a way in."

"And then what? They beat the shit out of you? Maybe kill you?" Fists on her hips, Emma glared at him. "That's the dumbest thing I've ever heard. Besides, what makes you think you could play a gay guy well enough to pick someone up?"

"Hey, give me some credit," he spat back. "I've got years of undercover work under my belt that I'm damn good at. Not once did the motorcycle clubs I infiltrated even suspect I was an ATFE agent. Besides, your cousin thought I was cute—"

Before he could finish his sentence, her hands were on his shoulders and Emma yanked him in for a kiss. Bronco's brain turned to mush, and all the blood in his body raced to his groin. His hands moved of their own volition, running through her hair, pulling those lush lips into his, his tongue seeking entrance, his hips crushing against hers. She grabbed his butt and pushed his erection against the vee of her crotch, his desire and hardness growing with each thrust of his hips. He moaned, reached for her breast—and she shoved him away.

Like two gunmen in an old Western town, they stood with their hands at their sides, breathing hard and staring each other down. Confused, he looked around wildly to see if someone or something had interrupted her display of passion. "What just happened?"

"A test. There are some things our body *can't* pretend." Hair wild around her flushed face, lips swollen, she rasped, "Do you *really* think you can pass

48

yourself off as gay?"

Stunned, he stared at her, his mind racing, grasping for thoughts, but all he could think of, all he could see was her in his arms, up against a wall with her legs around his waist, their moans of passion filling the darkness. A shout cut through his miasma of pheromones and lust.

"Get in here," Lucius called from the back door. "It's Bert. Says it's urgent."

Whistling for the pug, Emma stomped back to the hotel with Bronco and Gaucho pulling up the rear. Her fine ass addled his mind even as he tried to clear it of the sex-drenched fog.

What the hell was that about? A test? He hadn't planned to do the bump and grind with every guy in the club, just hang out at the bar and get the lay of the land—so to speak. Truthfully, he'd never even considered the possibility that he'd have to *prove* he was gay to play the role. *Dammit. She's right.* Well, that plan was out. He shook his head and stomped up the back steps, angry at himself for being so stupid.

Steph was no longer in the kitchen, nor was Tallulah. Lucius held a cordless phone out to Bronco. "He said to put it on speaker."

"I tried to reach you both for ten minutes," Bert's voice boomed. "I forgot your cell phones aren't worth the plastic they're packed in out there. No cell towers. We need to get both of you satellite phones."

"Speaking of satellites, boss, can you get eyes on the area around the Mustang Ranch, look for off the grid communities? We're looking for a Neo-Nazi installation, the American Schutzstaffel?"

"Ugh. Those scumbags. Yeah, I can do that. But I

have some more bad news for you guys."

The three exchanged glances and Emma chewed her lower lip. "Thirteen bald eagles have been found dead in Northern Montana. All shot with .308s."

"Ohmigod," Emma breathed and turned pale. "That's horrible."

"Yes, it is. It means the terrorists are escalating their attacks against symbols of America. First the Mustangs, now bald eagles, next it's—"

"The buffalo," Lucius exploded. "They'll be coming after them next!"

****

Staggering backward, Emma fell into a kitchen chair, overwhelmed by the enormity of the attacks. The bald eagle was not only the symbol of the United States of America, but also *the* sacred bird to the Crow and many other Native American tribes. The only thing that kept her from bursting into tears was knowing that her brother was safe in Washington, D.C., away from the terrorists who would take down sacred animals—and the shape-shifters among them.

"You can't come out here, bro. You know that, right?"

"I hear you Emma." Bert expelled a long sigh. "I'll be here in D.C., working our military and intelligence grapevines to get whatever information I can."

"If we can get a line on where they are," Bronco added, "we might be able to jam the signals they're using to control the drone."

"I'll get a request into our friends at MILSATCOM."

"Speak in English, bro. I may have been USMC, but don't know your alphabet soup."

Bert sighed. "Short for Military Satellite Systems Communications Directorate. I'll see what they can pull up for us."

"And, boss one more thing. We've sort of got a situation here. Tallulah is more than a little hormonally challenged. And regardless of what talent Lucius has, I don't think it's fair to drag him into this when his wife is about to deliver any moment now."

Lucius gave Bronco a nod and thumbs up.

"I'd like to request we move our consultant into the field."

"Our consultant? You mean my sister?" Bert's voice blasted out of the speaker. "In what capacity? What do you think she can do that you can't do?"

"She's a damn good fighter and soldier, sir, and on top of that she's got a secret weapon." He paused and gave her a significant look.

Emma wondered what was coming out of his mouth next. *Good kisser?* Because he was one damn fine kisser, and she still hadn't recovered from that dizzying, bone melting lip-lock and embrace.

"Well?" Bert yelled. "What is it?"

"She's a woman. And a damn good looking one."

Livid that her female attributes were being discussed with her brother and her ancestor, Emma rose to her feet and launched herself at the phone. Snatching it out of an open-mouthed Lucius's hand, she shouted, "I don't know where this is going, I wasn't in on this, bro."

Bronco yelled, talking over her. "These attacks are too organized, too methodical, and too well-funded to be a lone wolf lunatic. My gut is telling me the Neo-Nazis are behind these killings." Reaching for the phone and grabbing air, Bronco continued. "A single guy is too suspicious. But a couple—that's a perfect cover. I want us to go in undercover as a couple, boss. I want to gut these bastards from inside out."

"Have you lost your mind?" Bert roared. "She's my sister. I won't allow it."

"Bert, you're my brother, and I love you with all my heart, but I'm a big girl. I'm already involved. You can't keep me out. I want in. I've wanted in all along and you've shut me out. Now your guy is telling you the same thing."

The phone went silent for a long time. At last Bert said, "I don't like it."

"I know, boss, but unless you've got that Fury demi-goddess headed here…"

"Not available," Bert responded. "She's on an undercover assignment in the Middle East with her mother. And before you even go there, all our shifters are out. They'd be target practice for these goons."

Exactly why Emma had told her brother to stay in D.C. He'd suffered enough for his country.

In a soft voice, she called his brother by his Crow nick name, *Duuptakoische*, Bald Eagle, and added in English, "Bronco needs me on this case with him."

And God help her, she needed him, too.

Chapter Five

Bronco pulled his sweat-soaked do-rag off his head and ran his fingers through his hair. *God, I need a shower.* After a bit more brow beating, Bert had reluctantly approved adding Emma to the team with the proviso that Lucius be looped in on everything—just in case he was needed in an emergency. After wrangling about how that would work, Bert clarified, "Emma can get a message to me, and I can call Lucius."

Bronco mulled over that little puzzle piece for about a minute, then decided his boss worked in mysterious ways, ones he had yet to discern. Perhaps he and Emma had a similar connection to the one she had with dogs and horses? He shrugged. As long as it worked, who cared?

Lucius came into the kitchen and handed Bronco a room key. "Here you go, pardner. You're gonna need a place to stay and make plans. No way can you stay at Emma's place. The Indian telegraph will have you married by the end of the day, if not sooner."

Emma laughed. "He's right. Our clan has been yapping at me about getting married, settling down and having babies. You can come home with me long enough to grab your bike and leave. Otherwise, the elders will be planning a wedding feast by sundown tomorrow."

"I'm confused," Bronco said scratching his head.

"How are we going to make plans if we're not together?"

"We can't do anything in the absence of good intelligence, which if I understand how remote viewing works, means you do your best work when you're rested and in a quiet space. The LaBelle is much quieter than my neighborhood, trust me. While Bert is working on his end, we can get organized. You can head back here and get cleaned up, while I connect with my ranch hand, Hank, to arrange for him to take care of my horses and my dogs. Plus, I'll be packing a few girl things, since you said that was my secret weapon, and all."

Mouth working like a fish, Bronco's face flushed with embarrassment. "Sorry, I didn't mean to make you feel like a beauty contestant. I just know how those groups think. Women are objects to be used, arm candy, baby makers, sex objects, and tools of hatred. Die hard Neo-Nazis need their counterpart females to breed and create the New American Reich."

She cocked her head and threw a quizzical look at him. "Hey, Lucius, is it just me, or does our friend sound like an encyclopedia of Neo-Nazi harangues? I thought you were an undercover biker, or is this your third alter ego? Who were you before you were with Alcohol Tobacco, Firearms and Explosives?"

Bronco ducked his head to avoid looking Emma in the eye. Why'd she have to be so damn perceptive? Was *she* a mind reader? The best cover stories were constructed from truths—and half-truths. He shrugged. "I had some relatives who fell under the spell of a charismatic White Supremacist cult leader. They tried to recruit me, but I didn't buy their bullshit."

Her face softened. "I'm sorry to hear that. Where are they now?"

"Last known whereabouts was on a survivalist compound in Idaho. If they kept going down that violent path, my guess now is that they're six feet under." He could only hope. The last people he wanted to run into ever again were his abusive father—and his fraternal twin brother, Jack. Even though he'd only been a little kid, he remembered too well his father's descent into madness and hatred. It was imprinted on Bronco's soul.

His parents' marriage had always been tumultuous, but when his father, Terence, aka, Terrible Terry Craig lost his job in a Detroit auto factory, he blamed his boss, the company, and everyone but himself. "The Mexicans took my job!" was his oft-repeated rant. Between drinking bouts, his father began meeting with like-minded men who decided it was time to head out West to the last frontier of White America. His father dragged his mother and the twin boys, Brandon and Jack, and began to home school them on the Neo-Nazi creed, along with survivalist living and paramilitary training. By the age of seven, both boys were able to field strip weapons and hit targets on a par with adults. Jack, the center of his father's attention for once in his life, loved it.

Brandon hated every minute and prayed for a way out. One day his prayers were answered.

"Boys," his mother called, "we need to go into town. The state's been all over my case about getting you your vaccinations. Need to do it today or they'll make trouble for us."

Brandon leaped to his feet and ran for the door.

Any excuse to get out of the compound, even for a doctor's appointment, was a good one.

"Does Daddy know?" Jack hung back in the doorway, a suspicious look on his face.

"Yes, of course he knows. Now come on, the doctor said he could see us right away, so we've gotta go." His mother strode for the door, the keys to the pick-up jangling in her hand, a large bag slung over her shoulder. "I've got just enough money to buy you boys some ice cream. You'd like that, wouldn't you, Jack?"

"I don't want no needles."

His mother hopped into the truck and turned the engine over. Brandon jumped in and shouted to Jack, "Beat you to the truck. I got shotgun." He held the door open but Jack didn't budge.

Jack bellowed from the door, his face contorted with rage, "I'm telling Daddy!"

White faced, his mother turned to Brandon and screamed, "Shut your door!" She hit the gas, and they blew out of the dirt driveway, past the shocked expression of the sentries dressed in camouflage, trying to close the gates to freedom.

When Brandon/Bronco was old enough to understand, his mother revealed that during the time they'd been living in the survivalist compound, she had been secretly meeting with undercover federal agents posing as hunters camping in a wooded area outside the enclave. In exchange for insider information on the survivalists who were amassing an arsenal large enough to blow up Boise, she arranged for new identities for her sons and herself. When Jack refused to come with them and threatened to tell her husband, she had no choice but to run. Had he caught her, he would have killed her.

"Bronco?" Emma's voice brought him back to the present and the kitchen covered in Tallulah's post-it notes. "You okay? Did you slip into remote viewing mode?"

He shook his head to clear the memories and tried to seal the hole that had been ripped in his heart. An aching void that had never been filled, because his other half was gone, swept up by hate. "No. Just thinking about those relatives and wondering what happened to them." He shrugged. "Nothing to worry about, I'm sure they're long gone now."

"Grab your cat and let's go."

Gaucho, who was lounging in a spot of sun on the kitchen floor next to the pug, raised his head and glared at Bronco. *You dare to interrupt my nap?*

"I'd love to leave you here with your new playmate, but you know the drill."

Looking more like a truculent teen than a bobcat, Gaucho slouched over to his partner and turned his head.

"Oh, so it's gonna be like that, is it?" Bronco sighed. "We'll be back in a little while, then you and Franny can play, snore and eat together, until our mission is clear."

The cat shook his head and began to stroll toward the door, dragging his leash behind him.

Lucius chuckled, "See you later, pardner. We'll leave the lights on and have a nice dinner in the works by the time you get back."

Pocketing the room key, Bronco wished they had a better sense of where they were going and what they were doing. Emma was right. He needed a good night's rest and a quiet space for his remote viewing, minus distractions—like the very provocative Ms. Emma Horserider and her searing kisses.

****

Emma plastered a grin on her face to cover the turmoil beneath, bid farewell to Lucius, and jogged for the truck at a pace her old drill sergeant would have approved. *What was I thinking?* She tried to convince herself that the kiss had merely been a test, like they did on TV at night for the emergency broadcasting system. But she knew she was lying—to him and herself. From the moment she set eyes on Bronco, she'd been drawn to him, a bedazzled moth to his sizzling flame. While his rugged good looks were a large part of the attraction, something more pulsed beneath those muscles and tattoos. Like the waves on a moonlit lake, darkness rose and fell in his eyes, turning them from bright blue to granite gray when it overcame him. She wanted to tell him his secrets were safe with her, no matter how bad they were. What had happened to him? How had he chosen this dangerous line of work—or had it chosen him?

Gaucho folded onto Bronco's lap and resumed his napping. A short time into the ride, Bronco's head fell back onto the headrest, and he too began to snore lightly. Emma drove on autopilot, the undulating green hills hypnotic and soothing.

Where had that earlier intense erotic vision come from? Definitely seared into her brain, when she closed her eyes the afterimage appeared, haunting her with its intensity and power to arouse her. Were Bronco's remote viewing ability and her animal telepathy creating a subconscious link at the primal level? Would it happen again? Her biological clock was ringing its alarm loud and clear—but the timing? It wasn't just bad, it was dangerous. She had to keep that man out of her head and her life. When the assignment was over, he'd get on his bike and ride away, just like every other romantic interest she'd ever had. No use getting involved with a man who didn't understand her or her identity and heritage. She was her own woman, not some man's appendage. Taking a deep cleansing breath, she envisioned a bullet-proof Plexiglas barrier around her thoughts—and her heart.

When the truck ran over a pothole on her street, Bronco jerked awake and looked around in confusion. "Did I fall asleep?"

"If you call snoring for the last hour sleeping, then yes, you did. Even Gaucho passed out." She nosed the truck up to the curb. "Are you going to be okay to drive back to the hotel? Or do you need me to get someone to put the bike in a van and take you back?"

Shaking his head, Bronco said, "Nah, give me a cup of coffee and I'll be ready to get out of your hair."

"You're exhausted. Bert would never forgive me if I let you become road kill. A waste of tax dollars."

He yawned and scratched Gaucho's head. "Okay, you convinced me. I'd still love a cup of coffee."

"You got it. Come on in, I'll give Jimmy's mother a call."

"Two-toes?"

"Yes, but her name is Marjorie Longjaw." After placing the call and getting the woman to agree to pick Bronco up after dinner, she opened the door and was greeted by an eye-watering stench. "Taláashiile, your name fits you just right. You have butter for brains!

That skunk doesn't want to play with you." The yellow lab mix wagged her tail and pranced. "I'm not kidding around. You must love that tomato and vinegar bath."

At that the dog in question curled her lips and whined. "Outside. All of you." The pack trooped out the back door, and the German Shepard mix named Bishké, or Dog, cast a long sad look over his shoulder. "I know it's not your fault, Bishké, but you *all* stink now."

Gaucho sniffed and sneezed, and Bronco coughed. "Wow. Nice welcome home."

"Happens about once a month. She never learns." Emma opened windows and turned on a ceiling fan. "I'll put a pot of coffee on. I can use a cup, too." She rummaged in the cabinets, pulling out mugs. "Milk and sugar?"

He nodded, sat in a kitchen chair, and winced.

"Oh, dear. You're still saddle-sore, aren't you?"

"You could say that." He rolled his eyes. "I love my bike, but—"

"Hold that thought." She had something in her garden that would help, assuming the skunk hadn't sprayed the plant with his noxious fumes. Her fenced in back yard was part raised bed planters, part dog park, and completely her making. One side of her yard was lined with railroad ties and rebar boxes filled with loam. Protected from grazing deer, yarrow, sage, basil, bee balm, parsley, rosemary, dill, and other plants grew in profusion. She pulled some yarrow, or chipmunk tail, out and brought it into the house, placing the long green stems with lacy leaves into a pot of boiling water.

"What's that smell?"

"Yarrow. It's good on burns and sores. It will help

your raw skin." An image of applying compresses to his cute butt flashed into her mind. She pushed it away. She assumed a clinical tone. "I'll pack up a container of the solution and some washcloths for you to take with you. After you take a shower"—*Lord that was an image!*—"apply wet compresses soaked in the yarrow tea to the affected areas. It will help."

He crinkled his nose. "You're saying the stuff that smells like cabbage is going to help my butt?"

"Yes." She leaned on the edge of the sink to support her weak knees. *His butt. Good grief.* She had to get the man out of her house, but in the meantime. "Back in a bit. I need to take care of something. Enjoy your coffee."

Emma strode into her bedroom, closed the door, threw herself on her bed, and screamed into her pillow. So much for her mental Plexiglas wall to keep her romantic thoughts at bay. What she needed was some distance. Or an armed perimeter. If her grandmother were here right now, Emma knew she'd be pushing Bronco into the bedroom, slamming the door shut, locking it and throwing away the key.

She could almost hear her saying. "He's a good man. Why are you running away from him? Don't you want children? You're not getting any younger." Emma bit her lips to keep from yelling back at the memories of her elder worrying about whether she'd ever find true love. Her grandmother had gone to her grave disappointed. No little ones to dandle on her knees. Was she really bullheaded in her independence?

The phone rang, and Emma rolled over. A county office phone number showed on the caller ID.

"Hello?"

"Emma, this is Tommy. There's a motorcycle parked outside, and the neighbors are telling me a strange man, covered in tattoos is in your house. Is everything okay?"

"I'm fine," she said through clenched teeth. "He's a friend of my brother's. In for a visit."

"Seems pretty suspicious to me—and a lot of other folks, too," he said in his little whiney voice. "I'm outside your door, happy to send him on his way if you need me to get rid of him."

She stifled a moan. A high school classmate, Tommy Otterlegs, of *all* people, was the one her grandmother had favored and had kept pushing her to date. An ambitious bantam rooster of a man, he now worked as a sheriff's deputy and had at one time tried to railroad Lucius into prison for attempted homicide. That hadn't gone well for Tommy. Not that it kept him from still being a persistent suitor and nuisance. The short-legged man showed up at the most inopportune times, like now, sticking his nose into her business, as if he had a right to be there. Well, fine, she'd let him in. Get it over with, or he'd just pester her to death. "Be right there. Don't mind the skunk smell."

She strode past Bronco who nursed his coffee. Gaucho was spread across the rag rug like he lived there, playing with a dog toy. "One of our local constabulary has decided to stop in."

Bronco quirked a brow. "Because…?"

"Indian telegraph." She yanked open the front door, and the cocky little man sauntered in wrinkling his nose. "Tommy Otterlegs, meet Bronco Winchester. Bronco this is Tommy."

The bobcat leaped to his feet and growled, a low,

angry thrum ending in a hiss. He did not like this man, not one bit.

"It's okay, Gaucho." Bronco petted the cat's head. "He's harmless."

Tommy bristled and put his thumbs in his belt loops. His index fingers pointed at his crotch. "You got a permit for that wild animal?"

Every freaking time she had a male caller the little snot had to show up and posture like a tiny cave man.

"Of course I do." Bronco reached into his back pocket and pulled out his wallet which was secured to his pants on a chain. "Here you go. Federal and state."

Tommy inspected the document as if examining it for forgery. "Where'd you get this *thing*?"

The cat hissed.

"His name is Gaucho, and he was an orphan. I bottle raised him." Bronco tossed Emma a puzzled look and shrugged, as if to say, *What's his problem?*

The little man frowned and handed the paperwork back to Bronco. "I'll be on my way, but just so you know—" he glared at Bronco—"I've got my eyes on you. You better keep that cat under control."

Bronco stood and stretched, towering a good foot over Tommy. "I'll take that into consideration, Officer Otterlegs."

Tommy flushed and blustered, "Deputy Sheriff Otterlegs."

Bronco nodded. "You got it."

Emma stood with the door open. "Good night, Tommy."

As he strutted past her, he whispered, "Keep your phone handy. I don't like the looks of this guy."

"Point taken." She slammed the door behind him.

She didn't like the looks of Bronco either. No, she *loved* the looks of the sex-up-against-the-wall biker man and that was just the start of her problems. Emma had to get him out of her house before she did something she regretted.

As if in answer to her thoughts, a horn honked outside.

"I think that's my ride." He scrambled for the door. "Hate to leave you with the stink, but—"

She laughed. "Sure you do."

She'd have more luck de-scenting that skunk than she would getting him to stay after the assignment was over.

He grinned and gave her a two-fingered salute. "See you back at the hotel."

As the white van pulled away from the curb, Emma closed the door and leaned against it with a sigh. *Oh, my aching ovaries.*

Chapter Six

Bronco did not enjoy the ride to the Hotel LaBelle with Marjorie Longjaw as much as he had the one with Emma. For one thing, Mrs. Longjaw had earned her name. From the minute he climbed into the van, the extremely nice, incredibly kind, and exceedingly excitable mother of Jimmy Two-toes maintained a non-stop stream of chatter peppered with questions that she didn't let him answer. He'd met a lot of talkative people in his life, but this woman's hot air was off the charts with wind gusts up to one-hundred miles per hour.

"Oh, so nice to meet you. My son, Jimmy, he has a motorcycle, too, and he just loves it. Scares me sometimes, but he's my only son, had him when I was thirty-five and family is everything, you know." She took a breath, then kept going, "What about you, how do you know Emma?"

He opened his mouth to respond, but she talked over him.

"Oh, that's right, Emma told me you know her brother. We're all very proud of him. His work is important, but he never forgets his family and his people. You know, I can't tell you how many times he's bailed Jimmy out of scrapes." She shook her head. "That boy. Anyhow, if Bert ever decided to move home permanently, give up that big job in Washington, he could run for office, be Mayor of Billings, he's that well-known, you know? He's quite the fisherman, too. Wins the big trout tournament every time he enters. We call him the fish whisperer."

Bronco decided nodding was his best option in this one-sided conversation. Bert was so close-mouthed—except when it came to work related things—he was pleased to find out more about Bert's virtues, like his boss's love of fishing. *Fish whisperer.* He chuckled and tucked that little tidbit away in his mental file folder for use on a later date.

"Emma, on the other hand," Marjorie rattled on, as she glanced in the rear-view mirror to change lanes, "she's too shy to be mayor, you know."

Emma and shy? In the same sentence? Now that was a shocker.

"I've known Emma ever since she was a little girl, hiding behind her grandmother's skirts. Her great-grandmother was a powerful Medicine Woman and so was her grandmother. Lost her mother when she was just a little bit of a thing, but that's another story. Anyway, being a grandmother's grandchild, and all, everyone thought she'd be following in her grandmother's ways, become another great Medicine Woman. Runs in families, you know. But she didn't show a lot of interest in the herbs or healing ways."

The cooler full of yarrow tea in the back of the van on his bike said otherwise, but he didn't disagree. He grunted what he hoped was an "Oh really" sound.

"But, horses and dogs? You couldn't keep her away from them." She chuckled. "The dogs followed her wherever she went on the reservation. That girl was never alone, never afraid. She had her pack. And once she got her first horse? Well, let's just say, she was all over the place."

She sighed and turned on her blinker for the highway.

Oh, thank God, is that the sign for the turn off?

"That camping trip she took with her best friend her senior year in high school? I think that was a turning point in her life, you know. She joined the Marines right after graduation, after she healed up from the bear bites, and all."

He finally got a word in edgewise. "Bear?"

"Oh yeah, we've got a lot of bears around here, black and Grizzly." She nodded and for once on the entire trip, fell silent.

"How did Emma...?" He wanted to scream in frustration, but Gaucho shot him a warning growl from the back.

"Oh, so she and her best friend, Jessica, went out by the river, set up a teepee and were enjoying themselves—some say they were drinking, but I don't believe that—anyway, a Grizzly bear shows up, sees them, and attacks Jessica." She shook her head. "That Emma, who would have seen it coming, such a surprise."

He ground his teeth in frustration. "What happened?"

"Well, the bear was gnawing on Jessica's leg and according to Jessica, Emma went crazy, jumped on the bear's back, stabbed its throat with her hunting knife. Got the bear off Jessica, but the crazed beast went after Emma with a vengeance. She got clawed up pretty bad. Jessica lost her leg."

"How'd they get to the hospital?"

"Well, Emma must have been paying attention to

Sharon Buchbinder

her grandmother, after all. She tied a belt around Jessica's leg, got both of them up into her grandmother's pick-up truck—and drove the two of them back to the rez. EMTs rushed them to St. Vic's." As the sky turned from blue to gray, she nosed the van into the entryway to the LaBelle. "Well, here we are."

Here we are, indeed. He didn't just get a partner. He got a super heroine. Bronco stepped down from the van, and pulled the portable rear entry ramp down to the ground. Gaucho sat on the saddle of the bike, looking for all the world like an Egyptian statue of Bast waiting to be worshipped.

"Come on your highness." Bronco unclipped the leash from the cat's harness. "Go for a run, but don't go far. Come back when it gets dark."

Gaucho wasted no time leaping out of the back of the van and running into the long grasses while Bronco unloaded the bike and put the ramp back in the cargo space. As he walked the bike around the van and balanced it on the kickstand, he called to the driver, "Want some coffee? Lucius has a great machine."

Marjorie leaned her head out the window. "Nah, gotta get to the store, grab a few things, you know, and then head home to ride herd on Jimmy and his homework." She put the car in reverse and waved. "You take care, now."

"Thank you for everything," he shouted. As the van pulled out of the driveway, he said to himself in a normal tone of voice, "Especially the intel on my new partner."

"That Marjorie." Lucius's voice made Bronco jump. "She's a talker. Gave you all the deep dish on Emma, did she?"

"Couldn't stop her if I'd wanted to." Bronco shook his head. "The bear story. Is that true?"

"If you saw the scars on her back, you'd know it was." Lucius glanced around. "Where's your cat?"

Bronco closed his eyes and focused on finding his feline companion. He had a fat field mouse trapped under his paw. "Just grabbing a quick bite."

"Speaking of which, time to put on the feed bag. The guests are in the bar, if you want to join them for a drink."

"A shower first, then a cold one." Bronco whistled for Gaucho who came bounding out of the darkness. "You look satisfied with yourself." The cat chirped and head butted his leg. He clipped the leash on the harness. "No scaring the guests."

Lucius smiled. "I sure appreciate that. We have two couples staying with us. They fished all day, caught their limit. Hope you like trout almondine."

"My best recipe is a peanut butter and jelly sandwich. My second best recipe is drive through. This is a treat."

Lucius led the way into the hotel. "Your room's at the top of the stairs, to the right. We might have a few scraps of fish left for your friend. I'll go check the kitchen."

****

Bronco admired his room. The updated bathroom, king sized bed, and flat-screen TV brought the place into contemporary times, but the carved wood-paneled walls spoke of its rich history. Gaucho immediately leaped onto the four-poster, rolled onto his back, stretched his legs out and fell asleep. Never let anyone say that cat wasn't pampered.

Every muscle in his body screamed for a long hot bath, but with a cold drink waiting for him in the bar, a quick shower would have to do. Bronco pulled the white cloth curtain around the tub, cranked on the faucets to let the hot water run, and stripped out of his denim cut, T-shirt and jeans. He'd blown out of Colorado so fast, all he had with him was one set of spare jeans and a T-shirt in the bottom pouch of his back pack. He'd forgotten to pack underwear. *Perfect. Guess I'm going commando.* He set the recycled mayonnaise jar of yarrow tea on the edge of the sink, along with the dry washcloths Emma had provided. He stepped into the shower, yelped, and adjusted the spray of hot water. Lathering shampoo into his hair, he put his head back under the flow of water, and sighed.

Clean at last.

The only thing that would make this perfect would be if Emma was in here with him. He'd be careful washing her back—and her front—and using slow gentle movements. He'd be happy to show her *exactly* why this bucking Bronco was a ride she'd never forget. Soap bubbles slid down his chest, and he slowly stroked his pecs and lower abdomen in a dreamy state of relaxation. As his hand headed toward his groin, the toilet flushed.

"Dammit, Gaucho! I'm going to kill you!"

He snatched the curtain back—and no one was there, not even the cat. He stepped out of the shower and stomped into the bedroom. Gaucho, still sprawled out on his back, was apparently deep in sleep because his feet were running in the air.

Shaking his head, he went back into the bathroom. The jar full of yarrow tea sat *in* the sink with the top off, a cloth soaking inside. "What the hell?"

He glanced up at the steam-covered mirror. A pair of dark brown eyes stared back at him. When he swiped at the condensation, they vanished.

****

Emma packed her coyote colored rucksack with enough clothing for a week. After stuffing the side pouches with travel sized toiletries, protein bars, nuts, dried fruit, and bison jerky packets, she took the Mossberg 500 out of its rack, slid it into her tactical shotgun scabbard, and placed everything by the front door. Her glove compartment was packed with ammo, as was the ammo reload carrier pouch attached to the scabbard. Hunting knife strapped to her hip, she pondered for a moment, tapping her chin, feeling like she was missing something.

Her olive drab first aid kit sat open on the kitchen table. She didn't recall putting it there. Shaking her head, she said, "I must be losing my mind." Along with the usual scissors, scalpel, compress dressings, adhesive bandages, adhesive cloth tape, hydrocortisone, antibiotic ointment, antiseptic wipes, aspirin, acetaminophen, gloves, roller bandages, gauze, triangular bandages, and tweezers, she also packed injectable lidocaine, suture, needles, syringes, and an assortment of plastic containers filled with medicinal herbs and compounds.

The now clean and less stinky canine patrol came bounding through the doggy door, yipping and dancing around the kitchen. "Hey, who said it was dinner time?"

Panting, Baaíishiíaliche the Labrador mix threw herself on the floor in front of the refrigerator and gazed at the door as if in love. Hisshe, or Red, the rescue beagle, howled mournfully while Bishké, the German shepherd mix sat in front of the backpack and whined.

"The three of you can knock it off. I'm not going away forever." A rap at the door set the dogs into a frenzy of barking, yowling, and yipping. She put her hand up. "Stop!"

Shaking, Hisshe stopped howling, but continued to whine.

Thinking her ranch hand, Hank, had decided to stop by for any last minute instructions, Emma yanked the door open.

Tommy Otterlegs stood on her front step in his black uniform, hat in hand. "Good evening."

"What on earth are *you* doing here again?" She glanced at the moon halfway on its journey to the night sky. "And late, at that."

He craned his neck, trying to peer around her. The dogs sat alongside her, forming a canine wall. "Just checking to see if everything's okay." He glanced down at the dogs, and his gaze snagged on her rucksack. "Going somewhere?"

"Not that it's any of your business, but yeah, I'm going to be away for a while."

"I'll be sure to have a patrol car come by your house and keep an eye out."

"My ranch hand will be here, no need for that."

"He can't be here twenty-four/seven. Don't you have horses for him to look after, too?"

For the most part, Emma loved her tribe, but this was one member she could really do without—especially now. "I'm good, it's all good. You want to send a cruiser, knock yourself out." *But no more than that, you officious twerp.* "As you can see, I'm a little busy."

"Happy to check all your windows, make sure everything is buttoned up." He put one foot in the door, as if to come in, and Bishké growled. He pulled his foot back. "Or not."

Smiling to herself, she sent a mental thank you to her protective canine.

"Where are you going?"

Damn, this guy just won't take a hint.

"Not that it's any of your business, but I'm going west, taking a friend to see the Lewis and Clark Caverns." She knew that would provoke him, but she couldn't help herself. "So, see you in a week or so."

His lip curled with anger. "You mean that biker? Seriously, what do you see in him? He's no good. I looked him up in ViCAP, the Violent Criminal Apprehension Program. He's got a rap sheet as long as your arm. Assault, battery, auto theft, possession of dangerous drugs, possession of weapons, attempted murder—and that's just the surface." A smug expression crossed his face. "Yeah, I did my homework, that's what I do. I find the bad guys and I Lock. Them. Up."

Emma put her hand on her right hip, the one with the knife holster. "Well, if he's so bad, why's he out on the streets?"

"I—I'm—not sure. I'm trying to find that out." He frowned. "His complete records are hard to access. I could only see the charges, not the details."

"Hmmm." She shrugged. "Unless you have more than that, I strongly suggest you leave him alone. You wouldn't want your boss to find out you've been harassing someone, would you?" His radio crackled to life. "Who's closest to the Hardin Burger Barn? We have a D and D—Owner says her husband's drunk as a skunk and harassing the customers."

"I've gotta get going. Duty calls!" Speaking into his radio, he spun on his heel and sprinted for his car.

Wheels squealing, Otterlegs' car peeled away from the curb as if in a high-speed pursuit.

Chuckling, she returned to her packing. Bronco's cover was so good, it even fooled the local Keystone cop. The next time she saw him, which would be very soon, she'd have to compliment him on his nice "resume."

Another rap at the door, this time in code, told her Steph had arrived. She swept in, and the dogs wagged their tails and jumped on her in greeting. "Yes, yes, my loves. Good to see you, too."

Throwing her arms around Emma, she lifted her off her feet in a breathtaking hug.

"Steph, I'm not going away forever, just a few weeks."

"Well, I'm worried about you. I know you're a powerful warrior woman and all that, but seriously, you don't know who you're up against."

"My brother is going to send a detailed report to me shortly, and Bronco's got his own investigative tools."

Steph batted her eyes. "I'd love to see his tool, but I have a feeling you'll see it before I do."

Heat burned Emma's face. "You have the dirtiest mind. If you weren't my cousin—"

"Your life would be dull and boring!" Steph twirled her hair. "I do have a little bit more information on the brown-shirts."

"What? Tell me!"

Steph pulled a kitchen chair out and seemingly floated into it. Her cousin was exceedingly graceful. Emma sat across the table from her.

"I saw my friend, Babs, you know the one they beat up. We were at the Garrett, having a drink, and we were talking—"

Emma covered her face with her hands and moaned. "You did *not* mention this investigation!"

"Give me some credit, girl! Trust me, I'm a regular Mata Hari."

Emma grumbled under her breath, "Matted Hairy."

Steph slapped her hand. "While I was talking to Babs, a really cute young blond guy with a crewcut came over to our table and asked us if we were from Billings and if we were looking for a good time."

A lump formed in Emma's throat. "No."

"Yep." Steph smiled like a Cheshire cat. "So, I said, maybe, maybe not, have a seat, we'll talk about it."

"And?"

"He was adorable, but way too young for me, so I told him we'd be like his big sisters, keep him out of trouble. He says, 'Oh, I've been warned already' and I said, 'Do tell' and he told us there's a website with travel advisories for LGBT folks telling them to stay out of certain parts of the country."

"I'm going to kill you. Spit it out."

"He said, 'A bunch of Neo-Nazis have been posting crap online about how they're going to *own* Montana, make it a sovereign nation, make the state racially pure again, like it was back in the good old days,'" Steph wiped a tear away. "They're here. In *our* state. Up north. I think that's who attacked Babs."

Emma's head spun. *Neo-Nazis trying to take over Montana? Were they really that widespread?* She wasn't totally naïve about the ultra-right-wing groups. In fact, for a short stint in the Marines, she'd spent some time as a recruiter. In preparation for the role, she'd been taught to be on the lookout for controversial tattoos and symbols. Some people, she'd been told, attempted to penetrate the military to try to recruit people for their extremist causes. Tattoo identification had been part of her training. Gang and prison tattoos were a red flag, as were any of the Aryan Nation, Skinhead, White Power Warheads, or any other White Supremacist or Neo-Nazi groups' tattoos. Not only did these groups want to infiltrate to recruit members, but also to learn military and tactical training to take back to their paramilitary compounds to prepare for the coming war of the races.

What if a group decided just obtaining the usual military weapons training wasn't enough? What if they went high tech, going after the latest technology, including unmanned weaponized drones that could attack without anyone seeing it coming? These Neo-Nazis *had* to be responsible for the drone attacks on the mustangs and the eagles. Killing the sacred animals had been symbolic—and probably practice for bigger targets. She and Bronco had to stop them before they moved onto attacking people.

Steph waved a hand in front of her face. "Hello? You in there?"

Shaking her head to clear the black clouds lingering in her thoughts, Emma said, "Yeah, sorry. I had to process everything you said. Great job, Steph.

You *are* Nancy Drew."

"Mata Hari. I'm too exotic to be Nancy Drew."

"You've got that right." Emma stood. "Before I forget, here's the arnica compound I promised you. Rub it in at bedtime. If you can put some heat on that, too, it will help." She handed her a container of white ointment.

"Thank you, baby." Steph stood and clutched Emma's hand. "You know, I never used to believe in this stuff about us Two Spirit people having the gift of prophecy. But, just this once, baby, please, for the love of your family, your tribe—me—please, please, please be careful. I have a really bad feeling about what's coming."

Hugging her cousin, Emma tried to shake off a feeling of dread—with no luck.

"If I don't do this, others will be hurt. I can't let whoever is doing this kill any more horses or eagles— or buffalo." She almost said people, but kept that fear to herself. Instead, she plastered a grin on her face, lightened her voice and threw out, "Listen. Tonight I have a meeting at the Hotel LaBelle with a guy named Bronco who has a smart bobcat and looks like hot sex on a stick. I'd be crazy not to chase that cute little butt, wouldn't I? What could possibly go wrong?"

Chapter Seven

Bronco quaffed his cold brew and made small talk with the other guests of the Hotel LaBelle. His mind kept wandering back to that kiss and wondering what Emma was doing now. Belatedly, he realized they hadn't really discussed the next steps and timelines. But he was grateful for the ride from Mrs. Longjaw, although he found it difficult to socialize with normal people. Like now.

Long-time friends, the foursome dining in the saloon with him probably traveled together everywhere. The men had been friends as children, and now forty years later were still connected. The good news was they had each other and could "talk amongst themselves." The bad news was when all four of them turned their focus on him, he felt as if he was being interrogated by Senator McCarthy and the House Committee on Un-American Activities.

"So." The forty-something blonde named Claire tossed her hair over her shoulder and stared at his uncovered arm with the screaming eagle diving toward his wrist. "What does that tattoo symbolize?"

Paul, her balding, portly husband, whom Bronco pegged at a hair over fifty, put his hand up. "Claire, that's a personal question. I work with these people and I've been told each one has a story—none of which is my business."

"Hmm." Bronco frowned. "Not sure what you mean by 'these people.' Can you clarify that for me?"

Paul flushed as red as his glass of Merlot. "I just meant all these youngsters, the millennials, and what's your generation—the Gen X's? The ones I work with are covered in these things—and body piercings."

Claire grimaced.

Lisa, a woman who either had cancer or anorexia—and his money was on the latter after watching her push her food around on her plate—had what he dubbed a Skunk-Do—black hair striped with thick lines of bleach blonde hair, chimed in. "Yech. Those things on the lips? The brow? And the nose? What do they do when they get a cold? I mean, doesn't that thing catch a lot of—well, you know."

"Snot?" Bronco filled in, loving the expressions on their faces when he dared to use the four letter word. "The people I know who have nose piercings remove them when they get an upper respiratory infection. And tattoos? They're not new. Tattoos date back to Neolithic times."

"I'm not so sure about that," drawled Lisa's husband, Mark, who was on his fourth scotch—and that was just since dinner began.

"Hold on." Pulling out his phone, Bronco connected to the hotel Wi-Fi and searched on tattoos. "Smithsonian Magazine had an article on it." He displayed a photo of a mummy with a tattooed hand that dated back to over five-thousand years old.

Mark snorted and took another swig from his half-empty glass.

"Come to think of it," Claire said, "my grandfather had a ship tattooed on his chest. When I was a little girl, he'd take his shirt off and make it ride the waves for me."

"That's completely different," Paul sputtered. "He was a Navy man, a patriot. Not this…" He pointed at Bronco and stopped speaking.

"What he means is," Claire interjected. "Your generation."

Once again, his secret identity was good. Too good. As long as people were willing to judge others on appearance and not action, he'd never have to worry about having his cover blown. Bronco had said nothing nor had he done anything to offend the foursome— except show up in his own skin. He wondered how Lucius put up with guests like this, then he recalled the innkeeper came from a meaner time.

"My generation? My guess is I'm no more than ten years younger than you folks. Not that big a difference in age. But clearly a difference in opinions." He rose. "It's been nice meeting you. I've had a long day, so I'm going to say good night." The women's high-pitched voices drowned out the men's lower pitched mumbles of responses. He wondered how much later they'd be up drinking and if Lucius would have to carry Mark up to his room.

He found Lucius wiping the kitchen counters. "Where's your bride?"

"In bed with her feet up." He glanced at the kitchen clock. "She's usually asleep by nine-thirty these days. Has more energy in the morning. What can I get you?"

"Wondering if you have those fish scraps for Gaucho. If not, he'll scare up a meal on his own."

The tall innkeeper dried his hands on a tea towel. "I sure do." He rummaged in the large refrigerator and pulled out a plastic baggy filled with white chunks. "So, what did you think about the guests?"

"You really want to know?"

"Wouldn't ask if I didn't."

"Not a fan." Bronco shrugged. "But they're your bread and butter, so I'm not going to be a problem, if that's what you're thinking."

"Quite the opposite, pardner." Lucius handed him the baggy and then reached overhead and pulled down a package covered with buckskin. "Been doin' a little investigating while they've been out." He began to unwrap the bundle. "This here is Beautiful Blackfeather's medicine stick." He pointed to a plain looking twig with a wispy white feather at the tip. "You and I haven't had a chance to talk about what I can do." He put his hand up. "I know you don't want me going out what with Tallulah being about to pop. Just watch."

He reached over, and grasped the rod—and disappeared.

Bronco could scarcely believe his eyes. He scanned the room looking for a trap door or other exit. As he moved next to the spot where Lucius had disappeared, the stick fell to the counter and he and the other man stood nose to nose.

"Well?" Lucius's mustache quirked with his grin. "Whadya think?"

"Holy crap. Do it again."

Lucius picked the rod up and disappeared instantly. Like a light switch, he flicked in and out. Touching. Not touching. Pick it up, disappear. Hand off, reappear. On. Off. On. Off.

After the tenth time, Bronco said, "Stop. Please. You're making me dizzy."

"I have that effect," Lucius smirked.

"Tell me about this. How…"

"When Beautiful reversed the curse, we think she felt pretty bad about what she'd done. I'm guessing this was her way of trying to make it up to me. Gave me a piece of her medicine which allows me to become invisible."

"Amazing." Bronco shook his head. "So what did you find out about those bores in your bar? That Mark has a drinking problem and that Lisa has a terrible stylist and an eating disorder?"

"Hold your horses. Now I'm going to ask you a couple questions. What is the one big thing that makes this hotel unique?"

"Is that a trick question? Location, location, location. Real estate one-oh-one."

"Exactly. We are right on the Yellowstone River, home to the best trout fishing in the world. And these guys are all about fishing, tell me they want to go trout fishing." He pointed at the calendar. "They asked when the season was, and I told them it was year round, they just needed a non-resident fishing license."

"Okay."

"I told them it was illegal to dump game fish, that they had a choice to catch and release or eat it. Like tonight." He shook his head. "Like talking to aliens. No idea what I meant. So I hooked them up with a terrific local guide and they said, no, they had their own. When I asked for a name, they were cagey."

"Just sounds like just a bunch of obnoxious tourists to me."

"Well, I thought so at first, too. You get these greenhorns out here, they've seen a movie about trout fishing, so they think it's easy." He shook his head. "But these guys? Pardon the pun, but there's something fishy about them."

"I didn't like them, but that's not enough." Bronco closed his eyes and groaned. "Tell me you have something more substantial."

"They paid with cash. No credit cards, which is unusual these days."

"Unusual, but not illegal," Bronco pointed out.

Lucius nodded and stroked his mustache. "I asked for ID, so everyone pulled out shiny new drivers' licenses for the State of New York, all saying they're from Albany. When I commented about how new they were, Mark gave me a story about how they'd been robbed at gunpoint in New York City."

"I don't suppose you got copies of their IDs?"

"Tallulah made sure I did. She wasn't buying their buffalo chips, either."

"Seems like they have answers for everything." Bronco tapped the counter with his index finger.

"There's more." Lucius pulled out his phone. "While they went out fishing, I pulled out my trusty medicine stick and did a little snooping. Look here." He extended the cell to Bronco. "What's that look like to you? A little light reading?"

Bronco read the titles out loud. "*ICD-10, The Complete Official Code Book, CPT Current Procedural Terminology, Special Ops, 1939-1945: A Manual of Covert Warfare and Training, Operation OSS: Simple Sabotage Field Manual/Provisional Basic Field Manual/Maritime Unit Field Manual* and *The Official CIA Manual of Trickery and Deception.*" He looked up at Lucius.

"I don't know what the first two are for. The last three? Maybe one of them is writing a book, doing research?"

"I looked the first two books up. Those are for medical billing." Lucius snorted. "When I asked them what they did for a living, they all said 'business' and got busy talking about other things. My gut is telling me these people aren't what they seem."

"I can run their names and IDs through my databases tomorrow, see what I find," Bronco offered.

"I make a living on tourism and that river out there is a big draw." Lucius pointed toward the back door. "I've been attending Montana Fish and Wildlife seminars and learning about aquatic invasive species and why we don't want things like Zebra mussels and silver carp in our waters. If someone were to poison the well, biologically or chemically, they could ruin half the economy—maybe more."

"If they're not who they say they are, they were very convincing. They conned a con artist. They just seemed like a bunch of uptight accountants to me." Bronco rubbed his neck and yawned. "If something's off when I run their IDs, I can dig a little deeper."

"How about you try using your remote viewing to see where these people came from? They say they're from upstate New York, but their accents tell me otherwise."

"Let's see what the usual sources tell me before I jump into that mode. I'm beat. I don't do my best work when I'm exhausted. I promise I'll do it in the morning."

"Probably a good idea. They'll be out driving around, seeing the sights, or so they said. I suggested the Pictograph Caves and the Little Bighorn Battlefield. They said they'd think about it." He shook his head. "Why come all this way and not go to one of the most important historic sites in the area, if not the country?"

"Some people aren't interested in history. Doesn't make them security threats." He put his palms up. "I hear you. I'll work on it tomorrow. Promise. If they played me, you'll hear me kicking my butt all over my room."

A thought occurred to him. "Do your toilets ever flush on their own?"

"Didn't you say your cat uses the toilet?"

"Yes, but he was asleep at the time." He paused. "I could have sworn I saw someone staring at me in the bathroom mirror."

Lucius gave him a slow smile. "Well, it *is* a looking glass, supposed to reflect your face."

"Brown eyes. Mine are blue. Is this place haunted?"

"Aww, we don't like to talk about our relatives that way. We call them *Beings without Bodies*. Not supposed to use their names, according to the Crow."

"Relatives? So you know who it is?"

"Of course I do." He began to wrap up the medicine stick up. "Same person who gave me this gift. Beautiful Blackfeather. She returned to reverse my curse and decided to stick around. I thought only Tallulah had visions. Have you always seen spirits?"

Bronco shook his head. "No, never. First time in my life."

"Welcome to Big Sky Country, home of sacred spaces. Looks like you've been adopted by one of the strongest Medicine Women, alive or dead. Welcome to the tribe."

****

As the moon rose, Emma parked her pick-up truck next to the hotel shuttle van and killed the engine. Feeling like she did when she was a teenager with a crush on the captain of the varsity basketball team in high school, she took a deep breath and tried to lower the rate of her hammering heart. Hadn't she learned long ago only a foolish girl followed her heart instead of her head? Her mind went back to that terrible night during her senior year, the night Jessica lost her leg and nearly her life. It was all her fault. She'd been a foolish girl who followed her heart and not her head.

That year, Johnny Blackwolf, tall, dark, impossibly handsome and popular had finally asked her out on a date—but not to the movies or a dance. No, he wanted to take his new pick-up truck and go camping at Cooney State Park. The thought of being with him alone under the night sky, doing who knew what, made her dizzy. She had practiced kissing her arms just for this moment. She'd let him get to second base, for sure. But not third and certainly not a home run. Johnny wouldn't respect her if she went all the way on the first date. No, the first time she went all the way, it was going to be special. Maybe prom night. Not before then.

Of course there was no way her grandmother would allow her to go camping overnight with a guy. If Grandma were in charge of the world, there would still be menstrual teepees where the women went to live at that time of the month, separate from the men so they wouldn't contaminate their food. In June, after the prom, everyone would graduate and either stay on the rez or go away to the military or, if they were lucky, college. Johnny had a full ride to Bakersfield on a basketball scholarship. One night could lead to another and another and then prom and then he'd leave her to pursue his dreams. After that, she'd never see him again.

While complaining to her best friend about how unfair it was that she couldn't spend time alone with the love of her life, Emma had a brain storm. She'd tell her grandmother she was going camping with Jessica. Nothing unusual. They did it all the time. Emma would pack food, bedding, and a teepee, put the horses in the trailer, and take her grandmother's pick-up truck and head to the state park. The girls would meet Johnny there, along with the love of Jessica's life, Noah Littlebear. The plan had worked like a charm. Grandma bought the story. Why wouldn't she? Emma had never lied to her in her life. Until that night. And it was truly a lie of omission about the guys.

The boys showed up with two six-packs of beer, a bottle of whiskey, and a box of condoms. Too late, Emma realized her terrible mistake. She should have never concocted this scheme, never allowed Johnny to charm her. His name should have been Johnny Coyote, the Trickster, not Blackwolf. While the girls wrestled separately with their respective drunken suitors, a grizzly bear intrigued by their food, which they had not put into a bear safe away from the campfire, ambled into their party. And all hell broke loose.

The boys jumped into Johnny's cherry red truck and took off. The horses bolted, racing for home, and the girls faced the bear alone. Jessica screamed—and the rest was a blur of blood and pain. To this day, Emma could not recall how she'd gotten the two of them home. Emma was sliced open by the bear in so many places, her back looked like a road map. But, Jessica. Oh, dear God. Her best friend, who loved to dance, lost her leg. Although Jessica forgave Emma, she couldn't forgive herself. The boys—the cowards—never spoke of that night. If anyone had found out, Johnny would have lost his scholarship. His chances of getting off the rez and making a life in sports would have evaporated in the mountain air. Indian boys so rarely made it to Division One schools, much less on a full ride, that even a hint of impropriety would tank his chances. Drinking and leaving two girls to fend for themselves were not positive character traits when it came to resume building.

From May to June, Emma spent every moment she wasn't in school at Jessica's side. Immediately after graduation, Emma drove to the Marine Corps recruiting station and enlisted. That same day Noah Littlebear proposed to Jessica and she accepted. Shortly after, Noah took a job in Pryor, and Jessica went on to have five boys—her own basketball team. Johnny, the teenage heartthrob and Mr. Popularity, left town in a blaze of glory, a shooting star that burned out in the big city in a car crash some said involved alcohol.

As for Emma, if it hadn't been for the Marine Corps, she might not be alive today, sitting in the pick-up truck she inherited from her grandmother. The woman had gone to her deathbed never knowing her granddaughter had lied. Despite the passage of time, Emma felt ill every time she recalled the event. She read somewhere that we are only as sick as our secrets. If she could go back in time and undo the harm, she would. Instead, every day of her life she woke up with scars that throbbed with the pain of guilt to remind her. No matter how much arnica compound she rubbed on her back, she could never erase the shame. Each day she rose, burned cedar to drive away evil spirits, and prayed for the strength to make the world a better place and to prove she was good enough to make up for that awful night.

Thanks to her days in Camp Pendleton, she was no longer a virgin, however she hadn't connected with anyone on the same level of passion as she felt with Bronco. The intensity of her desire for him was so electric, so primal, and so visceral, she wasn't sure she could trust herself alone with him. If she had half a brain, she would listen to her brother, sit this dance out, and watch from the sidelines while Bronco and whoever else her brother sent solved the case. But if she did that, she would dishonor Indigo's sacrifice and her promise to herself to seek justice and do the right thing, no matter how hard.

As she climbed out of the truck and ascended the hotel stairs, she reminded herself that he was just like Johnny—hot as hell and a coyote trickster. No way, no how was she falling in love again.

Chapter Eight

Bronco awoke the next morning to a not-so-gentle tap on the head. He opened one eye, expecting to see Gaucho parked next to him, paw poised mid-air for the next jab. The cat, however, was not to be seen. *Odd.* He yawned, stretched, swung his legs over the edge of the bed and glanced at the open bathroom door. Gaucho sat on the sink, lapping at the water Bronco had left dripping.

Shrugging, he ambled into the bathroom, grabbed a quick shower, and applied more of the yarrow tea. True to Emma's word, the solution had soothed his inflamed derriere, and the bright red color was now rosy pink, almost back to normal.

He snapped the leash on the cat's harness. A brisk walk outside, then breakfast. Coffee, pancakes, and eggs would hit the spot right now. Nearly eight-thirty. He hoped the kitchen was open. Maybe he could grab a mug on his way out. As he hit the bottom step, he heard Emma's voice, and his heart stuttered. *When had she arrived?*

"So, I told him he could send a car around if he wanted, but I was sure everything would be fine." She chuckled. "Little twerp."

"You talking trash about me?" Bronco grinned and strode into the sunny kitchen. "Coffee? Please, pretty, please? Is the coast clear?"

"We can talk amongst ourselves." Lucius poured a piping hot cup and handed it to him. "The tourists are out for the day, said they'd get dinner in town."

"My ever so protective buddy, Tommy Otterlegs, stopped back by yesterday after you left." Emma continued, her eyes crinkling with mirth. "Said you have a long rap sheet, and he's going to Lock. You. Up."

"He's on to me." Bronco raised the mug. "To good police work."

"Speaking of which…" Lucius said with a meaningful look.

"Gaucho and I need a quick walk first, then you need to feed us. We can't work on an empty stomach."

"Gotcha covered. What's your pleasure? I can have it ready in twenty."

Emma broke in. "Let me guess. Pancakes and lots of syrup."

Bronco stared at her. "How'd you know?"

"Your phone, remember? Try to keep it away from your plate this time, okay?"

"Ya want sausage or bacon with that?" Lucius asked.

Cup in hand, he headed for the back door. "Whatever's easy."

"Okay if I join you?" Emma asked.

"Sure." He reached for the doorknob, and the mug wobbled. Hot coffee sloshed over his hand. "Shoot."

Emma opened the door and motioned for him to go ahead of her. "You still have that yarrow tea? It's good for burns, too."

"Yup. I got a reminder to use it last night."

"A reminder?" She frowned. "Who did that?"

"Lucius tells me it was Beautiful Blackfeather." He set his cup on the porch railing and unsnapped Gaucho's leash. "Go on, have a nice run." The cat leaped down the stairs and into the grasses. Bronco walked down the steps and headed for the path along the river.

"I don't understand. What does she have to do with this?"

"Well, according to Lucius, she's hanging around the hotel." He described the flushing toilet, the re-positioning of the washcloth into the jar, and the brown eyes in the mirror. "I got a good rap on the noggin this morning, which I'm beginning to think was her, too, telling me to get up and get to work."

"That's so odd." Emma strode next to Bronco, keeping up with his pace with ease. "I used to feel rooms that were cold when I was cleaning the hotel, but never saw or felt anything else. On the other hand, I'm sort of not surprised, because I'm Crow. We're raised to believe that when our loved one is gone, she's gone, and to call out a Being without Body's name is to invite trouble."

"I'm not sure about the trouble part. If it's Beautiful, she's seems to want to be helpful. But then again, I'm no expert on spirits. Unlike Tallulah, I've never had any experiences like this before." He chuckled. "Lucius seems to think your ancestor has adopted me."

"Hmmm." She placed her fingertips on his arm. "Look over there."

Across the river, half a dozen mule deer stared at them and chewed, their long ears twitching.

Their ears weren't the only thing trembling. His

cup shook, and she glanced at his face.

"Good thing that mug's almost empty. Why so jumpy, Jittery Jones?"

"What's with these cartoon nicknames? First it's Rooster McFusspot, now Jittery Jones." He forced a laugh. "What's next? Wiley Wolf?"

Truth be told, her proximity unnerved him. Her voice alone put his body on high alert. Her touch escalated his heart rate and breathing from normal to near fight or flight levels. The kiss yesterday had left him in a daze and every inch of his skin tingling. He wanted more, a whole lot more. At the moment, he fought the urge to throw Emma over his shoulder and drag her into his king-sized bed. He longed to bury his head between her quivering legs and lap at her until she shuddered screaming his name—just for starters. Visions of stroking her breasts and sucking at her nipples until they became rock hard and tender with his lavish devotions clouded his view of the river and demanded his attention. After that he planned to introduce her to his not-so-little friend Bronco, Jr. and take her for a long, hard ride. He looked forward to being her personal mustang, bucking in bed, out of bed, in the shower, up against the wall, over the desk, on the balcony, on his bike, alongside the river, and under the stars. And when they were done, exhausted by lovemaking, he'd kiss her scars and drive away the memories of the bear mauling and any other thoughts she had beyond wanting to start all over again. He shook his head to clear the testosterone haze and prayed his body's reactions to his lust filled fantasies weren't too obvious.

"Worried about the assignment, that's all." He

sipped his now cold cup of Joe. "We haven't heard from Bert. Remote viewing is assisted when it's accompanied by hard data, like aerial photography. That way I don't spend all day trying to figure out where to focus my energy, and I can get in and up close to the area of interest."

"You should be worried," she agreed. "There's a lot riding on this."

"Plus, Lucius has a lot of concerns about the quartet of stiffs staying at the hotel." At her raised eyebrows, he added, "The tourists. They seem like a bunch of uptight CPAs, but I have to agree with him, there's something off."

She nodded. "Tallulah took me aside this morning in their private office. Showed me their IDs, and the photos of the books. Gotta say the medical coding and billing books alongside the vintage spy craft manuals made me want to sing 'One of these things is not like the other.'"

"Exactly." His feline partner came bouncing up, a still wriggling rabbit in his mouth. "Aw, for me? You shouldn't have." The cat set the live animal at his feet, his paw on the hapless creature's neck. "Let him go and I'll get you some sausage. Is that a good trade?" Gaucho lifted his paw, and the stunned rabbit lay in front of them, his eyes bugging. "Good boy. Let's go in. He'll recover."

Emma blocked his path and put her hand up. "Stop, please, I need to say something." She took a deep breath and looked him straight in the eye. "I'm sorry I kissed you yesterday. It was completely inappropriate and unprofessional. It won't ever happen again."

As if to mirror the chill falling between them, a

gust of cool air swept off the river and into his heart. "Sure. Message received. Incident completely forgotten." He frowned and ground his teeth. "Now, if you don't mind, I hate cold flapjacks. I'm going to grab a bite to eat and get to work."

He whistled for Gaucho and took off for the hotel as if racing his cat, but in reality he had to get away from this woman who had charmed and captivated him and just now, crushed his hopes for any type of involvement outside of work. Actually, she'd just done him a huge favor. Bronco liked his job. If he screwed up an assignment, it was one thing, but if he screwed around with Bert's sister? He'd probably be a dead man.

****

Surprise and hurt had flashed in Bronco's eyes just before he shuttered his emotions and switched into the other persona, his cold, professional, ruthless double. As he retreated into the hotel, Emma wished she could recall the words from the air, pull them back into her mouth, and stuff them down her throat. Shoving her hands into the pockets of her denim jacket, she kicked at a rock and sent it sailing into the grasses.

Unprofessional? Inappropriate? Absolutely. *Unwanted?* Never. Whenever she was near Bronco, she wanted the man in a way that frightened her, made her worry she'd forget her vow to herself to bury her heart. She couldn't restore Jessica's leg, but she could use her head instead of her heart—and her pheromones—to guide her actions. Shit, this was a lot tougher than she thought it was going to be when she gave herself that pep talk last night. If his icy reaction to her apology was any indicator, she did the right thing. No need to make things any more complicated than they already were.

"Emma?" Hand on her lower back, Tallulah stood on the porch with Franny prancing at her feet. "Are you eating? Lucius made enough for ten people."

"Be right there."

Tallulah and Lucius had overcome a century of differences to be together and seemed to be blissfully happy in their marriage. How had they found their true mates in the face of these obstacles? Yes, she'd been there, watched them fight and fall in love and fight to stay in love. But what had made Tallulah toss aside her hesitation to take a leap of faith and go with the man from another era? She sighed. It didn't matter now. After effectively setting clear cut boundaries in the relationship, cutting off any romantic avenue of approach, Emma would think twice—maybe three and four times—before touching Bronco, much less kissing him again. And based on his response, she thought he'd probably do the same.

Emma entered the kitchen and found only Tallulah present, sliding eggs out of a frying pan onto a plate already occupied by a short stack and bacon. "Orange juice on the table, along with flatware and napkins. The boys are in the office, working on the computer, jabbering on the phone with Bert. Bronco took his food with him."

Between gulps of juice, Emma said, "Hope he doesn't touch the computer screen—or keyboard."

"Lucius ate earlier." Tallulah placed Emma's plate down. "My guess is he's doing the typing—one letter at a time."

"For someone who didn't see computers until a little over a year ago, he's doing well."

"Yes, he is." Tallulah traced a circle on the table top in the condensation from the juice decanter. "What about you, Emma. How are you doing?"

"Fine," she lied. "Why do you ask?"

"Oh, maybe because Beautiful Blackfeather is standing next to you, and she's frowning."

"For heaven's sake. That's not fair. You know I can't see her. Are you telling the truth or are you teasing me?"

"Not kidding. Oh, there she goes. Sign talking and pissed at you. Beautiful says she likes this guy, and you shouldn't be so fast to get rid of him. You're not getting any younger."

"Tell her I'm not going for two horses and a rifle."

"She heard you just fine. Now she's really angry, talking so fast I can barely keep up. Slow down, please, Beautiful." Tallulah nodded. "She says you're smart and beautiful in so many ways, but in the ways of the heart you're as stubborn as a government mule."

"Nice. Now I'm a mule." Emma shook her head. "Any other advice? Ow!" Emma grabbed her ear. "What was that?"

"She said to listen to your heart and your dreams." Blushing furiously, Tallulah shook her head. "No, I'm not telling her that."

"Now what?" Emma stared at her friend.

Covering her bright red face, Tallulah whispered, "She said he earned his horse name."

It took a moment for the meaning of the comment to sink in. "Ohmigod! I can't believe she said that."

"She may be dead, but she's not blind." Tallulah snorted in laughter.

Against her better judgement Emma started

giggling, too.

Holding a plate in one hand and a computer print-out in the other, Bronco chose that precise moment to walk into the kitchen. His gaze went from Emma to Tallulah, back to Emma. "Did I miss something?"

Coughing, Emma grabbed the glass of orange juice and chugged. Not only was her ancestor a powerful medicine woman, but she was trying to be a matchmaker from the other side, too. One glance at Bronco's cold expression told her that wasn't happening.

"No," she sputtered. "Got a piece of bacon stuck in my throat, that's all."

Tallulah took the dish and fork out of his hands and ran water in the sink.

"What do you have there?" Emma asked. "Is that from my brother?"

Eyebrow quirked, he gave her a long stare, then nodded. "It's an aerial view of the Neo-Nazi compound in northern Montana, four or five hours away from here by car. And it's worse than I thought." He placed four pieces of paper down on the table in front of her plate. "This—" he pointed—"is an electric plant. I'm guessing coal. From the steam, it appears to be operational. Those long, low buildings look like warehouses. And over here, those appear to be housing." He paused. "But the scariest part is this." He pointed to long white lines across the black and white photo. "These are runways—and there's a Christmas tree—where planes can park at forty-five degree angles and take off down the runway in fifteen second intervals. At the end here you can just make out a mole hole, the concrete bunker for the officers in command."

"Holy crap. It's the old Hawkhead Air Force base, one of the Strategic Air Command or SAC bomber bases. Shut down after the Cold War in the late sixties, early seventies. I read some shadow corporation bought it at a government auction for back taxes ten years ago. Caused quite a stir in the town next to it, then things seemed to settle down."

"Guess whoever bought it was biding his time, building up his army." He tapped a large building. "I bet this building next to the runway is where they create the parts and assemble the drones. I'm going to do a remote viewing, get a better look at the place so we can start to make a plan to get in there."

Coming up behind Bronco, Tallulah cleared her throat. "What about our businessmen? Any luck with their story?"

He turned his head and spoke over his shoulder. "The IDs are fake."

Tallulah gasped. "What do we do?"

"Right now, nothing. It's good you made color copies of the drivers' licenses. Bert's running those through a facial recognition program. He's going to call when he gets a hit."

"Honey," Lucius said as he strolled into the kitchen. "If those people try to harm a hair on your head, they will pay for it." He pointed at his leg. "Between the medicine stick and Old Betsy, my Colt Six-Shooter, we've got you covered. Plus, Bronco's going to look for them when he gets into his remote viewing routine."

Bronco looked at Emma, "Since Lucius is going to be occupied with guarding the house while I'm in my altered state, I need you to take notes while I talk.

Think you can handle that?"

"Yes, of course I can 'handle that'," she said testily. "I'm not illiterate."

"Just checking, making sure you're still on board."

Heat rose in her cheeks, but this time the source was anger, not attraction. "This is my mission, too, Bronco. Don't you dare forget."

"Message received," he snapped. "Over and out. Let's get going. We can use my room—unless you have an objection?"

"That's fine," she ground out between her teeth. "Do you plan to take Gaucho with us?"

"Not necessary."

"Good, because he and Franny are snoozing in a patch of sun over there," she barked. "They had a lot of sausages. Is that okay? Lucius can look after him while we work."

"Good," he snarled. "If I were any better, there'd be two of me."

Lucius put his fingers on his lips, and a dimple grew in his cheek.

Emma glared at him, "Not a word."

"I didn't say a thing, did I darlin'?" He turned to Tallulah. "But come to think of it, don't they sound like we did not too long ago?"

Tallulah poked him in the ribs. "This is not the time."

"I'm just sayin'," he protested and smirked.

"We have work to attend to in the office. The books won't keep themselves," Tallulah said as she dragged her husband out of the room.

Emma grabbed a notepad and pen from the kitchen counter and pointed to the door. "Lead the way. I'll be your scribe."

Bronco sauntered ahead of her, his altogether too cute butt in his tight jeans and Beautiful's comments reminding her of what she was missing in her life. Too late now, she'd closed that door good and tight, and he was unlikely to open it from the inside.

Chapter Nine

Bronco stomped up the steps and yanked the door open. The king-sized bed that he'd been day-dreaming about ravishing Emma in just a short while ago taunted him. This was a bad idea. Yes, he needed a quiet space and he needed a scribe. But this space and this secretary? Terrible idea. He turned on his heel and glared at Emma. This was all her fault. If she hadn't kissed him, he wouldn't be having all these fantasies.

"I think we should do this elsewhere," he growled. A floor away, Gaucho barked and gave him a mental jab. *Dammit.* Even the cat knew he was full of BS.

Emma shrugged. "It's your viewing. Tell me where you want to do this? Just so you know, Tallulah has some workmen fixing the furnace and the vents on the first floor today."

"That rules out the parlor and the entire first floor."

"And the maids are cleaning the other guest rooms," she added. "At least here you can put out the 'Privacy' sign and close the door. I can sit behind you, stay out of your view."

Was she completely oblivious to the implications of being alone in a bedroom with him? Was she that good at compartmentalizing her feelings and shutting down her emotions? With that impassive expression, he bet she'd be a good poker player. *Fine. Two can play at this game.*

"I use an eye mask and sound-proof head phones to decrease ambient light and noise."

"Great! You get set up and I'll be sitting over here on the side. Let me know when you're ready." She busied herself removing the nightstand from the side of the bed and dragging a wingback chair into the same corner. "Ready whenever you are."

He stalked over to the nightstand, pulled out a pouch and sat on the edge of the bed. The pillows were wrong. He got off the bed. Rearranged the bedding. Sat back down. Pulled his boots off, laid back, and realized he needed to pee. *Well damn.* He sat up and shook his head.

"Everything okay there, Fidgety Fred?"

"Enough with the cartoon names. I'm a grown man. That's completely unprofessional." Smothered laughter followed him when Bronco stomped into the bathroom and slammed the door. He used the toilet, washed his hands and face, and then looked into the mirror. An elderly woman with long black braids wearing a buckskin dress covered with elk teeth glared at him. *Beautiful Blackfeather.* Her hands moved, and although he didn't speak Plains Indian sign language, he understood she was not pleased with him. He threw his hands up and walked out the door.

"If I'm not mistaken, your feisty ancestor is not pleased with me." He described the apparition in the mirror. "I have no idea what I did, but she looks pissed."

"Don't blame me," Emma objected. "I can't see her or hear her. I have no idea what she's saying. We have a job to do. Can we just get to work, please?"

"You're right." He threw himself onto the bed,

opened the pouch and made quick work of putting on the sound-deadening ear covers and black eye mask, placed his hand on his diaphragm, and took deep slow breaths. Counting backward from one-hundred, he allowed his mind to go blank, floating free. When distracting thoughts arrived, he noted them without engaging them, and wiped an imaginary white board with an eraser. After a while, the bed and room fell away, and he was floating, moving to the latitude and longitude of the defunct Air Force base. When he saw the runways, he knew he was in the right location and began to swoop down toward the ground.

"I have the site," he intoned. "I see the Christmas tree. The runways are clear, no planes present. I'm doing a fly over. The roofs are red, blue, green, and brown. As I get lower, I see how decayed the housing is. It's a ghost town. Broken windows, boards off the side of houses. They look like a good stiff wind would knock them over." He rapidly scouted the residences. "No sign of life in these. I'm going to the center of the base."

He took a deep breath and dove down closer.

"Horse corrals, lots of horses—all different colors. What the hell do they need with a herd that size?" Barns, watering troughs, and hay feeders. He floated back to the horses, and got close enough to see the brand. "The Nazi SS bolt—of course. I should have known."

He rose and floated to the next area of activity.

"Mess hall. Lots of activity there, mostly women in black T-shirts with red, white, and blue shields on the front, swastika in the center." Long tables filled the huge room. How many people were they planning to feed here? "This place could hold a thousand people, easily."

A fair-haired woman waved good-bye and left the food hall. He followed her to a nearby building where children played on swing-sets. His stomach roiled at the thought of what poison these young minds were being fed. Two identical little tykes—they couldn't have been more than two years old—ran up to the blonde and hugged her knees. One at a time, she swung each of the children into the air and kissed their necks as each one threw their head back laughing. After she placed the second one on the ground, they grabbed her hands and skipped away. Grief grabbed his chest in an iron grip, and a lump filled his throat. The woman, so like his dearly departed mother, clearly cared for the boys. Love, not detestation, filled her face. How could this be? The love she showed her children contradicted the actions of the hate group she lived with. Couldn't she understand that people of other skin colors and religions loved their children, their families, too? How could any woman participate in such a perverse world?

"Families live here, too, not just soldiers. Women, children."

Pick-up trucks idled near a large outbuilding. "There's some kind of activity. Trucks, mostly old pick-ups, their beds filled with stuff...can't make out what it is. I need to get closer." He dropped to the ground and began walking toward one of the vehicles. "Tarps covering the cargo, I can just make out the shape of boxes." Movement caught his eye. "Forklift coming out, let's see what's in this thing. Must be a dozen men, all in camouflage, hanging around. They seem excited. Back-slapping."

He floated to the back of the crowd and spotted another officer. Bronco slipped alongside him. "Bald-headed guy in khaki uniform, looks like he might be an officer of some sort? No insignia. Jagged scar on his chin, bronze color skin, high cheekbones, swastika tattoo on the back of his left hand—wait—is that a feather tattooed on the side of his neck?

"Truck's sitting low to the ground. Must be a heavy load. Two underlings are untying the ropes keeping the desert camouflage tarp in place. They're pulling it back, exposing the cargo space. Everybody's giving a Nazi salute." He didn't need to hear them to know they were shouting "*Sieg heil!*" Using a crowbar, a minion ripped open one of the wooden boxes stamped with a well-known manufacturer's label, inducing a frenzy of salutes and back-slapping. "Oh, great. AT-4 shoulder mounted rocket launchers. One of the asshats is posing for a selfie. These guys love to brag. Wonder if he has a Facebook page? We can get on that later."

The crowd swarmed the boxes, tearing at them like a pack of wolves. Each one grabbed a weapon, some staggering under its weight, others lifting them above their heads like a boxing championship belt. "It's a feeding frenzy. Every one of these nutters has to have a chance playing with the toys. They are dangerous, but don't appear to be particularly organized. Who's in charge here?"

Almost as in answer, the crowd parted like the Red Sea, and a man in a Nazi officer's uniform—black peaked hat with a death's head, black jacket with red armband and black swastika in a white circle on his left arm strode through the minions. Black pants—jodhpurs really—tapered into jack boots. "I think the boss just showed up. Lightning bolts and an oak leaf cluster on his lapels—he's the *Reichsführer*, the leader."

All the other faces were sharp as photographs. He could have picked each one of those guys out of a line-up—except the one in the SS uniform. "That guy's face is a blur. I can't make out a single identifying characteristic." He tried to hover closer, but something pulsed, pushing him away and out of his remote viewing session.

He sat up, ripped his headphones and eye mask off, and turned on Emma, shouting, "Did you just do something?"

Emma stared at him, her mouth open, pen poised over the pad of paper on her knee. "I have no idea what you're talking about."

Dripping in sweat, he leaped out of the bed and strode into the bathroom. "Are you in here? What did you do? Why did you pull me out?"

Nothing appeared in the mirror, not even a pair of brown eyes.

Someone pounded at the door like a jackhammer. "Everything okay in there?"

Bronco yanked it open. Gaucho chirped in concern, stood, put his front paws on his thighs.

A red-faced Lucius gasped, "Your cat dragged me upstairs. Is there something wrong?"

Dazed and confused, Bronco petted the bobcat's head and rubbed his ears. "I—I don't know. Something strange just happened. This has never occurred before. A force of some kind—like a pulse of electricity or magnetism—just threw me out of my remote viewing session. Tossed me like a bunch of rags. The guy in the SS uniform. He knew I was there."

What the hell?

****

Emma snapped the notepad shut and rubbed her temples. This was scary stuff. Every fiber of her body screamed "Run away!" but her honor told her she had to continue on this path.

"You're drenched. Let's get you something to drink."

Lucius frowned. "You look terrible." He thundered down the steps ahead of them.

She grabbed Bronco's hand and led the glassy eyed man down the stairs into the cheerful kitchen.

Lucius passed an ice cold bottle to Bronco. "Sit down before you fall over. I'm gonna go check on Tallulah, make sure she didn't get any of those bad vibes."

Falling into a chair, Bronco chugged the liter of water. "This is a first. I've never been detected before."

"It sounded like a lot was going on. Crazy people generate a lot of negative energy. Maybe your mind pulled you out because it was too much for you? Maybe it had nothing to do with the guy in the SS uniform."

He glared at her. "Please."

"Just saying." She drummed her fingers on the wooden tabletop. "I never made it overseas, but many of those who do come back with Post Traumatic Stress Disorder, PTSD. You might have a form of it. Maybe something triggered an old memory?"

Bronco swallowed hard and sat across from her. "Perhaps."

She raised an eyebrow, "And?"

"There was a young woman with twins. She was very loving. Reminded me of my mother. She died last year. Cancer."

"I'm sorry for your loss. Your mother must have been a great lady."

"She was incredibly resilient. Overcame a lot of obstacles in her life, until the last one."

"Shitty disease." It came out a little more vehemently than intended. But, for her own reasons, Emma hated cancer, too. Her mother had died of one of the most treatable cancers, for God's sake. Her mother had hated going to doctors, hated having her female parts examined, even by a woman doctor. If only she'd gotten screened earlier, Emma would have had more time with her. Instead, at the age of ten, her mother was taken away from her. If not for her grandmother, who knew which relative would have raised her.

A look of surprise crossed his face. "You, too?"

"Lost my mother to cervical cancer."

"Sucks, doesn't it?"

"Yup. And grief has a lot of ways of showing up when least expected. Kinda sneaks up on you." She sipped her now tepid coffee. "I'll be braiding my hair and just like that, I'm a kid again, and it's my mother's hands, soft and gentle, stroking my head, repeating, 'Under and over, under and over' teaching me." She brushed a tear off her cheek. "Jeez. Here I go again."

He reached over and squeezed her hand. "I'm sorry for your loss. And, I'm sorry I was a jerk earlier. My ego—"

She turned her hand over, holding onto his larger one, enjoying the comfort of his warmth and maybe something more. "Ego, what ego?" She chuckled. "I think we both have enough to go around. I wasn't exactly a paragon of virtue. I'm sorry. I'll try to be easier to work with. This—stuff—it's all pretty overwhelming."

He nodded. "You got that right."

"By the way, the feather on the neck tattoo?"

"Yeah, I've never seen that before."

"I have." She relayed her training as a Marine recruiter. "Native Americans who have served prison time like to get those. If he served time, I'm guessing he came from out of state, because that's usually found in Texas, Arizona, and Missouri state prisons. Each feather stands for the commission of a crime against white society." She paused. "Of course, he may just be some idiot kid who doesn't know what it stands for."

"What the hell is he doing with a bunch of Neo-Nazis, much less as an officer?"

"White supremacists aren't the only ones who advocate for racial purity," she said pulling her hand back, but he held tight. Her heart lurched and stuttered. He just needed comforting. Nothing more. "There are some Native Americans who want to cut ties with the United States, bring back the old ways, and have their own country. They want independence, self-government. Sovereignty. Some of those kind of people could be attracted to the Nazis."

Disbelief etched in his face, Bronco asked, "And they really believe the Nazis would embrace them?"

"Remember, if it suits their purpose, the Nazis will do whatever they need to do. Means justifies the end. The enemy of my enemy is my friend and all that." She took a deep breath. "I have a little confession to make."

His brow quirked. "Oh?"

"Before I insisted on joining you on the mission, I did some research and became a card-carrying member of the Neo-Nazi Party."

"You did *what*? How is that even possible?"

"Well, if you go to their website, you will find an application form for Non-Aryans." She laughed at his open-mouthed expression. "Yes, even I can become a Nazi—not one that can vote, mind you, but I'm permitted to support them."

His face twisted with disgust. "You're joking. Why would you do such a thing?"

"Thought it might be helpful." She shrugged. "It was simple. All I had to do was give them a minimum of ten dollars and my affidavit that I wanted to become an official sympathizer for the Neo-Nazi Party and state that I'm in basic agreement with their aims and that a Neo-Nazi success will end the dishonesty and mistreatment that affects people of all races."

"I can't believe this."

"Nope, all true. There are even lots of photos on the Nazi website of Der Führer with Arabs, Asians, and, yes, even Jews. The poster child is a *mischlinge*, a mixed blood, half-Jewish military man, Field Marshall Edhard Milch. He had a Jewish father and an Aryan mother. Adolf Hitler liked him so much, he had him reclassified as Aryan."

"This is all so messed up. The world is turning upside down, I swear." He rubbed his temple with his free hand. "I have a splitting headache."

"You've got a lot going on," she said in a low voice. "This is a stressful assignment. No one knows that better than I do."

"No, this is different. I feel hungover, without having a drop of booze."

"Did I hear you say you needed an espresso?"

Lucius strode into the kitchen. "You are in luck, I was just getting one for me, happy to make one for you." He glanced down at their hands and smiled. "Did I interrupt something?"

Bronco pulled his hand away, and Emma immediately missed his touch. She wondered what it would be like to be with him, skin to skin, head to toe. Would they be separate or one? She shook her head. *No point even going there.*

"Espresso sounds good to me, too," she said. "We've had a hell of a day—and it's not even lunch. Got any aspirin in the house? My friend here has a doozy of a migraine."

"I sure do." He reached into a cabinet, pulled out a green and white bottle, and handed it to her. "Any word on those tourists?" Lucius asked as he ground coffee and twisted knobs.

"I haven't checked my phone all morning," Bronco said. "Five missed calls. How did that happen?" Pressing buttons, he put the cell up to his ear.

"Service is pretty spotty out here." Lucius placed two steaming cups on the table along with a plate of fresh homemade oatmeal cookies. "My wife's in a baking mood today. Got all tuckered out, now she's taking a nap. Wonder if that means anything about the baby?"

"My grandmother said if a pregnant woman starts hanging curtains or cleaning, that means it's gonna happen soon. The nesting instinct kicking in." Emma bit into a caramelized raisin and moaned. "These are my favorite."

Bronco put the phone down and reached for a sweet. "Maybe my blood sugar is too low."

"Were the voicemails related to the case?"

"Cases." He chewed thoughtfully, then dipped the baked crescent in the tiny cup. "The tourists are wanted robbers. Bert found them using facial recognition."

Lucius fell into a chair. "You don't say. They sure don't look like the violent type."

"White collar crime. These four have been embezzling from a large medical insurance company in Chicago called BestHealth." He grinned. "And they really are accountants. So, we nailed that. They've been at this for a while. But they got greedy and dumb, their goals exceeded their grasping hands."

Fascinated by criminals, especially stupid ones, Emma asked, "How'd they do it?"

"Dummy medical corporations. They set up clinics in the poor parts of Chicago and employed a shady physician to order blood tests, X-rays, that sort of thing that can be done on location, even a crappy one." He sipped his coffee.

"BestHealth is the largest provider of insurance for the elderly, poor, and disabled in Illinois. A huge corporation. Since these guys worked for BestHealth and had access to all their billing information, they knew who was covered by the company. They recruited insurance recipients to participate in phony medical tests. The patients received ten percent of what BestHealth paid. So if BestHealth paid one hundred dollars for a blood test, the patient received ten dollars and the crooks got ninety."

"How long have they been doing this?"

"As far as the feds can tell, it's been going on for seven years, maybe longer. On the one hand, they were smart to set up dummy corporations. On the other hand, they were stupid and misjudged the people they hired to pull it off."

Emma reached for another cookie. The hell with the calories, she'd skip lunch. "What happened?"

"Never underestimate the power of a woman scorned. Seems the sleazy doctor promised the receptionist he was going to leave his wife right after he got a big payout from our buddies, the CPAs. He told her he was going to marry her." He laughed. "Instead, he went to Reno and returned with a divorce—and a different wife. Not the receptionist."

Emma spewed coffee and couldn't speak because she was laughing too hard.

Lucius choked out, "Hot damn, that was dumb."

"But wait, there's more."

"No." Emma slapped the table. "Stop."

"The reason your guests have been so cagey with you about fishing guides is because they've been driving around with a realtor, looking for a location for a new clinic. They figured if they moved out of town and changed their names, all would be forgotten. And they might have gotten away with it. Thanks to you, Lucius, they are currently under arrest."

"Whoo-hoo," Emma whooped. "Lucius for county sheriff. You and Otterlegs can be a team."

"Bert told me they're going to be guests of the Yellowstone County Detention Center."

"Oh, I know that place. I hope they like the accommodations. A bit different from Hotel LaBelle." Lucius snickered. "When I was there, they were over-crowded, had three-hundred more inmates than they were supposed to have. The roof was leaking, the toilets weren't much better than outhouses, and there were no

solitary cells. Even the women's areas were full up—
female inmates were sleeping on portable beds in the
day room. And the smells." He shuddered. "I still have
nightmares about the stench in that place."

"I seem to recall you said the food was good,"
Emma smirked. "Powdered eggs and stale bread."

"Nice company, too." Lucius guffawed. "The
gangs will welcome them with open arms."

"A job well done." Emma clapped him on the back.
"But you said cases."

"Wait a minute. What were all the spy books
about? If they were paper thieves, not real robbers,
what were they going to do with that stuff?"

"You won't believe this." Bronco smiled. "The one
who drank too much, I think his name was Mark?"

Lucius nodded. "That would be the one."

"Seems he fancies himself the next best-selling
male adventure novelist. He has self-published ten
books, some of which have the lovely titles of *The Spy
Who Came in from the Heat, Silver Finger, Doctor
Maybe, Wunderball,* and, my favorite, *The Alien Who
Loved Me.* As I suggested, those spy craft books were
research for his next thriller."

Lucius snorted. "I can't wait to tell Tallulah when
she gets up from her nap."

"Come back a minute," Emma insisted. "Did Bert
have intel for us on the Nazis?"

"Yes." Bronco nodded. "Not sure what I think of it.
Seems the FBI has a guy in deep undercover with them.
Been there for a couple of years. They won't tell us
who, of course."

"Does that mean we're out?" Emma wondered
what would happen to the horses, eagles, buffalo—who

would be their protectors?

"Bert still wants us to go in, feels the other agency is playing it too close to the vest. Telling him it's only horses and eagles, not humans, so not terrorism."

He drummed his fingers on the table—again. Emma was tempted to call him Fidgety Fred once more, but held her tongue. "These crazies are escalating. It's only a matter of time before they go after people, maybe even hospitals or schools."

Bronco nodded. "Bert agrees. Homeland outranks all the other alphabet soup agencies, so he has the upper hand. Even if he didn't have the upper hand, we're a clandestine agency, so the rules aren't quite the same for us. He said, as of this moment, unless we hear otherwise, we should still go in."

Cotton-mouthed, she asked, "What do you want me to do? What's the plan?"

Bronco stood, got down on one knee, and said, "Emma Horserider, will you marry me?"

Chapter Ten

Emma burst out laughing, and Bronco's dismayed expression made her snort. "Ohmigod, where is Tallulah when we need her? Lucius, go wake your wife up and tell her to get down here. Beautiful Blackfeather needs her for this special moment."

"She did ask me to wake her in an hour." Lucius ambled out of the room, mumbling, "I knew they were sweet on each other…"

Standing with a sheepish expression on his face, Bronco stood and rubbed the back of his neck. "Sorry for the surprise. It just occurred to me that it would make a better cover if we posed as a married couple."

"Yes, yes, I understand completely." She wiped tears of mirth from her cheek. "The problem is, my ancestor has been, shall we say, riding me like a stubborn mule, telling Tallulah I wasn't getting any younger, and I needed to get hitched."

"Oh jeez." He glanced around the kitchen. "Is she here now? I don't see her."

"I have no idea. I can't see or hear her, remember?" Emma shook her head. "You are in trouble now, my friend. You had better find some horses and a couple of rifles soon, or she's gonna be all over you."

"How about we go out shopping today? Find cheap wedding bands? Take some photos of the two of us? We can send them to Bert so he can get one of our master forgers to create our wedding day, at the same time he gives us a wedding certificate. I'm thinking Vegas."

"Oh, yes, perfect," Emma chortled. "With an Elvis impersonator as the chaplain, please, pretty please? That's my dream wedding."

"Consider it done."

"There's just one thing."

"What?"

"I have to keep my maiden name, the one I put on the Neo-Nazi sympathizer application."

"Horserider?"

"No, that's much too tame." She grinned. "Emma Bearkiller. And if they ask, I've got the scars to prove it."

"Damn, you're good." He shook his head, "That's a great cover. We need to add another layer now and make sure everyone in this area knows we're a couple. Since they're only half a day's drive away from us, my guess is they do some local recruiting. Just in case they've got some spies hanging around Billings, let's go find some rings, shall we?"

Tallulah stood in the doorway, her glowing face wreathed in smiles. "They said love at first sight wasn't real. Now look at you two."

Emma rolled her eyes at her friend so hard, she thought they'd snap out of her head. "It's a sham marriage, for our cover. Didn't Lucius tell you?"

"Beautiful is so happy, she's crying. She wants to know when you're having the wedding feast and what you'll be wearing. She wants you to put on the buckskin and elk teeth dress, the one you have in your closet and have been saving for your—"

"Shut up!" Emma rushed to put her hands over her friend's mouth. "Do you have to repeat everything she says?"

Something pulled on her ear.

"She's not happy with you," Tallulah muttered through Emma's fingers.

Taking her hand away, Emma said, "We're going into town, getting rings and other stuff. Need anything?

Tallulah shook her head and whispered, "You'd better not come back without a ring on your finger."

Emma grabbed Bronco's arm. "C'mon, we've got a wedding to plan and some phone calls to make without nosy relatives butting in."

"Ready whenever you are." Bronco led the way out the front door. "Truck or bike?"

She chuckled. "Sure your butt's ready for the ride?"

"Thanks to your yarrow tea, yes."

"Then let's take the bike. I have a helmet in my truck."

Amazement crossed his face. "You ride?"

"I've been known to pop a wheelie or two."

His eyes narrowed. "You taught Jimmy Two-Toes, didn't you?"

"Maybe." She shrugged. "Not that different from riding a horse—an iron one."

He shook his head. "You are one surprise after another."

"No. I'm a riddle, wrapped in a mystery—"

"Inside an enigma," he finished. "One of my favorite Churchill quotes."

"Me, too," she said snapping her helmet into place and wriggling into a well-worn black leather jacket decorated with fringes and feather patterns. "Now let's see how she rides."

He stared at her a beat too long, his mouth open in an O of surprise.

Her heart stuttered at the intensity of his unshuttered gaze, and lust sparked between her denim-clad thighs. *Get a hold of yourself.* "Ride with your mouth open like that, you're gonna catch a lot of flies."

Shaking his head, he pulled his helmet off the back seat. "You want a ride, you're gonna get a hell of a ride."

"Ooo, I'm so afraid." She shimmied her shoulders. "Bring it."

He lifted the helmet. "Okay, fender fluff."

She slugged his arm. "Better not call me that undercover."

"No, I'll call you worse. Otherwise, we won't be believable. Now let me get my lid on, so we can get engaged." He snapped his helmet, and the engine started with one-kick. "Ready to rock and roll, Ol' Lady?"

Snorting at the term of endearment, Emma threw her leg over the passenger seat—what little there was of it—of the rumbling machine. Was it just the vibrations of the growling metal beast that were setting explosions off in her core? Or was it the fact that she had a good reason to wrap her arms around Bronco's waist and hold on tight. No back rest or sissy bar meant nothing to catch her if he popped a wheelie to prove his point or—

"Holy sh—" She grabbed onto him for dear life and shrieked with laughter as he pulled a one-eighty and rocketed out of the driveway, onto the asphalt highway, and back into her heart. *Dear God, how she loved an inked-up wild man on a bike.* As the road hummed beneath their feet and the engine throbbed, she hugged this hard bodied man, put aside worries and fears about the upcoming days, and allowed herself, just this once, to enjoy the ride.

****

Bronco savored how tightly Emma wrapped her arms around him when he surprised her with his bike trick—but she surprise him when she lay her head on his back and continued to hold him tighter than necessary. His heart sputtered like a bike in dire need of a tune-up. Since when did he get this agitated over a woman? *Never.* He'd seen the effect of undercover work on enough marriages to know not to go down that aisle. The long hours, not knowing where your spouse was, the jealousies when women worked an operation with a male partner. His rule had always been no entanglements.

Now all he could think about was entanglements— under the sheets, in the shower, and yes, even in a Vegas wedding chapel with an Elvis impersonator. A writer for a bride's magazine would have a heyday with all his fantasies. No. He had to pull those hormone-laced cobwebs off his brain and clean up his mind. This was strictly business, and he was going to keep it that way. As soon as they got off the bike, he would make sure they were on the same page. No need to have her thinking he was *really* interested in marrying her.

He pulled into an upscale mall near the heart of Billings and parked the bike. She dismounted, pulled her helmet off, and shook out her long raven black hair. Laughing, she looked up at him with a wide smile that went up to her eyes and crinkled her face. "I haven't

121

had that much fun on a bike since I was at Camp Pendleton and dated a guy with the Mongols."

"You what?" Just when he thought she couldn't surprise him anymore, she pulled yet another cat out of the bag. "You dated a one-percenter?"

"Well, he did have that outlaw patch, but I kinda doubt he killed anyone. Although he did have some especially scary-looking dudes in his club." She quirked an eyebrow, "Jealous?"

"No. I was just, er, surprised," he said attempting to erase the deer-in-the-headlights look he was sure he had on his face. Alongside the Hell's Angels, the Mongols was one of the most notorious MCs, or Motorcycle Clubs, in the country. That club had a history of drug trafficking, motorcycle theft, and conspiracy to commit murder. The fact that a Mongols MC member shot and killed the President of the Hell's Angels in 2008 sealed their badass reputation in history forever. "I'm curious—how did that fit with you being a Marine?"

"Actually, there are a lot of leathernecks in Motorcycle Clubs. When I became a recruiter, the guy who was leaving the position I took invited me to a party at his local club. That's where I met Danny." She looked down. "He was cute in a very bad boy way."

"He sounds great." *Dammit.* Even he knew he sounded jealous. "What happened?"

"Oh, the usual. Boy meets girl, boy meets another girl, girl meets another boy…"

"So he dumped you?"

"Yes," she said in a low voice. "For a bleached blonde with a bigger bra size and a lower IQ. Also, he didn't like it when I decked him for calling me 'my bitch.'"

"I will make a note of it and promise never to call you that." He shook his head. "His loss." And a surge of happiness filled his chest. *My gain.* "Let's go find some rings. Nothing too fancy, but just flashy enough so they don't look like they came out of a gumball machine."

"Ah, no secret decoder rings for you, I see." She grabbed his free hand and dragged him into the entrance. "Come on. I know just the place. Family business, very classy and affordable. I know the owner."

"Of course you do. You know everyone in Billings."

She flashed him a heart-melting grin. "Not really, I don't know the out of town students at the university."

"Well, maybe you need to rectify that."

"Another day."

A small midday crowd wandered in and out of stores. Some window shopped, others raced to get to the food court on lunch break. The stone and wood décor, clearly a recent renovation, added a high-class touch to the array of brand name stores. If you needed anything, even a movie, this was the place to go.

"Enigma Fine Jewelry," he said when they arrived at the store. "Why am I not surprised?"

"They call it that because it's a mystery how they produce all these custom pieces and keep their prices reasonable," she said pointing at the sale sign. "This is what we want. Forty-percent off everything works for me."

"You know that's because jewelry is already marked up two-hundred percent, right?"

"Buzzkill."

A distinguished looking gentleman with graying temples and tortoise shell glasses emerged from behind another counter. "May I help you—oh, Emma, it's you. So good to see you."

"Hi Mr. Ernest, this is my fiancé, Brandon."

He flinched at the sound of his real name. Why had she done that?

The older man extended his hand. "Nice to meet you, Brandon."

Bronco offered a firm shake in return. "Likewise. My bride-to-be has spoken highly of this store."

"We carry a number of Stephanie's designer handbags and accessories." He looked at Bronco brightly, his cheeks turning slightly pink as he spoke Stephanie's name. "I trust you're familiar with her work?"

Oh, Steph was a piece of work, all right. He gave a polite smile and nodded. "I've heard of it, haven't had the pleasure of seeing it—"

"We're not here for that, Mr. Ernest," Emma broke in. "We're in a bit of a hurry. Heading to Vegas for a wedding chapel with an Elvis impersonator. We need a set of wedding bands. Something simple, but appropriate."

He touched his chin and looked pensive. "I wonder why Stephanie never mentioned this to me."

"Because I didn't know!" Stephanie flew out of the back room and hugged Emma, lifting her off her feet. "Why didn't you call me? We can go trousseau shopping together. I'll be your Maid of Honor. Damn, girl, you caught him!"

His face hurting with a grin plastered in place,

Bronco mentally smacked his head. How did Stephanie show up in time to hear half a conversation and launch herself into the middle of it? The timing was so bad, it was almost ludicrous. Almost.

Speaking to her cousin in low tones only Stephanie could hear, Emma finally extricated herself and spoke in a louder voice. "We wanted to tell everyone at the same time, back at the hotel. What do you suggest? Your taste is better than mine."

Steph waved a hand at Bronco, "Pfft. Your taste is just fine. Look at this man. Gorgeous."

She winked at him. "With a dash of danger on the side. Mmm, mmm, mmm."

"Steph?" Emma pleaded. "In my lifetime, please?"

"Okay, forget all those diamonds, emeralds, rubies, and sapphires." Steph slid a manicured finger across the glass counter, stopped and tapped over a specific set. "Mr. Ernest, could we please see these?"

"Of course." He pulled a set of keys out of his pocket and slid open the back of the case. Placing a velvet display board on top of the glass, he set the rings on the black surface. "Exquisite."

Stephanie oohed and ahhed and gave a ten minute dissertation on why these rings symbolized the history of this woman and her connection to the land, and the rocky power of this *fabulous* man. She sounded like she was about to say, "I now pronounce you man and wife."

Against his better judgment, Bronco agreed with Stephanie. The Black Hills gold rings with the signature leaves and pink, yellow and white gold *were* perfect. Twice as wide as the woman's, the man's band fit his left hand without any need for adjustment. Her ring needed to be enlarged, something Mr. Ernest said he could do easily in the store, on the spot.

"Well, honey," Bronco said squeezing her shoulder and kissing the top of her silken head. "What do you say?"

"Yes!" She stood on her tiptoes, wrapped her fingers in his hair and pulled him in for a hard, hot kiss. She whispered, "How's this for a good act?"

His lips and hips flared with passion, and he pulled her close, pressing against her in a suggestive manner. "Two can play this game," he whispered and licked her lower lip. Her breath hitched, and her tongue darted into his mouth in response.

"Oh. My. God. You have *got* to be kidding me."

Bronco unhooked from his faux fiancée. There in the entrance to the store stood a red-faced, out of uniform Tommy Otterlegs, with his fists on his hips. In all his bantam glory, he looked like he was about to dig at the barnyard dirt and pick a fight.

Otterlegs stomped over to Bronco and poked him on his chest. "You get your hands off this woman, you, you, reprobate!"

"What a big word for such a little man," Bronco said pushing Otterlegs stubby finger aside. "Take a hike, my friend."

"I'm not your friend, and *you're* not about to marry this woman. You aren't worthy of Emma Horserider." Otterlegs reached over to pull at her hand. "Emma, please, you're not using your head. You're thinking with your—"

"Tommy!" Emma shook him off. "This is none of your business."

"As a sworn officer of the law, it is my *business* to serve and protect the good people of Billings,

Montana." He puffed up his chest. "I am saving you from a terrible mistake. This man is a criminal."

Bronco snorted, "Says who, short stuff?"

"Says ViCAP, the Violent Criminal Apprehension Program. You have a rap sheet as long as your"—he looked Bronco up and down—"legs."

Bronco shook his head slowly. *How could he get this stupid little man to shut up?* This was supposed to be a quick trip, an in and out of the mall, followed by some digital photos for the document division in D.C. How had everything gone sideways? Running into Stephanie was one thing. She sold her designer duds here. But Otterlegs? "Have you been following us?"

Otterlegs crossed his arms over his chest. "I have a right—no—an obligation to be aware of suspicious people in my town. You are a person of interest."

"So you're saying there was a crime and you think I have something to do with it?"

"In a manner of speaking." Otterlegs bobbed his head. "Yes."

"Can you tell me the nature of this crime? Did I steal something—or *someone*?"

Otterlegs turned beet red. "You, sir, are a fraud. I know you have a deep secret and a terrible history. I'm the man who is going to reveal you for the con artist that you are. You will not involve this woman in your crimes. I will not allow it."

Bronco struggled to keep from laughing. The little twerp had nailed him, he just didn't know it. *Jiminy cricket.* Too dangerous to bring into the real story, too loose of a cannon to be trusted, the guy had to be shut down. Bronco stroked the side of his nose with his finger, "Ya know, those are fighting words."

The short man put his fists up. "Let's take this outside, you outlaw."

Bronco smiled and peeled Emma's grip from his bicep, and gave a deep bow. "Rooster McFusspot, at your service. Let us adjourn. "

He turned and walked right into Stephanie. "Let me handle this one." She wheeled on Otterlegs. "Listen, Mr. Tommy Otterlegs. If we always got into fights over who we want to love us, I would be a bruised mess." She towered over the little man by at least eighteen inches and tapped the top of his head. "When we were in high school, you were my heartthrob."

Otterlegs visibly blanched. "Steph—"

"You were so feisty, such a fighter. I love that when you entered the Indian relay races and people gave you crap because you were so small, you not only won, you won three years in a row. I can still see you, shirtless, sweaty, grabbing the horses, becoming one with those stallions—well, I digress." She fanned herself.

Otterlegs studied his feet, his hands flexing and unflexing into fists. "He's a bad guy, Steph."

"I get it. You want to protect her." Steph patted his head. "I wanted to protect you, too. We were best friends, remember? I looked out for you. Kept the other boys from stuffing you into lockers or hanging you on coat hooks—or worse."

Tommy ground out, "Stop, please, just stop talking."

"When I came out, I told you first. And you, you supported me. Told people to shut up, leave me alone. Even stood up to that jackass on the basketball team— and he was taller than me." She wiped a tear off her cheek. "I loved you for that, Tommy. You are a brave, handsome, smart man. I know you can't ever love me back the way I love you. The point is, we don't always get what, or who we want. You need to let go, just like I let you go, Tommy. Please."

Otterlegs blew out a long hard breath, threw his hands up in the air, and stomped out of the store. Bronco shook his head. "You're a Twerp Whisperer, Steph. Thanks for defusing the little hand grenade." Despite his words, however, he didn't think they'd seen the last of the inquisitive little man.

Chapter Eleven

Emma dragged Stephanie into a quiet nook outside the store. "Thanks for doing that. You saved Tommy from losing more than his high school secrets. I need you to keep an eye on him for us. Can you do that?"

Steph twirled her long hair and narrowed her eyes. "Why? You afraid he'll follow you to Vegas? Hell, I'll go with you, be your bodyguard."

"Yes. No. You can't come." Emma blew out a long breath. "Please, trust me when I tell you this is very important to me."

"Honey, a girl's wedding should be special. An Elvis impersonator? *Really?* I don't understand the rush. You know the clan is going to be put out if they can't throw a big feast for you and Handsome."

"If everything goes well, you and the entire Crow Nation can throw a party for us." Emma grabbed Steph's hands in hers, "I can't tell you everything, but trust me when I say it's *critical* for Tommy to stay away from us. Use your charms, tackle him if you must, but don't let that man follow us."

"I promise to keep an eye on him," Steph said. "You're scaring me. Whatever you are doing, please come home safely—with that lovely beefcake, eye candy of a man."

Emma hugged her cousin. "Who knows, maybe Tommy will come around."

"GFM—Gay For Me?" Steph shook her head. "That only happens in romance novels, my darling."

Arm in arm, Emma and Steph strolled back into the store. Steph made a show of handing her cousin over to Bronco. "When the preacher says, 'Who gives this woman' think of me."

After settling up the bill with Mr. Ernest and hugging Stephanie goodbye, Emma pulled Bronco through the mall to the portrait photography boutique, Glam-More.

Eying the purple neon sign, Bronco asked, "Is this the only place in town?"

"It's the closest and the quickest for what we need." She strolled over to the counter and told the teenager with the puce hair and sparkling nose ring they needed the wedding package.

"Of courth." A flash of a steel ball confirmed the tongue piercing as the source of the girl's lisp. "We have theveral." Pointing to a tablet, she swiped left. "Thith is the hippie, flowerth in the hair package." A woman in a rainbow sundress holding a posy of daisies looked adoringly at her beau, a bearded man in a matching T-shirt and bell-bottom trousers.

Emma quirked a brow at Bronco. He shook his head no.

"What else do you have?"

"Medieval Knighth." A buxom lass with her breasts spilling out of a burgundy tasseled gown wearing an elaborate headdress gazed at a chubby fellow who wore a white shirt with billowing sleeves, a black cape and a sword. "Very popular."

"Not my style," Bronco said and rolled his eyes at Emma.

"Hunting?" Man and wife stood side by side, he in a classic camouflage deer hunter outfit, she in a camouflage wedding dress, each armed with what appeared to be authentic Weatherby deer hunting rifles. "They brought their own gunth."

If there had been a dozen horses in the photo, the bride price would have been complete, Emma thought. "Very tempting, but not quite right."

The girl kept swiping. "Cheerleader and team captain?" The teal and orange uniforms brought flashbacks of Johnny Blackwolf, her high school crush and that awful night. Jessica's screams mingled with the bear's roars. Emma shook her head so hard to dispel the sounds and images, she got dizzy.

Breathing deeply, she focused on the salesgirl who pointed to an image of a couple in black leather. The woman wore thigh high boots, fishnet stockings and a corset. She held a black flogger in her hand poised over a man's exposed buttocks, as if about to strike him. "Dominatrix and thubmithive?"

Bronco covered his mouth with his elbow and coughed convulsively.

The teenager frowned, "You okay? Want a drink of water?"

He shook his head and wiped his eyes, "All choked up about the big day."

Emma discreetly kicked his shin, "As you can see—" she lifted her helmet—"we're really into bikes. Do you have a package for that? Say with Vegas wedding chapel backdrop?"

A huge grin creased the girl's face. "Why didn't you thay tho to begin with?" She waved them into the studio. "Come in back." They stepped past dressing tables outlined in light-bulbs, make-up kits, a multicolor array of wigs on stands and rolling coat racks of one-size-fits all costumes with long cords dangling down in the back for easy on and off. She paused in front of a door, as if re-considering. "Did you want me to do your hair and make-up?"

Emma shook her head. "Nope. What you see is what you get with me."

The girl nodded, flipped a light on in a darkened room, and pointed to a large green screen. "We're going to do it with a computer. Go over there."

Rummaging in a nearby plastic bin, she retrieved a silk nosegay and handed it to Emma. "Your flowerth." Then she pinned a white carnation boutonniere on Bronco's denim cut and maneuvered him into position. "Don't move." She placed Emma in front of him. Stepping back the young woman surveyed her subjects, then pointed at Emma. "Hold the flowerth up higher, like you're thmelling them."

The girl ran to the front of the room and picked up a digital camera.

Emma began to giggle, and Bronco chuckled. As the receptionist/stylist/photographer flashed her digital camera repeatedly and yelled, "Thmile! Be happy!" their chuckles turned to outright guffaws. Knees buckling, Emma could barely stay upright for the shoot.

"Done." The girl grinned and gave them the thumbs up as she left the room. "Grab a water bottle while I work."

Emma reached up to unpin the fake carnation, and he caught her hand. "You really should smile more. You're quite beautiful when you do."

A flush warmed her face and neck. "We're not on

camera now. You can stop faking."

He stroked her cheek as if she were a quivering horse that needed calming. "Not pretending."

"Why, Mr. Bronco, whatever shall I do with you?" She gazed into his eyes, half-worried he'd morph into the monster with the flat affect, the one that scared the bejeezus out of her in the truck. Instead, to her surprise, he regarded her with a mixture of sorrow and longing—which almost frightened her more than his killer persona—almost, but not quite. If she'd been a teenager, she would have said she heard her heart melting. She swallowed hard to push the confusing emotions down, the words away from her lips, away from an untimely confession that maybe, perhaps, perchance, she fancied something more than a professional relationship.

"Here we are." The girl reappeared with her ever-present tablet. "Check it out."

There they were, indeed. She had placed the couple in front of an Elvis impersonator decked out in a white jump suit covered in rhinestones. Two big metal choppers covered in white flowers flanked them on either side. And the expressions on their faces? Either Bronco and she were the best actors in Montana, or the girl with the pierced nose had sniffed out a chemical signal that alerted her and her camera to record the non-verbal communication between the two. For all intents and purposes, the couple in the photo getting hitched in the chapel of love by the King was truly, madly, deeply in love. And just looking at the photos made Emma's eyes well up. Too bad it was all a sham.

****

Bronco paid cash for the digital collection on a

DVD, thanked the girl for her time, and slid her a fifty-dollar tip when Emma wasn't watching. He'd had so much fun today, it should be illegal. As they exited the mall, he whistled Wagner's Bridal Chorus.

Emma shot him a cutting look, "That's enough."

"Really? I thought you'd enjoy hearing your wedding music, maybe start practicing throwing the bouquet—" He dodged a fist aimed at his chin. "What did I do?"

"Nothing," she grumbled. "Let's just get this show on the road."

Her mood had gone from sunny and happy to glum and annoyed. "What's up with you?"

"I'm worried about getting out of town before Tommy has a chance to change his mind and starts trailing us again."

"You have a point there." He duck walked the bike backward, out of the parking spot. "When do you propose we leave?"

"You have to send those pix to Bert, right? Get whatever last minute info we can. We're going to be off the grid." She paused in the process of putting her helmet back on. "I wish we had a satellite phone."

"Your wish is my command." He grinned. "As soon as we started down this path, I asked Bert to have one over-nighted to the hotel. Should be there today, I hope."

A look of relief crossed her face along with a tentative smile. "Great minds. We'll also need to load your bike onto my pick-up truck. I have a ramp, a wheel chock, and tie downs. I'll need your help taking the tail gate off, so we don't fold my old truck like a taco—and break your bike."

He kick started the engine and shouted over the noise. "You've been thinking about this a lot, haven't you?"

"Marines don't like to go into battle unprepared." She hopped onto the passenger seat and wrapped her arms around his waist. He liked how Emma leaned against his back. A mental image of spooning in bed with her naked leaped into his mind and burned itself into his retinas. Good thing they were just *pretending* to be interested in each other, otherwise he could really get in over his head.

A short thirty-minute ride later, he pulled onto the driveway to the hotel. The felonious accountants' vehicles still sat in the parking area, awaiting impounding by the sheriff's department. The wheels of justice would grind their way out here—eventually. Parking alongside Emma's truck, he flipped the kickstand down and removed his helmet.

"About time you got here," Tallulah yelled. She stood on the porch, shielding her eyes from the sun. "Beautiful has been quite agitated." She stepped to the side and pointed to an empty rocking chair swaying back and forth at a furious pace.

"Great," Emma muttered. "As if we didn't have enough to deal with, my dead ancestor is pissed off."

Bronco led the way up the stairs, Emma one step behind.

"And the problem is?"

Tallulah looked at the chair and said, "I know, I know, hold on." She latched onto Emma's left hand and stared at her fingers. "Where is it?"

"Hold on." Bronco reached into his pocket. "Got it right here." He opened the black velvet case and held it toward the rocker. He couldn't see anyone in the chair, but that didn't mean he was a nonbeliever. "See. Wedding bands."

The chair stopped moving, and an invisible iron grip clenched his wrist. His hand and the box turned this way and that, glinting in the fading light.

"She's seems to like them," Tallulah said in a soft voice. "You happy now?"

All eyes focused on the space in front of Bronco, waiting for some sign of satisfaction. His hand fell without warning, and he nearly dropped the rings. "Now what?"

Tallulah laughed. "She wants to know where the horses and rifles are."

"I'll get right on that," Bronco said with a shake of his head. "Tell her she drives a hard bargain."

"She can hear you just fine," Tallulah said. "She said you're getting a valuable woman. Emma's worth a case of rifles and a herd of horses."

He glanced at the woman in question. Despite her attempts to duck her head and shield her face with her long hair, he could see a blush bloom on her cheeks.

Husky voiced, she finally spoke, "Tell my ancestor she's embarrassing me in front of my man. He has given me more than the required bride price. He makes me happy."

Stunned into silence, he mulled over the words she'd just uttered. Was it part of her act to keep the peace with Beautiful? Or did she really mean them? When was the last time he had made someone happy? He'd bedded a lot of women, and they all seemed to enjoy their time with him. Some hung around longer, especially when he'd been undercover. Over time, each of the fender bunnies had wandered off to find a better ride, or a man with fewer secrets. The last time a woman had told him he had made her happy, he'd almost killed someone.

He'd been deep undercover for the ATFE. After surviving his prospective member time, a miracle in and of itself, he'd been made a full member by one of the baddest clubs of all time. With his cover as a debt collector who worked as an enforcer for a Vegas crime boss, the club had decided he'd make a great bodyguard and enforcer. Most of the time, all he had to do was show up with a snarl, a bad attitude, and his metal baseball bat, and the transgressor in question gave up anything of value—drugs, guns, money—and in the last case he worked humans. Nearly wetting his pants when Bronco appeared at his door flanked by two of his club brothers, the meth dealer in question had quickly offered up his trafficked wares.

Unlocking a dark closet that reeked of human waste, the sweating chemist dragged out a terrified woman and twin girls. Clearly under the influence of his own brew, the meth cooker chortled, "Lookie here, I've got you a three-fer. I was gonna sell the little girls, save the mother for me and my crew. But, I'm feeling generous today. They're all yours—" The maggot never finished his sentence. Bronco's bat hit a home run into the man's teeth—and head.

His brothers at arms tried to peel Bronco off the crumpled piece of excrement, but he was not having it. Sirens shrieked in the distance, and the men at his side went up in smoke. Panting, he looked down at his blood-spattered pants. As if coming out of a fugue state, he realized the woman was sobbing and shielding her screaming children with her body. She was afraid of him. No, not afraid, *terrified.*

He dropped the dented aluminum rod and put his hands up in the air. "Not gonna hurt you. *Tranquila, no voy a hacerte daño,*" he said in a low voice. "*Va a estar bien.* It's going to be okay."

"*Está muerto?*" Tears streamed down her face.

Bronco placed his fingertips on the dealer's neck and searched for a pulse. "*No. No está muerto.*"

Her face twisted in rage, the woman grabbed the bat and before he could stop her, slammed it down on the meth head twice. Just as he yanked the instrument out of her hand, she smiled.

"*Ahora el bastardo está muerto.*"

He grunted. Yes, now the bastard was dead. What the hell was he going to do when the cops showed up—which judging from the sirens would be any minute now.

She wiped her hands on her filthy jeans, knelt on the floor and pulled her twins in for a tight hug. Looking past their shoulders, she stared straight into his eyes and said in heavily accented English, "You make me happy."

From a distance, a woman called his name. "Bronco? Are you okay?"

He blinked, "Yeah, I'm good."

"Where'd you go?" Emma put her hand on his cheek. "You weren't here with me. I called your name three times before you heard me. Did you slip into remote viewing mode?"

Only if you counted flashbacks as remote viewing, he thought.

"No. I'm good, honest." Laughing, he kissed the

back of her hand and then her palm. He was delighted to see her blush—again. *This is fun.* "Did Beautiful like everything?"

"You could say that." Tallulah snickered. "She wants a baby. Thinks you two should go work on it now."

Crimson-faced, Emma pulled her hand away. "Too much information, my friend."

"I'm just the interpreter." Tallulah laughed. "Oh, here comes the delivery man. I was wondering when he'd get here. I know you're expecting a few things."

The big white and green van pulled into the circle, and a man in navy shirt and shorts hopped out. "Howdy, Mrs. Stewart. I see that baby hasn't come yet." He pulled up the back door of his vehicle and began to ferry boxes, large and small to the porch. "I see you have some help, so I'm gonna leave this pile here, if you don't mind. I've got about ten boxes for you."

The truck pulled away, leaving a mountain of cardboard boxes, each addressed to Bronco. The return address was a PO Box in the Midwest. No one would ever find that address, a decoy for the Anomaly Defense Division.

Wiping his hands on a red-striped kitchen towel, Lucius appeared in the doorway and gave a low whistle. "Looks like Christmas has come early."

"If I'm not mistaken, Bert has thought of everything. We'll just need a place to do inventory and get this stuff packed up. I bet he even sent duffle bags."

"You can do that after dinner. I've got some nice steaks on the grill to celebrate your engagement." The pug yipped, and Gaucho chirped. "See? Even the animals say it's time to get the feed bag on."

Bronco placed Emma's hand on his arm. "Well, my beautiful fiancée, shall we adjourn to the dining room and toast our nuptials?"

Emma smiled and batted her eyes. "Nothing would give me greater pleasure, my handsome warrior." Her next words were whispered, "Academy Award performance. You'd better watch out, or someone's going to believe you."

Heart battering at his ribs, for that moment, he wished that someone was Emma.

Chapter Twelve

Later that evening, long after Tallulah said her good nights and good-byes, wiping her eyes and pleading, "Come home safe, please."

Emma stood in the office behind the registration desk and watched as Bronco uploaded the photos from Glam-More onto the secure Homeland server. "How long before we begin popping up on the Internet as man and wife?"

"Based on past experience with the documents team, I'd say two hours, four hours at the most."

"Wow. How is that even possible?" The thought that the world would see them as married by the time they got into the pick-up truck and headed north, if not before, was hard to believe.

"Our cyber hackers can clone these images and the marriage certificate will be placed in the Chapel of Love and Las Vegas Vital Statistics records. News outlets and social media sites will be fed short descriptions of our whirlwind romance and marriage. By tonight, each of us will have a fully filled out Facebook page that says "Married" to the other one. Of course, our pages, likes, dislikes, and newsfeeds will provide a rich source of Neo-Nazi propaganda, as well, to ensure when the geeks at the American SS looks us up, we look legit."

She paced the small office, stomach roiling at the

idea that her Crow cousins would be seeing this hateful spew. "Is that really necessary?"

"Absolutely, standard operating procedure. Spycraft one-oh-one. Build an airtight cover before you hit the field. No different from the Marines, just from an intelligence perspective."

Emma glanced at her phone which was vibrating—probably with rage, based on what she heard. "You underestimated your team. Our Facebook accounts are alive and already under attack for our hate speak." It buzzed again. "Seems we're trending on Twitter with our rants about racial purity."

He rubbed his hands with glee. "Excellent. The game's afoot, my dear Watson."

She glanced at her watch. "Sure you're up for driving this late at night? We could wait until tomorrow?"

"Nope, nope, nope. We wish to make an entrance, my love." He grinned. "It's going to be fun."

"We're just a couple that wants to be part of the New World Order, remember?" She wanted to do this, but hoped to get out alive. His devil may care attitude concerned her. Undercover work drew adrenaline junkies like moths to a flame—that much she knew and understood. Who else would be crazy enough to take these risks? "If we go in, guns blazing, we won't last a day."

"We will arrive at dawn, a metaphor for a new beginning." He tapped the tip of his nose. "These people can smell a lie. If I don't believe it, they won't. You're going to have to get used to seeing this side of me. If I don't appear to be arrogant and full of myself, they won't believe I'm one of them."

She released a long breath. "You had me fooled. And scared the crap out of me."

"Excellent. Now you just be yourself and everything will go fine." He folded his arms across his chest and leaned back in the desk chair. "Now, let's prepare. What's your name, and what are you doing here?"

She shook her head. "Not here. If you think Beautiful was pissed off before—"

"Point taken." He stood. "Okay, let's get our things packed up. After that we should grab some sleep. It will take us five hours to get there, so we need to leave here at midnight."

Lucius popped his head into the doorway. "I packed a big thermos of coffee and a cooler full of food for you. They're on the kitchen table. Grab it when you go. I'm heading up to bed, taking Franny with me. Gaucho's snoozing by the refrigerator. I think he's waiting for a chicken to fall out."

Hugging him hard, Emma said, "We'll keep you posted as much as we can. If there's a problem—"

"What? With your Marine training and his bad ass attitude, you'll fit in just fine." Lucius shook his head. "Just don't get lost in there. Evil can be seductive and powerful, and power can ruin the most ethical man."

Lucius left the room, and Emma continued to put their supplies into a backpack. A thought struck her, and she started laughing.

He cocked his head. "What?"

"Just thinking about my ancestors and their hunting parties. I'll be following in the footsteps of some brave women warriors who fought with Custer. You and I will be counting some coups."

Bronco emptied boxes of .308 rounds into an ammo can. "George Armstrong Custer?"

"The same. I bet you didn't know that Crow warriors served as scouts and soldiers alongside General Custer's troops in the fight against their old enemies, the Sioux, Cheyenne, and Arapaho. And that at least two Crow women served as warriors in this battle, Osh-Tisch, which means Finds-Them-and-Kills-Them and The-Other-Magpie. The-Other-Magpie fought because the Sioux had killed her brother. All she had was a stick and spit. She rode into battle with Osh-Tisch, who could shoot like a demon. The-Other-Magpie hit the enemy with a stick and spit on them. While the warrior was wondering what the hell that was all about, Osh-Tisch shot them."

"Like tag-team wrestling?" He chuckled and dumped more ammo into the can. "These are going to be super heavy."

"Well, if we can't shoot them, we can hit them in the head with the ammo cans."

"Good point." Bronco opened a duffle bag and began putting olive drab shirts and pants in it. "Interesting. What's this counting coup thing?"

"To become a chief, a Crow warrior had to 'count coup' by doing one of four things—striking an enemy with a bare hand or stick without killing him, leading a successful raid, stealing horses from an enemy camp, or grabbing a bow or gun in hand-to-hand combat."

"So if you do any of those things, you can be a chief?" He frowned. "Did they really let women do that? I thought Native American women were all Indian princesses or maidens—or drudges doing all the heavy work."

"Ohmigod." She put her fists on her hips. "Step away from the TV. You've been watching too many cartoons. Erase the Pocahontas myth from your mind, *please*. Women were—and are still respected members of our society. We owned the teepees and all the household goods. The men moved in with us. If we wanted to get a divorce, all we had to do was get up at a dance and say, 'I'm throwing my husband away. Anyone who wants him can have him.' That simple. It went the other way, too, but women had rights and owned property. Our descent is through our mothers, not our fathers. We were and still are a matrilineal society."

Bronco put his hands up in surrender. "Sorry. I'm a product of bad education."

"One more tidbit for you. At ten years of age, a child named Pine Leaf was captured in a raid on the Gros Ventre. Raised like a boy, she became a great warrior and ultimately a woman chief. She and Beautiful are both my ancestors. Don't mess with me or my family, or you will regret it."

He grinned. "I will never regret meeting you, Emma. Of that I'm positive." He glanced around the office. "I think we're packed. Now, let's go grab some sleep."

Emma took in Bronco's jaunty smile and wondered how he could consider closing his eyes when for all they knew they'd be dead by dawn. Did Pine Leaf sleep when she was fighting her enemies? Did Beautiful Blackfeather snooze when her daughter died in childbirth? Where was her inner woman warrior?

"Sleep?" She grabbed his collar and pulled him close. "Tomorrow we face a nation of insane people who will shoot first and ask questions after. Since you like metaphors, we're jumping out of a plane without a parachute. Before we go down in flames, there's one thing you and I are going to do."

"What?" he breathed.

She went up on her tiptoes, placed her lips on his, and kissed him as if there was no tomorrow.

****

As Bronco lifted her off her feet, she wrapped her legs around his waist, and he pushed her back against the wall. She gasped when he slid his hands under her T-shirt and found her unfettered breasts. He lifted the material and moved his mouth from her lips to her hardening nipples. She pulled his head closer, arched against him, and his erection rubbed against her jeans, aching to be set free. The thump of her butt against the woodwork reminded him they were in the office—with the door open.

"My room?" He gasped while licking her nipples.

She moaned and pressed harder against his groin, riding his bulge like a bucking stallion. "Don't stop."

"Now?" He slid his hand under her buttocks and nipped her neck.

She hissed and brought her lips down on his for a searing kiss. He bucked involuntarily at the connection, and she groaned.

"Make love to me as if there's nothing standing between us and death but the connection between our souls."

"Elevator," he murmured against her breasts.

"Yes." Slowly, she slid down his legs, over his throbbing erection. "Now."

Hands entwined, she leaned against his shoulder as

147

they walked toward the elevator, pausing every five steps to kiss, pull away, take a few steps, and kiss again. They stepped into the brass cage, pressed the up button, and the elevator shook into movement. She stroked the scar on his cheek, and he shuddered.

She whispered, "How did you get this?"

"Training accident," he lied. Now was not the time for his sordid family history. "I was chasing a 'bad guy', leaped without looking where I was heading, and landed on broken glass. Bled like mad."

He stroked her forehead. "You? How'd you get that?"

"Thought a bull would be as easy to ride as a horse." She giggled. "On a farm, not in a rodeo."

"Crazy woman."

"I was ten."

"Crazy girl."

He ran his finger along her lower lip, and she sucked the digit into her mouth. She drew it in and out, swirling her tongue around his index finger, giving him a heady preview of things to come. The elevator stopped. She removed his finger with a popping sound and smirked.

Hand in hand, they entered his room, lit only by the full moon. He held up a finger and peeked in the bathroom. *No eyes stared back from the mirror.* That was a relief. "We're alone."

He pulled his T-Shirt over his head and then without taking her eyes off his face, Emma peeled her own shirt off. Her breasts were full and round, high and perky, with dark pink nipples that made his mouth water. Above her right breast and below her collar bone sat a puckered circular scar. Two Gothic letters tattooed in black ink encircled the scar.

"MF?" he asked.

"Mother f—"

"Got it. From the meth head tweaker at the convenience store?" He guffawed. "You got him, not the other way around."

She drew closer. "And for this operation, MF will stand for Mongols Forever, should anyone ask. I took a bullet for my club. Street cred."

He grabbed her by the waist and lowered his lips to the nipple and pulled with his teeth as she moaned. He whispered, "Do you like a rough ride, Emma Bearkiller?"

"I like to ride real stallions. No little ponies for me."

Running his hands over her back as they kissed, he stopped and turned her around. "Sweet Mother of God." Scars crisscrossed her back like hashtags, some looping down and beneath her denim jeans. "Do they hurt?"

She shook her head. "Not as much as they did at first. I put yarrow tea on them every day. Speaking of which, I need to see how that worked out for your butt." She pulled at his belt. "Medicine woman's orders."

When he dropped his jeans and kicked them aside, his erection stood at attention, proud and free. Her eyes danced with admiration—and mischief.

"Turn around," she ordered. "I need to see where you were chafed."

He complied and felt a hand press against his butt cheek. "To your liking?"

"Oh, very much, but I need to complete my inspection." She stroked his buttocks with both hands, and he trembled as she skimmed her hands up and

Sharon Buchbinder

down his inner thighs, then feathered her fingers between his legs, tickling him.

"Do I get to return the favor?"

"Yes," she breathed. "Keep your eyes front." Material swished and her belted jeans thumped on the floor. "About face."

He turned. The moonlight shimmered on her skin, caressing every inch. Hands floating over her arms, his mouth hovered over her neck, breasts, and belly like a butterfly. A kiss here, a lick there, a nip in between, he kissed his way down her belly to the dark triangle between her legs. Feeling as if he was worshipping an ancient goddess, he knelt before her primal splendor. Palming her buttocks with both his hands, Bronco pulled her against his mouth and slid his tongue between her wet folds. Moaning, she pressed his head into her core and rocked against his mouth. She tasted like the ocean and confidences between lovers. Probing deeper he found her trembling nub, and then slid his fingers deep within her molten core. She gasped, and cried out, "Oh God!" and shuddered.

"You approve?"

Breathless, she finally responded, "Very much." She pulled him to his feet. "Your turn."

"In bed, my beautiful Indian princess." He pointed to the four-poster. "More comfortable."

"Me or the bed?"

"The bed for sure. We'll soon find out if you are."

Jumping onto the bed, she opened her arms and invited him in.

"A considerate lover, how nice." Hands on either side of her head in a modified push up, he hovered over her, then leaned in for a long, lingering kiss. "Did you

150

miss me?"

Smiling, eyes shining, she pulled his head back to hers. "Like the moon and the stars."

He lay on top of her, reached into the nightstand and withdrew his wallet. "Emergency stash." He rolled onto his back, ripped the packet open and began to slide the condom onto the tip of his penis. She grabbed his hand and helped him unroll the latex and stroked him.

She whispered, "Just want to ensure this is properly applied, medically speaking, that is."

"Of course. We don't want any slip ups—just slipping into something comfortable." He rolled back over and palmed her core. "If you're ready for me, that is."

"Let me show you how ready I am." Placing her thumb on the tip of his erection, she rubbed back and forth and his entire body quivered in response.

"You're killing me," he moaned. "But don't stop."

She drew her hand up and down his hardness and explored the contours of his maleness with her clever fingers causing him to shudder with delight. "I have to be sure this is the right fit." Emma gave a throaty laugh. After torturing him for what felt like hours, but was truly only moments, she finally said, "I think you're properly protected now."

He groaned as she guided him into her center, wrapped her legs around his back, and rose up to meet him. He plunged into her warmth, wrapped his arms around her warrior's back, and nuzzled his face against her neck, clutching her as if this would be their last embrace. With terrible timing, the enormity of the task before them hit him and regrets about dragging her into hell nagged him. What if he got them both killed? It was one thing to put his life in danger—but hers?

"Is something wrong? Are you okay? Or is it me? Do my scars turn you off?"

Damn, it was not her fault, none of this was.

"No," he croaked past a baseball sized lump in his throat. "You're the strongest, most beautiful woman I've ever met. I was taking a moment—to enjoy the pleasure of being so close to you." He kissed her, and she invited him into her mouth, tongues tangling. She nibbled at his bottom lip and raked her fingernails down his back and across his buttocks. Ripples of pleasure raced to his groin, and he slid back to thrust deeper into her core. She moaned and cried, "Yes," even as she rose again to meet him. Uninhibited, Emma's passion mirrored his until when at last they came together, he called her name and collapsed on her beautiful breasts.

He had never been so out of control in his life. Even in the sack, he had always prided himself on his ability to orchestrate each move in what he considered his symphony of lovemaking. He had not been in control from the instant she kissed him. This woman, this horse whisperer, had taken charge of his body and now his heart was following.

Deep in the heart of the house, Gaucho stirred and barked, laughing at him. His feline partner had been courteous enough to stay out of his mind during their intimate moments, but now he was all up in Bronco's business. He knew Bert was going to kill him for bedding his sister. But this one time, a little insubordination went a long way toward making him feel better about the fact that they were on their way to an armed camp.

Tomorrow might be their day to die, but tonight for

a short while was their time to live. They had a room, a soft bed, and a truckload of pent up craving. He'd be a fool to let it go to waste. Rising once again to the occasion, he rolled onto his back and pulled Emma on top, determined to mark her as his now and forever.

Chapter Thirteen

At midnight on the dot, having caught only an hour of sleep after a breath-defying lovemaking session, Emma climbed behind the wheel of her trusty pick-up truck and began driving into the unknown. Purring loudly, Gaucho curled into a ball on Bronco's lap, and fell asleep. Before long, his owner's head began to nod, giving her ample privacy and the opportunity to reflect on recent events.

The sex was amazing. Ethereal, possibly supernatural. *So what's the problem?* The very reason she was attracted to him should have been her first warning. Like a too stupid to live heroine in a horror movie, she'd not only gone into the house, but down into the pitch black cellar without a flashlight. The man was a loner, a trickster, an adrenaline fueled drifter whose only desire was to live on the edge. He was so used to working undercover, she wondered if any of his emotions were real. In the moonlight drenched hotel room, magic lit up every corner with love. In the front seat of a dusty old truck, however, the magic was gone, along with the irresistible combination of adrenaline, lust, and dancing with death.

The man had no clue, not a single shred of knowledge when it came to Native Americans. In her world, language, culture, history, and relationships were the glue that bound the family clan and the tribe together. He was an interloper, an outsider, uninterested in any culture outside his own—whatever the hell that was. While Bronco didn't appear to be a misogynistic racist, he could be keeping that under wraps—along with any other antisocial tendencies not worn on his inked sleeves.

Beautiful had it all wrong. For one thing, she'd been dead over a hundred years. For another, even when she was alive, she'd been one of four wives—all sisters. Emma was not the least bit interested in playing second, third, or fourth fiddle to other women. That era was long gone. Plus, Beautiful had been a shape-shifter, which had its own set of rules. Why did Beautiful have to stick her nose into Emma's love life, anyway? Seriously, no one else she knew in the tribe had this much interference from those who'd gone to the other camp.

Regardless of her ancestor's opinion, Bronco was wrong for her and she knew it. The sex was great, but there was no need to go any further. She would never allow herself to be some man's appendage. No, she was an independent woman with her own home, her own business, her own life, and her place within her tribe with all her cousins, aunts, and uncles. Just like Woman Chief, she would never give that up. As soon as this mission was over and the bad guys were caught, she was sending his adorable outsider's ass packing. She'd be firm, polite—wait—what if he didn't want to stay with her?

Slamming her palm on the steering wheel, she cursed herself mentally. *Stupid woman.* Aside from the impromptu roll in the hay, what made her think for even one nanosecond that *he* was that interested in *her*?

Here she'd been thinking about how she'd give him the tip of her cowboy boot, when in fact the man was probably just going to hop on his bike and ride into the sunset—alone. Well, that made things easier, didn't it? No need to get her tail feathers in a bunch, after all. The man had all the reliability of a coyote, a master trickster. She caught her reflection in the rearview mirror, gave herself a grim smile, and nodded her head. All's well that ends well, and soon enough, this little romance would be over and done.

A loud gasp from the passenger seat startled her. Reflexively, she jerked the wheel. The truck wobbled, and the bike jounced in the back.

"Stop!" Bronco shouted, and Gaucho growled and hissed.

Heart trip hammering in her chest, she slowed the vehicle down to ensure the bike wouldn't launch itself out of the bed of the truck and into the cab. At last, she pulled onto the shoulder of the road. Without looking at the man beside her, she yelled, "What the hell's going on?" When she turned the dome light on, her tongue stuck to the roof of her mouth.

Sweat poured down Bronco's face, and he shook so hard his teeth chattered. Clearly distressed, Gaucho yowled and put his paws on his partner's shoulders. Yellow eyes like twin searchlights, the cat looked at Emma as if to say, "A little help here, please?"

Dabbing his forehead and temple with the bandana from her neck, Emma tried to assess him. Pulse bounding and strong, skin cool and clammy. Hand on his chin, she turned his head to see his eyes. Pupils dilated. "Hey, can you hear me?"

No response, just a dazed expression and glassy-eyed stare.

"We're two hours away from the compound." She glanced at her watch. "Bronco, what do you need me to do? Should I turn around and go back home?" Giving his chin a gentle shake, she said in a low voice, "Lover boy, I need you with me. Now."

Bronco shook his head and wiped his face with his hands. "Things are much worse than I thought. Terrible."

"What's terrible? Tell me? Where did you go?" Pulling the thermos up from the floor, she poured him a half cup of the strong brew. "Drink this, then talk."

"Dream—not a dream. Remote viewing in my sleep." He put his hand on top of hers. "They killed people this time."

Frozen in place, she held her breath. "Who? Where?"

"Bighorn Canyon. They were after the mustangs— found some high school kids camping. Shot their teepees up. Killed them all." His eyes went flat. "Six kids. All Crow."

Numb, Emma dropped the coffee cup. "My tribe. My people. My family." Her vision blurred. "That's where I was when Jessica was attacked by the bear—" Unlike when she went up against a bear armed with her knife, the kids didn't stand a chance against a flying AR-15. If she had any lingering wisps of doubt about the importance of and need for this mission, they were blown out with the gulp of air she took to keep from bursting into tears.

"You don't have to do this." Bronco took her hand in his. "I'll go in alone, say we had a lover's quarrel, you were worried about not being accepted. I'll need the truck with the weapons. Take the bike, go home. Please. We're dealing with dangerous psychopaths. I don't want you to get hurt. This was my mission, not yours. Go home. Your family, your community needs you. I have no family, no real friends outside of work. Like a Pony Express rider, I'm an orphan, and I'm *expendable*. You're not."

Emma shook her head. "Now, more than ever, this is my fight. I'm not going home. Remember the women warriors I told you about? If they could ride into battle against their enemies armed only with a stick and a rifle, the least I can do is to honor their memories. I have guns, knives, you, Gaucho—and the Crow Nation and the U.S. government behind me. *Semper fi!*" She put the truck in gear. "I'm not giving up until every last one of these bastards is in jail or dead."

****

Bronco dared not voice what he'd seen. Past and present had blended together along with dream sharing with another person—his brother, Jack. His first emotion had been to rejoice that his fraternal twin was still alive, because where there was life, there was hope. After spending time in Jack's dream world, seeing his brother's past and present through his twin's eyes, Bronco's optimism faded to grief and fear.

Heartbroken, Jack watched his mother take his brother and drive out of the compound in her husband's beater pickup truck, leaving him behind. Running after the truck, he screamed, "I'm telling Daddy." Jack collapsed to his knees sobbing. A hole ripped in his heart because his other half was gone. Over time, he filled that hole with hatred and swore vengeance on his mother, brother, and any group that opposed his father's group. Time passed, and Jack watched his father's underlings bring a drunk and high chubby blonde, named Pam, back to the compound.

His father kept Pam as his slave, showing Jack how to treat women with his brutal and controlling behavior. He beat the woman when dinner was late, or not to his taste, when she didn't say "Sir"—basically for any small infraction. One day, she refused to obey. He killed her.

His father found out about the CIA's mind control experiments, MK Ultra, and used the same drug and torture techniques on volunteers in his group— including Jack. The boy almost died from an overdose of LSD. When revived he told his father he saw everything they were doing. He also told his father he traveled outside of the compound in his mind and moved objects with his thoughts. His father assumed the LSD was talking and didn't believe him.

When Jack turned eighteen, he enlisted in the army and became an unmanned aircraft systems repairer. He left the army after he learned all he needed to know about drones. Jack became the leader of the American SS. He used slaves to build the compound. A gifted tinkerer, Jack ultimately built his own unmanned drone from parts purchased from hobby shops and electronic stores. Over time, he built bigger drones with greater remote capacity, a visual guidance system and weapons—which he controlled with his mind.

Still cold and clammy from the vision, Bronco said in a shaky voice, "The attack on the kids is his latest victory. It was a practice run against human targets. He has a fleet of drones, and he's ready to go after a town, to begin to bring America to its knees. Not just any town, but a symbolic one—Helena, the capitol of Montana. He's practicing for his ultimate target—Washington, D.C."

Gaucho moaned and head-butted his partner.

One hand on the wheel, the other on Bronco's thigh, Emma asked, "Who are you talking about? Did you see who's in charge? Is it the guy you said saw you when you went in last?"

Sucking in a deep shuddering breath, Bronco nodded. "Yes. He was asleep, so I was able to get in under his psychic radar."

"Who is he? What's his name?"

"My twin brother—Jack."

Emma hissed. "Your identical twin?"

"Fraternal. He's fair haired, with brown eyes, like my mother." He covered his face and shook off the last vestiges of the dream. "He's a remote viewer, too."

"Shit. Shit. Shit." She pounded the steering wheel with the palm of her hand. "Could this get any worse?"

"Yes."

Gaucho yowled.

"Tell me before I have to pull this truck over and beat it out of you."

"He can control objects with his mind."

"Telekinesis?" She let out a low whistle. "That would explain why the things can't be jammed. No satellite or radio signals required. He's the remote viewer *and* the remote controller."

"Exactly." He stroked Gaucho's head and rubbed his ears to calm the cat—and maybe himself, if he was lucky.

"You never told me you had a brother." She glanced at him, her eyes wary. "You said you were an orphan."

"I thought I was. I didn't know my twin was still alive." He shook his head. "I—I didn't want to tell you about my family. I have feelings for you—wanted to see where this relationship would go."

"Really?" Her tremulous voice held a hopeful note. "I thought if we survived, you'd be on the next road out of town."

"You read that right. That was me." He grabbed her free hand and kissed it. "Not anymore. When I'm with you, I feel like I'm part of a huge, caring network. I never had a big family. My mother didn't have any more children—and we were in the witness protection program. So no one in our extended family knew where we were. They were told we died at the compound, no bodies retrieved, no funerals."

"Good God. If I didn't have my family, every crazy one of them, I'd feel like I'd lost my arms and legs—not to mention my heart."

"You and your family have begun to fill that hollow part of me. I hope what I'm about to tell you won't ruin my chances with you."

"Let me be the judge of that."

He took a deep breath and told her all about his father, his job loss, his descent into hate and attraction to the survivalists in remote rural Idaho. When he described how his mother escaped after attempting to persuade Jack to come with them, he stopped. Raw with emotion, he needed to take a breath.

"That's what you were afraid to tell me? That your father was a maniac and your mother escaped taking you with her? Your mother is a heroine. She rescued herself and you. Jack was clearly confused and didn't understand the consequences. If she had stopped—"

"My father would have killed her," he said in a flat voice. "He demanded blind obedience. She knew he'd not only murder her, but probably make her boys watch to 'teach us a lesson'."

"She did the right thing, a terrible choice, but the right decision," Emma stated. "I'm sure it haunted her to the end of her life."

He nodded, recalling his mother's deathbed request. "If you ever find Jack, please tell him I'm sorry and I miss him every day. Tell him I love him."

"It did," he said out loud. "She married the ATFE agent who helped her escape. Special Agent Thomas Winchester adopted me, raised me as if I was his real son. I joined the ATFE as soon as I could, started as an analyst, tracking hate groups."

"How appropriate."

"Yes, I was highly motivated and had personal insights on the brainwashing techniques. I was an excellent computer nerd employee. When Thomas died in the line of duty, I applied to be a field agent."

"And the biker persona?"

"They thought I was too close to the hate groups I studied, so they decided to put me undercover to get Intel on arms trafficking. I found Gaucho and discovered I had a latent talent—remote viewing. No drugs required."

She shot him a quizzical look. "Drugs? What's that got to do with it?"

"For my brother, everything." Relieved to be sharing his nightmare with someone, he told her about his visions.

She blew out a long breath. "Change of plans?"

He shook his head. "No. At dawn, we knock at the front door, just as we planned. If I read the scenario correctly, they won't bring us to him immediately. Jack has layers and layers of people between him, including slaves."

"What the hell are you talking about? *Slaves?*"

"When I was an analyst, we thought it was only an urban myth. But it's true. The American SS not only runs guns and drugs to raise money, it also traffics humans. Smugglers recruit desperate people from Asia, bring them in through Canada—some in seafood containers—then tell them the price of the trip has quadrupled. If they don't agree to be indentured servants, paying off their huge bills, they tell them their gang will kill their family back in Asia."

"I don't know what to say." She squeezed his hand. "Whatever you decide, I'm with you. You got that? One pissed off warrior woman coming up."

"Thank you for not pushing me away. I was ashamed to tell you the truth about who I was, where I came from. It's an ugly seam of my life, one I wish I could erase, but it's part of me and who I am."

Guilt, shame, and outrage battled within his chest. Guilt and shame for leaving his brother behind to the devices of his sociopath father. Outrage at being accused of abandoning his other half, the brother born two minutes before him, the one who taught him how to climb a tree, catch a frog, and cross his eyes. The brother who cried with him and bandaged his cheek when his father decided his son should learn how to spar with a knife, the real source of his scar. The brother he missed every day when he woke and when he went to bed at night. Once again, his rational brain reminded him that he had been a child of seven when they escaped from the compound. His mother had tried to save Jack, too, but the boy's emotions were in control that day. He craved his father's love and refused to leave. As a child, he had no control over the circumstances or the events leading up to Jack's abandonment. But as an adult, maybe he could save Jack from his own burning rage and hatred—if it wasn't already too late.

Chapter Fourteen

"We have entered SS country," Emma called out and pointed at the hand-lettered road sign.

NO TRESPASSING!

You are hereby notified that you are entering sovereign territory established by the rightful owners of this land. Public officials must abide by the law of this land and the Constitution of the United States of America and the Bill of Rights.

If you are interested in becoming citizens of the Sovereign Territory of the American SS, you are hereby advised to apply in person for inspection to be sure you are the right kind of people for our state.

All others may reach us via Post Office Box 1888, in Billings, MT.

"Isn't that special?" Bronco shook his head. "They requested and got, it would appear, the symbols for Adolf Hitler, Heil Hitler for their mailbox. Nice."

"Very classy sign, too. The illiterates must have had a dictionary at hand while they did the lettering." She slowed down to the posted speed limit of fifty miles per hour and jounced over frost heaved concrete and potholes. "Nice roads."

"No need to repair roads in a ghost town," Bronco said. "Look at these buildings. It's just like I saw back in the hotel."

Like watching a train wreck, Emma didn't know

which way to look first. She had taken notes as Bronco had completed the remote viewing, but nothing could prepare her for this post-apocalyptic town. Ramshackle houses, with paint peeling off the sides exposing wood beneath, and garage doors hanging at crazy angles, competed with tumbleweeds and rusted cars. Trees overran sidewalks, driveways, and lawns, as nature seemed intent on taking back the land. Behind the houses in the distance, a water tower leaned at a forty-five degree angle, as if waiting for a good blizzard to knock it down and put it out of its misery.

"How could the government just abandon all this property?" She slowed the truck down to avoid a missing paver. "There are homeless people, refugees looking for shelter away from war and conflict. They could use these houses, fix them up…"

"And do what?" He shook his head. "Once the base closed, there was no employment for the people living here. Shops closed, people took what they could and left."

"Internet based businesses don't require a local employer. Credit card companies have customer service bases in rural areas. Even healthcare can be conducted, in part, through Skype and other virtual applications. This is a total waste of resources."

"You're seeing it through your cultural lens of honoring the earth and not wasting anything."

Shocked, she turned on him. "How do you know about that?"

"I may be a product of bad education, but that doesn't mean I can't observe and learn." He waggled a finger at her. "I was a nerdy computer analyst, remember? Once a nerd, always a nerd."

She narrowed her eyes. "Tell me what you saw."

"Your home is an homage to your nation, from the kitchen to the bathroom." He smiled. "Each photo and decoration is from your tribe. You have herb gardens where you grow your own medicines, thank you very much, and your first aid kit is a composite of your encyclopedic knowledge of healing."

Face on fire, she could only nod. He was good.

"You don't just recycle, you re-use everything, including mayonnaise jars for herbal teas. The dogs play with deer antlers. Your freezer is filled with venison, but not overfilled. Your relatives do what you tell them to do, which tells me you are held in high esteem, which only comes when someone cherishes their family and community."

"You should go on stage, you're a mentalist." Truly, the man's power of observation was astonishing. She wondered what he had left out.

"In the field, my life depended on my being observant. If someone acted wrong, out of character, twitchy, it was time to get out of Dodge." He touched his nose. "Thanks to Gaucho, my remote viewing, and my ability to sniff out a stinky situation, I'm still standing above the dirt."

"And, I for one, am especially happy you are. Oh, look at that, we're at the gates of Hell." She nosed the car up to the red and white stop line and leaned back in her seat. Shiny new eight-foot tall fencing topped with a one foot of three strand barb wire rose up on either side of a closed four-foot high metal cross-bar entryway. Two men in olive drab camouflage uniforms, bearing large side arms raised their rifles, leaned over the entrance, and pointed the weapons at the truck. "With those ugly clowns, the stop signs posted on the gates are overkill, don't you think?"

"Heil Hitler," he whispered. "Time to get in the backpack, Gaucho."

"Yeah, heil effing Hitler," she responded and prayed to God they got out alive.

She smiled at him and took a deep breath. "It's show time, my new husband."

Bronco rolled his window down and waved a guard over. "Hey man, we're here to support the cause." He extended his driver's license.

The lookouts exchanged glances. "Who sent you?"

"We sent ourselves, man." He pointed at Emma. "My old lady here is a card-carrying member of the American SS." He grinned. "Show 'em your card, honey."

Emma waved her red and black card out the window. The men didn't budge.

Bronco kept talking enthusiasm spiking each word. "She convinced me to join up. We came straight from Vegas, drove all night to get here at dawn. Symbolic, don't you think? Our new beginning for an Aryan nation."

The man in camo on the left said, "What are the fourteen words?"

Bronco shook his head. "Dude. That is a shit password, but here it goes. 'We must secure existence of our people and a future for white children.'"

"She don't look very white," remarked the sentry on the right.

"Saw that coming," she muttered.

"She's racially more pure than a lot of other folks.

One hundred percent Native American." Then as if an afterthought, he threw in, "The most powerful medicine woman you'll ever have the honor to meet."

The sentries looked at each other and had a brief excited exchange too low to make out the words. Then they lowered their weapons, opened the gates, and waved them in.

She breathed, "What the hell?"

At one guard's upheld hand, Emma stopped the truck mid-way through the gates. The man with the nametag that said Leroy leaned into the open window, brown teeth displaying either poor dental hygiene, a lack of fluoride, or both.

"Thank you for coming, Medicine Woman. The children are sick, we don't know why."

"Glad to be of service." Emma dared not look at Bronco. She was clearly expected. Who told them she was coming? Was it the undercover FBI agent? She thought Bert had kept them out of the loop. "Please show us where to go. I have to unpack my supplies."

"Yes, ma'am." Leroy hopped on a three-wheel all-terrain vehicle, an ATV, and led them past a barracks to a smaller wooden outbuilding with a weathered hand-painted sign identifying it as the Clinic hanging over the door. The place looked like something left over from a 1960's TV Western. He pointed to a parking spot reserved for physicians, and she nosed the truck into the space.

As she climbed out with her bag in hand, an overhead speaker crackled to life. "Attention Aryan women. Bring your sick children to the clinic now."

Emma turned to Bronco, who had the backpack on his shoulder and said in a low voice, "Let me guess, only Aryan children get treatment."

He nodded. "Guess so."

"Leroy," she said in a louder voice. "Can I get inside, get set up?"

"Yes, it's open. We don't lock our doors here. This here is the safest place in the world."

She doubted that, but chose not to argue the point. "Thank you." Emma climbed the three steps, her boots clomping loudly on the timber. Bronco followed behind, his boots echoing hers. She opened the door and waited for her eyes to adjust to the dimly lit room.

Leroy said, "Light switch is over here." The room glowed with bright light revealing a reception desk, waiting room with chairs, and an open door to what turned out to be an exam room. Despite the antique exterior, everything inside was spotless and dust free. The chrome examination table gleamed, and a counter on the side held jars of tongue depressors, alcohol wipes, and adhesive bandages. An otoscope and ophthalmoscope sat in chargers on the wall and a blood pressure cuff and stethoscope, both shiny and new, sat at the side of the counter. She opened drawer after drawer, each of which held organizers and every variety of instrument a physician or nurse practitioner could want. Truth be told, she had no idea what half of these things did.

Leroy stood in the reception room, a worried look on his face. "Is everything to your liking?"

"Yes, it's beautiful. Where are your camp doctor and nurse? I usually work with Western medicine, not alone."

"They—um—well, never showed up." He took his hat off and scratched his head. "We offered a lot of money, too, but nobody would come. That's why when the Obergruppenführer said he saw you coming in a vision, we were told to make you welcome."

The Obergruppenführer—Jack—saw her coming? Her heart somersaulted down to her feet and stayed there. They were doomed.

****

Bronco hung back in the waiting room, giving Emma the space and opportunity to establish herself. The woman was a natural, she hadn't missed a beat. Time to ask a few newbie questions.

"So, tell me Leroy, when do we get to blow things up?"

The multiple gun-toting man favored him with a look reserved for idiots. "You don't get to do shit until we say so."

"You sure were happy as hell to see my old lady," he grumbled putting a hard emphasis on the last two words, as a righteously indignant real man would be.

The man gave him a hard stare. "We need her. Don't know about you."

"Man, we just drove all night, all the way from Vegas. We showed you how important this is to us. What else do we need to do?"

The man gave him a rotten toothed grin. "For starters, drop your pants."

Bronco shrugged. So the jerk wanted to see if he was circumcised. *Fine*. He did as ordered. "Happy now? Not Jewish."

Leroy nodded. "Okay. Good start. You can pull 'em up."

Shaking his head, Bronco wondered what test would be next.

"Open that backpack. I need to see what you're carrying."

Oh, this was going to be fun. *Not.*

"Sure. Just do me a favor and lower your weapon. Don't want you to shoot my cat by accident."

The man's face twisted in derision, and he lowered his weapon with a laugh. "Aww, the big man has a widdle biddy puddy-tat in his bag?"

"Um, sort of." He unzipped the mesh top. "Come on out, Gaucho."

In one leap, the bobcat was on Bronco's shoulder.

Startled, the guard reflexively lifted his rifle.

"Leroy!" Emma's voice cut through the tension. "That's my medicine animal. You hurt him and I lose all my power. You sure you want the Obergruppenführer to hear about how you took away my powers?"

The man lowered his rifle. "Sorry, Ma'am, I had no idea—"

"You be sure to tell all your pals if they harm one hair on that cat, they will be hearing from the Obergruppenführer, and not in a good way." She looked at Bronco. "I need Gaucho with me while I see the children." She pointed out the door at the front porch.

A line of blonde women in jeans and shearling jackets held pajama-clad children, wrapped in blankets, streamed up the stairs and into the waiting room. At the front of the line stood the woman Bronco had seen during his remote viewing. The twins, so active when he saw them, leaned against her, glassy-eyed, runny-nosed, and lethargic. Behind her children coughed and sneezed, and mothers wiped little noses and stroked small heads.

Bronco handed her the leash, telling the cat to stay at her side. Gaucho chirped, jumped down to the floor, and padded over to Emma.

"What do you want me to do?" Bronco had no idea what was going on, but it didn't look good.

"Are there any medical records for these children?" Emma asked Leroy.

He shook his head, "It's the mother's job to take care of their kids. They're supposed to keep a diary for each of their kids. Obergruppenführer commands it."

"Okay, we will need to see each diary so I can get an idea of what to use for treatment." She lifted her chin at Bronco. "Baby, would you go and collect the diaries please? Start from the back of the line. Leroy, go with him so they know he's legit."

Taking his backpack, he went outside, expecting the queue to end at the bottom of the steps. Instead, the line of mothers, toddlers, and infants, streamed down the road in front of the clinic over to the barracks. It had to be a quarter of a mile long. Shaking his head, he walked along the line, murmuring hellos and offering assuring noises to the stricken, weeping mothers. With each step, his heart sank a bit more. Like the twins in the reception room, every child had a runny nose and glassy eyes. Some coughed and sneezed, others were freckled with red spots on their faces and hands. He began to walk faster, practically jogging to the end of the line.

Leroy shouted at the terrified women, "Give this man your diaries. Drop them in his bag. Now. You'll get them back when you see the doctor."

Fumbling in pockets, tote bags, and purses, each woman dropped her black composition notebook into his backpack and whispered, "Thank you" as he passed by.

No matter how horrible the belief system of the parents, no child deserved to be without medical care. The sins of the father should not be borne by the children. He knew that first hand. What the hell was going on here? He'd never seen anything like it in his life. Along with many other things, as part of his transition to Homeland Security his training had included identifying the presence of germ warfare. Had his crazy brother been testing biological weapons on his own people? On babies and children? How could he do this to his followers?

Backpack filled to the brim, he raced along the line back up the stairs and into the reception room. Leaning the backpack against a wall, he stacked the last notebooks on top of the teetering pile. Emma motioned to Bronco to come inside the exam room. In a low voice she said, "Are your immunizations up to date?"

"Yes, I've got everything for germ warfare, including cholera. You thinking biological warfare, too?"

She shook her head, smiled at the mother with the twins, and said, "I just need to take a look at your diary." She plucked the top notebook off the pile, began flipping through the pages, set it down and went on to the next one, then the next.

"No," she said in a low voice. "Not warfare. Bad decisions. It appears these children have never received measles, mumps, or rubella vaccinations—or immunizations of any kind."

"What—is that even legal?" He struggled to keep his voice down. The idea of not immunizing a child in this era was mind-boggling. "How is that possible?"

"My guess is these women do whatever the Obergruppenführer commands—including not seeing doctors outside the compound." She turned to the woman with the twins. "Now, I need to start bringing in the children and figuring out what we can do."

Bronco stepped aside and smiled at the blonde woman who seemed so familiar.

Emma said, "Your name please?"

The blonde threw her shoulders back and said with pride, "Frau Obergruppenführer, the SS leader's wife." She stepped into the exam room with the twins, closed the door and gripped Emma's hand with both of hers. "Tell me now, what do you plan to do about this measles outbreak?"

Chapter Fifteen

After placing the sniffing, sneezing twins on the exam table, Emma motioned to the woman to take a seat in the only chair in the exam room. "Frau Obergruppenführer—"

"Call me Eva. It is the name I was given when I joined the American SS, a symbol of my rebirth in the movement."

"Eva." What a disgusting homage. Was her maiden name Braun? "Why do you think this is a measles outbreak?"

"Did you see the kids? Before I joined the SS, I was a registered nurse, worked at St. Vic's in Billings. Textbook signs and symptoms."

"Okay, I agree it looks like measles." She glanced at Bronco. "Any idea where these kids would get it? It looks like none have been immunized, is that correct?"

Eva nodded. "Yes, Jack was quite adamant. Said it caused autism. I tried to argue with him." She shook her head. "That's the day I learned not to disagree with him. Fortunately, he only broke my arm. I was able to set it myself, get it to heal properly, a little awkward given I was pregnant with the twins."

Sickened, Emma checked to see if she heard correctly. "He beat you while you were pregnant?"

Face blazing, Eva stared at the floor and whispered, "Yes."

Emma took her hand. "That's classic domestic violence. You know that, right?"

Eva looked up, and a tear trickled down her cheek. "I was such a fool. Two years ago I met Jack at a political rally for a local candidate. I didn't care about politics, I was there working the first aid tent, earning some extra cash. Jack and a couple of other men brought in an older man who fainted. It was hot as blazes, so no surprise."

Emma squeezed her hand.

"He was so handsome, so caring to that elderly man, so charming to me." Eva shook her head. "Fool that I am, I fell for him. He asked me to come here. I quit my job, sold everything, gave him all my money." She shook her head and the trickle of tears became a flood. "His men watch me like hawks. He uses the boys as pawns, threatens to take them away from me if I even look like I'm thinking of disobeying him. Please don't say anything. If he knows I told you all this—he'll kill me."

Seething inside at the abuse this woman had endured, Emma vowed to free Eva as soon as she could. "What you tell me is confidential."

Eva flicked the tears off her face and took a deep breath. "Thank you."

Emma kept a poker face. "So, no immunizations for the kids. What about the adults?"

"They've come from all over the country, so my guess is they had vaccinations. This is the only outbreak we've had in ten years."

"How many adults are in this community?"

"Aryans?"

"Yes." Emma bit her tongue.

Eva looked to the left, a good sign she was telling the truth. "About five hundred. But the compound is built to hold two-thousand. With the Internet, they've been able to increase recruitment efforts, so Jack anticipates more coming." She frowned. "Like you."

"Other than us—who are immunized, by the way—any other new people in the community?"

Eva frowned. "Asians—slaves Jack brought in to do the dirty work on the compound."

"Um-hmm." Now they were getting somewhere. "What kind of work?"

"They clean the houses, watch the children at daycare, take care of the horses, and serve food in the dining hall—that sort of thing." She glanced back and forth between Emma and Bronco. "Why?"

"How did they come here, if I may ask?"

"I'm not sure how they got here from Asia. They came in the trucks from Canada."

"Did anyone check to see if they had been immunized before they got off the trucks and began to work?" Disease didn't respect global boundaries or political beliefs. Most likely the trafficked victims brought measles with them when they got on the boat and headed to Canada.

Eva shrugged. "Jack never tells me anything that's not related to my assignments. My job is to work on the Internet, keep our website up to date, help recruit members, and keep the money coming in."

Emma weighed her words with care. "Frau Obergruppenführer—Eva—I need your help. I have no cell service here, I need you to get me on your computer so I can contact the appropriate medical personnel for help." The satellite phone in the truck was not appropriate at this time. She needed to co-opt Eva, get the woman to do her bidding.

Panic crossed her face, and Eva opened her mouth to protest, but Emma continued.

"You're a nurse. You know what happens after the runny nose, fever, and rash. Next comes respiratory distress and ultimately, brain infections which can lead to brain damage. Without proper medical care, kids can die from this." She pointed at the twins. "Do you really want to see your babies suffocate to death or have seizures and die in your arms?"

Tears filled the blonde's big blue eyes. "But Jack—"

"Are you prepared to go out there and tell every desperate mother standing in line that they must sacrifice their child for the SS?" Struggling to keep her emotions in check, Emma took a deep breath.

"He can be so mean. I used to love him, but he's gotten worse, crazier since I had the twins. I'm afraid he'll *really* hurt me this time—or the boys."

"Do you love your children?"

"Yes." Tears streamed down Eva's cheeks. "Very much. That's why I'm here today, to help them."

"What children will the Obergruppenführer have for the new world order if they go untreated? Some will survive. But many will die or be brain damaged. Will you be able to live with yourself knowing you could have done something?"

The blonde put her face in her hands and sobbed. "What do you want me to do?"

"Let me have access to the Internet. I will do everything I can to keep public officials away from the compound. They can tell us what to do and drop supplies at the front gate. Please, allow me to help you, that's why I'm here."

"Okay, but not now. It will have to be later, when all these people are gone." She gripped Emma's hand again. "Jack has eyes *everywhere*. Snitches like Leroy get rewarded."

"Allow me." Emma opened the exam room door and stepped out in the waiting room. Rocking their sick children, the mothers looked up expectantly. "Listen up, please," she said in a loud clear voice. "We have a measles outbreak."

A collective gasp filled the room and anxious, chirping voices sent the message down the line.

"First, you must all go home and keep your children isolated from other children. No one, and I mean no one is to go in or out of your home unless they have been vaccinated against measles." She took a deep breath. "This is a highly contagious disease. When your child coughs, the droplets are left floating in the room and are infectious for up to two hours."

She turned to Leroy, whose eyes were bugging out of his head. "Two hours?"

"Were you vaccinated against measles, Leroy?"

"I dunno. I don't think so."

"Then you can catch it, too."

His face drained of color. "I'm feeling a little feverish, now that you mention it." The rifle slipped out of his hand, and he fell to the floor in a dead faint.

Well, that was easy.

"Go home. Isolate your children. Give them lots of fluids. If you have children's acetaminophen, use it. If not, I will be coming house to house and bring medicines to you. I repeat, go home and isolate your children."

The orderly line, which had bunched up around the porch to hear her announcement, was now an unhappy, unruly crowd. A heavy set woman shouted at her, "Why should we believe you? You're not Aryan."

"Please, you need to listen to me. Your children's lives, your lives depend on taking these measures."

The women exchanged uneasy glances, but the mouthy one didn't relent. "On whose say so?"

Gaucho padded onto the porch and sat by her feet. The pack moved back two steps. Bronco came up behind her and murmured, "Eva is right behind you."

"Frau Obergruppenführer, would you like to say a few words?" Emma stepped aside for the woman to come through with her babies.

"My husband foresaw Emma Bearkiller's arrival. She is a powerful medicine woman. If you disobey her, I will report you to my husband. Now, do as she says. Go home, isolate your children and take care of them." She clicked her heels, gave a Nazi salute, and said, "We must secure the existence of our people and a future for white children. *Sieg heil!*"

Heels clicked, arms saluted, and a chorus of *Sieg heils* responded to Eva's shout.

Emma thought she would never live to see this on the land of her ancestors. It was all she could do not to vomit as she joined the chorus and saluted.

Eva turned and spoke rapidly, peeking over their shoulders, eyes on Leroy's inert figure. "Until they figure out how Bronco fits in, you'll be put up in the VIP visitors' quarters, not far from my house. The computer is in the office, on the other side of the compound, away from housing. Nothing is locked.

There is one night sentry at the office, Greg. He's loyal to me. Hated it when Jack broke my arm. I'll tell him to let you in." She paused and swallowed hard. "My life is over. Save my children. Please."

Leroy groaned. "What happened?"

"You fainted. I think you might have a fever. You need to go home and rest."

Bronco offered the man a hand to stand up, but Leroy swatted it away. "I'm fine."

Shrugging, Bronco said, "Yes, I see that. Would you like Emma to put a bandage on the gash on your forehead?"

Leroy put his hand up, and his fingers came away covered in blood. "I guess so."

"Good man."

Emma touched Eva's shoulder. "Hang in there. Your children need you."

Children did need their mothers—even when they were Nazis.

****

Despite the gash on his forehead and his fever, Leroy insisted on escorting them to their quarters. After a wobbly dismount from his ATV, the man demanded their car keys.

"This truck and this bike are now the property of the American SS. You can take your clothes and personal items, but that's all."

Bronco reached into the cab and flirted with the idea of stuffing the satellite phone into a pile of clothes—but Leroy came up behind him.

"Well, looky here," he chortled. "You brought a phone—we've been needing another one of these."

So much for that idea, Bronco thought. He hoped

182

Emma's psychic link with her brother was a strong one. Otherwise their last connection to the outside world had just been confiscated.

Leroy led them to a private cabin five doors down from the Obergruppenführer's residence, which he pointed out with pride. While not showy in the way of McMansions that dotted suburban landscapes, this house was twice the size of the others and had his name on a sign out front. A stone walkway led up to the stairs of a porch where four rockers sat behind a split log railing. Bronco doubted Beautiful would enjoy rocking on *that* porch.

Leroy opened the door to the cabin and pointed out the nice arrangements. A galley kitchen with a microwave, coffee pot and mini-fridge, a bedroom with a king-sized platform bed. A bathroom with a vanity and shower. A sitting room with a couch, loveseat, and recliner. On the coffee table sat a copy of *Mein Kampf,* along with American SS literature.

Gaucho strolled in, looked around, and hopped up on the loveseat. He promptly closed his eyes and pretended to sleep. The cat sent images of small metal buttons he'd spotted under the furniture as he padded around the cabin. *Listening devices!* Bronco sent him a mental thank you.

"This is beautiful, my brother."

Leroy stiffened. "Fellow Citizen, not brother."

"My apology, I meant no offense. In my biker club, we call everyone brother."

"Which club?" Leroy relaxed a bit.

"Mongols, of course. One percenters."

Leroy frowned. "Thought they had a lot of mixed breeds?"

"That's why I left. The Mongol Club in Germany has a Muslim leader, can you believe that?" He shook his head. "I had to get out. So my old lady and I, we turned our back on them."

"She was a Mongol?" Disbelief filled Leroy's face. "You're lying."

"Honey, show them your tats." He jerked his thumb at Emma's chest.

Leroy grinned. "Tits are good, too."

Emma rolled her eyes, pulled the neck of her shirt down and pointed to the tattooed scar. "Mongols Forever. I took a bullet for my club." She shook her head. "And then they let in people I don't want to be near, much less in the same club."

Leroy's eyes shone with admiration. "Wow. A medicine woman and a bad ass."

"Ha." Bronco guffawed. "You ain't seen nothing yet." He made a twirling motion with his index finger. "Turn around, Babe. Show him your back."

Emma glared at Bronco. "You know I don't like that."

"Bitch." Bronco raised a hand. "You'll do as I say." Emma flinched and turned around. Bronco lifted her shirt and pointed to the hashtag of scars from her neck down to her waist. "Now that is badass. My old lady killed a grizzly with nothing but her knife."

Gulping, Leroy whispered, "Did she really kill a bear? Or are you making that up?"

Emma snatched her hunting knife out of the holder on her leg and whirled. Before the guard could swallow, she had the sharp tip at his throat. "Yes, I killed a bear and I've killed a man, too. So if you're done ogling my tits and ass, you can put your eyes back in your head."

The man put his hands up in surrender. "I wish all our women were like you." He shook his head. "Lunch is at noon in the mess hall. Just go down the path and you'll see a big building opposite the horse barns." Clicking his heels and snapping off a Nazi salute, Leroy ran down the steps, apparently no longer feeling ill. Bronco was pretty sure the snitch of the SS was going to go straight to the Obergruppenführer and tell him all about the new arrivals. Good, that was exactly what he wanted. Now it was time to wait.

"Emma, my love." Bronco put his finger to his ear and pointed around the room. "We're on our honeymoon. Why don't we do what newlyweds are supposed to do?"

Eyes flashing, she looked as if she wanted to punch him in the nose, but played along. "Oh, baby," she cooed. "I thought you'd never ask. Let's go test drive this big bed."

Boots clumping with extra effort, they threw themselves on the bed, which squeaked like a giant mouse.

Bronco whispered in her ear. "Gaucho spotted bugs everywhere. I sent him a message to remove the bugs from the bedroom. While he's doing that, we'll give someone an old radio show, complete with sound effects."

She grinned, mischief dancing in her eyes. "Oh, baby, I want it rough," she yelled. "I've been a bad girl. Spank me."

He nearly choked laughing. "You're right. You didn't polish my shoes." His open palm landed on his thigh.

"Ow, that hurt!" she shouted and gave him the thumbs up.

"And you haven't cleaned that truck in a week." Another smack to his thigh, this one stung.

"Ohmigod, you're really hurting me. Do it again, you're making me hot."

He slammed his hand on his other thigh and winced.

"Oh, oh, oh, I'm gonna come!"

"No you don't, not unless I say so," he commanded. Pulling his belt out, the leather whistled in the air and slapped the bed. "Now, you can come."

"Ah ah ah! Omigod, Omigod. Baby, you're the best, you give me what I need." She wrapped her arms around herself and kissed her biceps. "I love you."

"I love you, too, baby, my turn now." He whispered into her ear. "Gaucho cleared the bedroom of bugs. It's just us." Exhausted from the drive and the tension of play acting to the unknown listeners, he flopped onto his back.

To his surprise she whispered, "Yes, it is your turn." With that she peeled off her T-shirt and jeans, pulled his pants down to his ankles and stroked him. Reaching into his wallet, she extracted a foil packet and deftly unrolled the sheath over his pillar of an erection. Climbing onto him, she brushed his face with her long hair, and kissed his cheeks, neck, and chest. At last, she brought her lips to his in a searing kiss, breaking the connection only to whisper, "Welcome back."

Chapter Sixteen

Emma woke up disoriented and stared at the ceiling, trying to recall where she was. A low rumbling purr next to her head brought her back to reality. She turned her head and came nose to nose with Gaucho. Golden eyes glinting, he tilted his head and placed a demitasse saucer sized paw on her chest, precisely at the spot where she'd been shot. He chirped and head butted her. "Is that your seal of approval?" He barked, and she swore he was laughing. One of these days, she'd figure out his language. But for now, she'd have to rely on Bronco to interpret. Speaking of the devil, where was he? She stood, stretched, and headed for the shower—where she found her missing man singing a tune about being happy. Damn, the man could whistle and carry a tune.

"Mind if I join you?"

He pulled her into the shower and dunked her under the warm water. "Time to lather up, Butter Cup."

Laughing, she pushed her hair out of her eyes and pulled him into a hug. "Ready for an encore performance?"

"If you insist, but pretty soon, we're going to run out of condoms." He quirked a brow at her. "Still interested?"

Lower lip out in a pout, she said, "Given we might die at any moment, I've developed a very keen interest in sex."

Mouth slanted over hers, he murmured, "I couldn't agree more."

An hour later, with clean clothes, dry hair, and at least one appetite satisfied, Emma dragged Bronco out the door following Leroy's directions to the mess hall. Gaucho strolled along between them, alert and handsome. The few people out and about, stopped, stared at the trio, and nodded. "Ah, it appears word is on the street about us. Hard to miss us, I guess we make quite a sight in this place."

"Or anywhere else for that matter," Bronco murmured. "There's the dining hall."

Had it not been for the Asian servers wiping down tables, the space would have been devoid of human life. Emma glanced at her watch. "Noon, right?"

"Yup, on the minute." He waved to a pale young woman in a white apron. "Can we get some food?"

She stared blankly until he mimed eating, then nodded and scurried off.

"Either she ran to get food, or she ran away. Either way, she's in a hurry."

A portly man with a light brown mustache in a cook's hat and apron emerged from a swinging door. "You must be the new folks." He extended a ham sized hand. "Welcome and thanks for coming, ma'am. What can I get you to eat?"

"Whatever everyone else was having. Leroy told us noon. Did we miss lunch?"

"Ah, no. Frau Obergruppenführer told me we had a measles outbreak. I used to work in a nursing home, I was the head chef. When we had any kind of outbreaks—norovirus was a big one for the old folks—

we forbid communal eating and congregating of any kind. Just good public health measures, ya know?"

Astonished, Emma agreed, "Yes, exactly. Good thinking. But what about the servers?"

"I don't have any say over those workers." He shrugged. "Above my pay grade. I was told to keep 'em working."

"The girl we saw didn't look very well." She bit her bottom lip. "She could be spreading the disease if she's preparing food to be taken into people's homes."

"She's an adult," the man blustered. "Measles is a kid's disease. She's *fine*."

Emma pressed on. "If she made the food for the Obergruppenführer's twins, would that be okay?"

His blue eyes widened, and a look of sheer panic came across his face. He flew through the swinging door and shouting followed. "Get out! Go back to your rooms! Stop touching the food! Go, just go!"

Crying and weeping, a stream of young girls— some couldn't have been over twelve years old—ran out of the kitchen. One stumbled, righted herself, and staggered out the door leaning on another girl.

"Happy now?" Bronco asked.

"Taking it one thing at a time." She glanced around. "I'm still hungry. Let's go in the kitchen."

The chef sat at a large metal table with his head in his hands, moaning. "I'm a dead man, he's going to kill me."

"Who's going to kill you?" Emma asked. "The Obergruppenführer?"

"Yes. You don't know him. Any infraction, any disobedience and you can be the next one shot as an example to the rest of the camp." A beseeching look on his face, the cook asked, "I obeyed the Untergruppenführer, his second in command. Please tell him I did what I was told to do."

Incredulous, Emma asked, "What makes you think he'll listen to me?"

"He foresaw your arrival and said you would save our children, help make things better."

She took a deep breath. "I'm honored and will do my best to make his words come true."

Bronco cleared his throat. "Not to be a nuisance, but if you have some canned soup, we'd be happy to take that to our cabin."

The man leaped to his feet. "Yes, yes, of course. I have to toss all these sandwiches. Come, pick out what you want. I'll give you a tote bag. You can take it all back with you."

Ten minutes later, laden with canned goods, frozen bread, jars of peanut butter and jelly and coffee, Emma, Bronco, and Gaucho headed back to their cabin. The cat strained on his leash and chirped. "You sure you want to be loose?" Bronco said in a soft voice as he unsnapped the harness. Gaucho's only response was to bolt into the underbrush.

"Must have seen a rabbit, his favorite fast food."

Emma smiled, glanced up—and froze. "Honey, I'm worried Gaucho might get hurt. Could you please follow my medicine animal? I can't do my work without him."

Bronco shot her a puzzled look.

On the porch of their VIP cabin two large men in black uniforms with red armbands stood at either side of the door and glared at them.

"Please. You know how much I need him." Under

her breath, she said, "Just go, for God's sake."

He glanced at the men, back at Emma and said, "Of course, my little fender bunny. Happy to keep an eye on *your* pet." He took off into the brush after the cat, calling, "Gaucho, where are you? Mommy's worried about you."

She muttered, "Fender bunny. Nice." In a louder voice, she approached the porch and said, "How can I help you?"

The door flew open and the black shirts clicked their heels and snapped off salutes. "There you are. I've been anxious to meet you. My wife has told me how *wonderful* you are."

Heart lodged in her throat, Emma nearly stumbled. There in the doorway stood a grinning, devastatingly handsome man in a black uniform with SS insignias on his collar and a death head on his peaked black hat. "Obergruppenführer, I presume?"

****

Watching from a discreet distance, Bronco saw his brother engaged in a lively conversation with his wife—lover—partner. *Damn.* He'd expected to see a wild-eyed lunatic, instead the man looked completely normal. No, he looked *terrific.* Handsome, dashing, he could practically feel his charisma pulsing at Emma, pulling her into his magnetic field with his smile. Jack took her heavy bag of food and led her inside the cabin. Was Jack planning to seduce her—or kill her?

Dream sharing with his brother had been traumatic, even at a distance. He hadn't relayed the scenes of abuse his brother withstood to Emma, all his crazy father's attempt to recreate MK Ultra, a top secret CIA project in the sixties and seventies. In the project's heyday, hundreds of physicians and psychiatrists, universities, colleges, pharmaceutical companies, and prisons participated in the most immoral and unethical practices previously known only in concentration camps of World War Two, including using children as research subjects. One of the most shocking projects had been the administration of LSD to unsuspecting subjects in bars, brothels, and CIA safe houses. One man was given LSD by his supervisor, after which he leaped or was thrown to his death. Finally shut down in 1973 after a Congressional investigation into the ethics of the program's brainwashing research, MK Ultra left a shameful stain on the history of the intelligence and medical community.

Bronco's brother's memories revealed that through the Freedom of Information Act, his obsessed, sicko father had tracked down all the publications and protocols related to MK Ultra and applied the same methods to his followers—and his son. The old man mixed and matched a psychotic cocktail of verbal abuse, sleep, and sensory deprivation, electroshock therapy, injections of psilocybin, and oral administration of LSD. His father's participants, not surprisingly, responded in the same manner as the CIA's research subjects. Some continued to have flashbacks, some died at their own hands, and others barely functioned above a vegetative level. How had his brother not only survived, but apparently seemed to have thrived, albeit in a Neo-Nazi world?

Emma had been in there a long time with Jack. What if he overpowered her? She was a smart, sassy, bold, beautiful woman. Any fool could see she was one of a kind, a keeper. Seething with jealousy and fearful for her safety, he rubbed the back of his neck. How could he rescue her without being seen? He needed ears in there. Where was his partner?

At the precise moment Bronco was about to whistle for him, Gaucho smacked his hand. "Oh, hey buddy." He put his head to the cat's forehead and asked him where he'd been.

Saw someone we know.

Out here in the middle of nowhere? Who the hell could that be?

He shot him an image of a short angry man in a uniform.

"Tommy Otterlegs?" Horrified that the little twerp would ruin everything, Bronco asked, "Are you sure?"

Gaucho hissed.

"Sorry. You're right, I trust you. Where is he?"

Bronco stood and gazed around the compound. How had Otterlegs found them? He must have followed them, but *how*? He would have noticed if they'd been tailed out to the SS compound. How had he gotten in? They'd been given the third degree—until the Medicine Woman worked her magic. Were they all distracted by the measles outbreak? No alarms rang, no shouts of intruder alert, not a peep. *What the hell?*

A herd of horses, all branded with the SS logo appeared in his mind. And the little bantam rooster was skulking around the horse corral coming this way. The last thing they needed was for that guy to blow their covers. Bronco considered wringing his neck just for the joy of shutting him up, but he knew the woman he was rapidly becoming very fond of would never forgive him.

Could things get any worse?

"There you are!" Emma called and waved to him from front porch. "Come on over, darling, I want you to meet the Obergruppenführer."

Apparently, they could get worse. And just did.

Stomach feeling like it was filled with a heavy stone, Bronco turned and faced his worst nightmare. From the black peaked cap to the tailored jacket with the oak clusters and SS bolts on his lapels, his twin brother was every inch the man he'd seen in his remote viewing session, right down to the shiny jack boots. And then he noticed the white stick with the red tip.

Jack was blind.

Chapter Seventeen

Emma grabbed Bronco's wrist and pulled his extended hand away from his twin. "Oh, dear, your hands—weren't you just out cleaning up after Gaucho?"

The cat chirped and Bronco said, "You are so right. Please allow me to wash my hands, Obergruppenführer." He strode into the cabin, glancing over his shoulder at her with what she thought was a look of gratitude—or maybe panic?

"Let's have a seat inside," the Obergruppenführer said. "While your husband gets his hands clean, you and I can discuss the measles outbreak."

A wave of relief washed over her. "I'm so glad we can talk in person. This is really quite bad, you know. It appears none of the children have been immunized for measles, mumps, rubella, polio, or influenza. Is that correct?"

"Yes, you are absolutely correct." He nodded and stared straight at her, his eyes clear blue, his face relaxed and smiling.

"It's a simple matter to correct. I can contact the public health officials for this county, get the needed supplies, and—"

He held his hand up. "There will be no vaccinations. I forbid them."

"I serve—served as a community representative to

the Indian Health Service, working to get kids immunized. Did you know measles is a leading cause of death for children?" Her voice rose, "Last year, world-wide, almost one-hundred and fifty thousand children died—that's four-hundred a day, or *sixteen deaths an hour*. You could lose all of your children in the community."

"Nonsense." He flapped his hand. "Bronco, where are you? I want you to hear this."

"Right here, sir." He sat down on the couch making a big production of drying his hands. Gaucho hopped up next to him, laid down, and closed his eyes. Emma had a strong feeling the cat was as perceptive with his hearing as he was with his eyes.

"Just so you understand, Eva told me all about your plans to save the children."

At Emma's sharp intake of breath, Jack grinned. It wasn't a warm friendly smile. No, it was chilling. Here was the face of evil beneath his veneer of charm. Her gut roiled. How much did he know?

"Eva just can't keep a secret, especially from me." He placed his hands on his cane and leaned forward conspiratorially. "Yes, she told me how she was going to get you into the office so you could contact the authorities for help." He shook his head and chuckled. "You would think she would know me better after all this time. Anyway, after this latest incident, I'm in the market for a new wife."

"I'm not sure what you mean? Did you divorce Eva over my suggestions, because I should be held accountable—"

"No, no. This isn't the first time she's sought to undermine me. You're new here, your education is just beginning. Hers is over."

A chill slithered down Emma's back. Eva had said he'd kill her if he found out. *Did he make good on that threat?*

"I think I'd enjoy *you* in my bed. You sounded very enthusiastic when I listened in this morning." He smirked. "Oh, did I shock you?"

Emma bit her lower lip and looked down at her hands. *Glad you liked the show.* "I must confess, I'm a bit surprised at this, especially with my husband sitting right here."

"Any SS member who lives in my compound has to be willing to share his wife with me." He chuckled. "Didn't you notice how many of the children looked alike? They're mine."

She shifted in her seat and looked to Bronco for help. His attention was elsewhere, staring out the side window. *Great.* She needed the man *here,* not off in space.

"Can we go back to the children, please?" Maybe she could appeal to his massive ego. "If we believe in the fourteen words—"

"Yes, yes, we must secure the existence of our people and a future for white children."

"If you don't have your children, how can you secure their existence?" Aside from massive sperm banks, she thought. Which for this guy wasn't entirely out of the question. "This is a serious disease—"

"And only the strong will survive." He nodded. "I'm in the middle of a grand experiment here. The Nazi eugenics program was just the beginning. I've already weeded out the schizophrenics, manic-depressives, epileptic, demented, the genetically blind and deaf, anyone with severe physical deformities, chronic alcoholics, and the feeble-minded."

Emma wanted to say he seemed to have missed Leroy, but bit her tongue.

"Now I will weed out those who are susceptible to contagions. Measles is just the first wave of diseases I plan to expose them to."

She gasped. "You did this on purpose?" The man was a monster, as bad as Hitler and his ilk.

"Serendipity." He shrugged. "When I heard the slaves I bought had an outbreak of measles, I immediately sent them to work in the dining hall, cleaning the barracks, and taking care of the children in the Brown Shirt Club."

"How could you do this to your own flesh and blood?"

"My father experimented on me," he said with pride. "The blindness was an unfortunate side effect, one he couldn't predict. But it matters not. Look at me now. I have powers you could not possibly comprehend. That is what I want for my children. Using better methods, more up to date technology, I am picking up where Goebbels left off. I am creating a Master Race. We will be Gods."

His words chilled her to her bones. Emma stood, rubbed her arms, and said, "I'm sorry I interfered in your plans Obergruppenführer, please forgive me. I was working from imperfect knowledge. I'm not sure what it is you want me to do."

"Use your Native American remedies on the children, nothing more, and nothing less. I have great admiration for your people. Aryans of course will be at the top tier, but Native Americans will make excellent breeding stock for our second tier. Your people have maintained your sovereignty with hundreds of years of attack from the U.S. government. And you have many wonderful traditions which I am bringing back here in our Sovereign Nation. Polygamy, concubines, slaves. These are good things that were tossed out when the missionaries came."

Pacing and hoping to catch Bronco's eye, she said, "You know, the Smallpox Epidemic of 1843 occurred after the US Army knowingly distributed blankets and rations contaminated with the contagious disease to my people. But we survived, using only our native medicine and herbal remedies." Pretending admiration, she almost gagged at her next words, grateful no one in her family, including Beautiful was nearby. "I think you may be onto something."

"See, I knew you understand. You are as smart as I foresaw in my vision."

She turned on her heel. "Do you go on vision quests?" She thought she knew the answer, but wanted to see how much he would reveal.

He laughed and shook his head. "Not exactly. When you come to bed with me, I'll show you how I do it. Then you will understand why in this compound, and in bed, I'm God."

****

Hating himself for his next words, Bronco cleared his throat and said, "Emma's her own woman. She can decide what she wants to do with her body, it's up to her."

His brother—the Obergruppenführer—filled him with revulsion. His father had twisted his body, mind, and soul, creating the vile monster before them.

Surprise crossing his face, his twin said, "You're an enlightened man. I underestimated you. Based on Leroy's reports, I expected a tattoo covered, macho motorcycle thug." His lips twisted in a sneer. "You sound like a feminist."

Bronco rubbed the back of his neck and stared out the side window again. There was something or someone moving about out there. Gaucho stirred and nudged him with his mind. The cat wanted to go out—he had heard something and wanted to investigate.

"Well." He chuckled and strode to the door. "I wouldn't go that far. You won't catch me changing diapers or taking care of babies, if that's what you mean. That ain't my job. She's in charge of family matters—and that includes taking care of her body so it looks good for me."

Bronco nodded at the men standing at attention on either side of the door. "Cat needs to go out." They glanced at the four-legged creature, and one man smiled. "Good by you?" They nodded, and he released Gaucho from the leash.

He closed the door and stood by the side window. "I'm just keeping an eye on him, making sure he don't get into any trouble."

"So back to my proposition. You're okay with my taking your wife to my house and having rough sex with her?"

He winced. *Shit. They did that act a little too well.*

"Like I said, that's up to her entirely." He thought a minute. "As long as you don't mind that she's on her time of the month. Some guys don't care for that."

Disgust convulsed the Obergruppenführer's face. "I can wait until she's clean again—in fact, I prefer my women to wait a week after their menses before I have relations with them." He tapped his cane on the floor and nodded. "It's a much more fertile time."

Bronco glanced at Emma, and saw her face regain the color that had washed out at the start of the discussion. "Sure thing. We'll let you know when she's ready."

He hated talking about Emma as if she was some cow waiting for rutting season with the head bull. What he wanted to do was beat his brother up right then and there, but he knew that would undermine all the work that had gone before to set up this mission. No, he'd have to set aside all his emotions, keep his undercover persona intact, or they wouldn't get out of here alive.

The Obergruppenführer stood. "This has been delightful. So refreshing to have an intelligent conversation for a change. My lackeys are so fearful, they dare not even speak to me." He shrugged. "The price of power." He turned toward the door. "Emma, thank you for agreeing to care for the children. I'll have Leroy come by in the morning and assist you in making rounds."

Emma nodded and said, "It would be my honor."

"Good." He reached out and seemingly without any problem found and then stroked her cheek. "Nice bones. I look forward to our time together."

Bronco opened his mouth and was jarred by the image of Tommy Otterlegs being tackled by two men in olive-drab camouflage. He closed his mouth and cleared his throat.

"And you, Bronco," the Obergruppenführer said pensively. "Leroy said you reminded him of me, for some reason. Couldn't put a finger on it." He paused and a look of sorrow crossed his face. "You know, I had a brother. We were inseparable. Loved him very much. We were fraternal twins. But he and my mother were murdered by the U.S. government when I was a child. My work here will avenge their deaths."

His brother's words pierced Bronco's heart like an ice pick. Deep beneath the maniacal exterior, a little boy grieved for the loss of his brother and mother. He, too, had a hole torn in his chest that day. How different life would have been if only Jack hadn't refused to get in the truck. If only, he could get through to that youngster, perhaps he'd have a shot of saving him from becoming more of a monster. It wasn't over until the fat lady sang—where there was life, there was hope. God willing, maybe he *could* be redeemed.

The door crashed open and Gaucho flew in and dove under the sofa. "Sir! We have an intruder!"

The Obergruppenführer's head snapped toward the officer. "Well, what are you doing here? Go after him!"

"We have him in custody, sir. Says his name is Deputy Sheriff Tommy Otterlegs, and he's here to arrest him." He pointed at Bronco. "Says he has a rap sheet as long as my arm."

"Rap sheet? No, my dear fellow. This man has a *resume* with skills and talents I can use." The Obergruppenführer grinned. "This is our lucky day. So many *interesting* people showing up unannounced."

Bronco's head spun. Was this maniac playing with them? Did he know Bronco and Emma were here to destroy them?

Emma jumped to her feet. "That stupid son-of-a-bitch. He's a jealous ex-boyfriend, always making trouble for me and Bronco. He can't stand the fact that we got hitched."

"Oh, yes, in Vegas." The Obergruppenführer smiled. "My sources told me you were married by an Elvis impersonator—very amusing, and so American."

Grateful to the documents division of Homeland, Bronco sent a mental note of thanks to the support team in D.C. What the hell were they going to do about Otterlegs? The man was like chewing gum on his shoe. The minute he opened his mouth, he'd blow their covers.

"Emma, let's go meet him and see how you dole out some American SS justice, shall we?" He paused. "That is, if you are the woman you say you are."

"I'm not sure what you want," she said. "As you've said, I'm learning about the American SS. I have no idea what you think I should do."

He spoke as if to a slow to learn student. "His name sounds Native American. He has violated our compound. What kind of justice do you think your ancestors would dole out for a transgression of this sort?"

Bronco's heart caught in his throat. It wasn't fair to put her through this sort of loyalty test. But if he spoke up and offered to do it, he'd deep six the mission. He had to let her play her role, or else he'd risk blowing both their covers.

Dumbfounded, he watched Emma's face light up in a wide smile. "I have just the thing. Take him to the horse corral, strip him to his underwear, and duct tape his damn mouth. I'll take it from there."

"Oh this sounds like fun." The Obergruppenführer thumped the floor with his cane. "You are just full of surprises."

She caught Bronco's eye. "I hope you enjoy the play by play on this show, too, Obergruppenführer. It's a special treat, just for you."

Chapter Eighteen

Emma sat in the back of the open jeep and held on for dear life. One of the Obergruppenführer's personal guards drove, yelling at his boss to hold on each time they approached a pothole or bump. Having no idea how much the leader of the SS was really capable of doing with his psychic abilities, she kept her thoughts hidden under a constant stream of insults for her so-called ex-boyfriend, Otterlegs.

"That little jerk is so small, he fit in the little lockers at school," she shouted into the wind. "Some days, his mother came to pick him up and she just tucked him in her purse, like one of those Chihuahua dogs."

Bronco guffawed, and even the guard sitting between them cracked a smile.

Good, my comedy routine is working, she thought, pulling out all the short people jokes she could think of.

"Otterlegs is so short, even when he was an adult, they wouldn't let him on the carnival rides." She snorted, caught Bronco's eye and nodded for him to chime in.

"He's so short, I could put a red pointed hat on his head and use him as a lawn ornament."

The guard between them laughed and slapped his thigh.

As the man bent over with laughter, she mouthed

to Bronco, "Keep going."

He frowned, and she mimed riding a horse. He grinned and nodded.

"He's so short," Bronco shouted. "He shops in the kids' section of the clothing store."

The guard wiped his eyes and pointed at the horse corral. "There's Shorty, half naked and his mouth duct taped, just like you said." He slapped his thigh. "Can't wait for this show!"

Emma took a deep breath, climbed down from the jeep and glanced around. "Where's my medicine animal?"

Bronco shook his head. "I thought he jumped up on the back of the jeep when we left. I could have sworn he was on the other side of you."

"Great!" She threw her hands up. "Just great. Probably chasing a rabbit. Great timing. Okay. I'm gonna have to use my other medicine. I was trying to hold off on that, seeing as how it's the old way." She shook her head and frowned. "Well, let's see how this goes. Not sure how this is going to go, so I need you all to stay out of the corral."

She stomped over to the gate, opened and closed it behind her, being careful not to shoot the bolt all the way through. Ears twitching, the horses nickered and whinnied. A few pranced in anticipation. Hands and ankles tied, stripped down to his boxers, Otterlegs glared at her over the silver duct tape. Pity filled her, but she had to stay in character, or they'd all be dead. Keeping her eyes on Otterlegs, she sent out a request to the horses to calm down. *Not yet, my friends, soon.* Their heads stopped shaking. They were listening. Good. *Now to find the alpha mare.* A nearby female stomped her foot and nodded. *Whoa, baby, nice to meet you. Hold on.*

Emma approached Otterlegs. "Oh, I know. You're good and pissed at me now, aren't you, Tommy?"

Leroy appeared on the other side of a roan about nine yards away from her.

"Hey, I specifically told everyone to stay out of the corral." She whirled toward the Obergruppenführer who leaned against the fence. "Did you or did you not expressly tell me I was in charge of this little jerk's punishment?"

Frowning, the Obergruppenführer said, "I did, indeed. This is your show, Emma Bearkiller."

"Get out of here, Leroy, get back to the barns. I've got some serious medicine to work here and you could get hurt."

"Sorry," Leroy stammered. "Just trying to help."

Hands on her hips, she glared at the man until he melted back into the outbuilding. *Good.* Emma hoped he stepped in a nice pile of manure on his way. Turning back to her task at hand, she watched Otterlegs' expression shift from hate to puzzled hurt. Heart wrenching in her chest, she prayed everything would fall into place. *Show time.*

"Hear me, Oh Great Creator, it is I, Emma Bearkiller, calling on your power to punish one of our own." As she spoke, she moved her arms up, down and around. Between nonsense motions and hand waving, she inserted Plains Sign Language. *Be ready.* "This man has trespassed where he doesn't belong." *Ride for your life.*

Blinded by rage, Otterlegs missed the message the first time, so she had to re-do it, repeating her first call to the great one in Crow, not talking to Otterlegs directly in their native tongue, lest one of these lunatics actually spoke the language. The second time, a glimmer of recognition lit his eyes. He took a deep breath, shrugged, and nodded as if in surrender.

Keeping a poker face, her heart danced with joy. *He got it!*

"Tommy Otterlegs, I hereby sentence you to be dragged to death by horses."

A collective gasp of joy went up from the crowd of men. Cheers and shouts erupted. "Go get 'em Medicine Woman!" "Awesome!" A chant of "Kill, kill, kill!" rose to the sky.

Sick to her stomach at the pure hatred pouring out of the mouths of those around her, she stomped over to the alpha mare and led her over to Otterlegs. As she walked she gave the horse instructions. *When I tell you to go, don't look back, just run. This gate is open. You will have to jump the metal gates.* The mare, a beautiful blue roan that reminded her of Indigo so much that tears pricked her eyes, nodded. Then with crystal clarity, Emma saw the mare running in a field, prancing with a foal, and then being lassoed and dragged into a horse trailer, her youngster screaming for his mother. These same men in camouflage, the ones cheering for Otterlegs' death, had taken her away from her baby and the life she loved as a wild horse. She was more than ready to extract her revenge on these monsters.

Shaking her head to clear her vision, she led the mare over to Otterlegs. Shouting over the crowd's jeers, she yelled, "Better start running, short stuff!" With one swift move, she yanked her hunting knife out of its sheath and sliced the bindings on his hands and feet.

Leaning next to his head, she said, "Get ready, Tommy. Remember your Indian relay race days." Then she tore the duct tape off his face, and he shrieked.

The crowd went wild, jumping up and down, cheering at his pain.

Eyes wide, Otterlegs grabbed a fistful of the mane and nodded at Emma.

Without moving her lips, she shouted, *Now you beautiful girl, run home to your foal, run free, and take your herd with you.*

Like a shot out of cannon, the mare screamed and flew toward the gate. Protecting their females, enormous stallions lined up along the fence, reared, kicked their legs and shrieked. The mob of bloodthirsty men fell off the fence railing like target practice beer cans. Kicking and stomping, the male horses managed to create panic and chaos, providing cover for the little running man and their alpha mare. Racing alongside the horse, Otterlegs got up to speed, threw his leg over the horse, and flattened himself along her back.

Frozen in time, dust swirled and clogs of dirt floated around Emma in a vortex. Protected within the eye of the raging storm, not a single horse touched her. Hands at her side, mouth shut, she closed her eyes and screamed at the great beasts in her mind.

Go, go, go! Run for your lives and don't stop running until you get to the Crow Reservation.

Chest resonating with the thunder of hundreds of hooves, she mentally urged the horses onward. Mind still connected with the alpha mare, she felt the weight of Otterlegs on her back, firm and strong. The metal gates came into view, and the mare didn't falter. Two men screamed and leaped out of the way, racing to escape the herd. Raising her front legs, the mare cleared the bar easily. Behind and alongside her, the rest of the herd joined her one by one. Heart thundering, the alpha mare shot a thought back to Emma. *Thank you.* The tears Emma had not shed since arriving at the SS compound fell hot and wet and free, like the great beasts she treasured.

Sounds began to penetrate her bubble of concentration as if from a distance. Blinking, she swiped at her face, as if dirt had flown into her eyes. The haze began to settle, and the cursing men dragged themselves out of the manure. Blood running down the side of his face, spittle flying, one of the manure and mud covered men stumbled over to her and shouted, "You bitch!" He lunged at her and grabbed her shoulder. Twisting, she ducked under his outstretched arm and placed the tip of her hunting knife at the base of his skull. Blood trickled to his collar, and he cursed using every vile name for women and Native Americans he knew.

"You can walk away, or you can be a quadriplegic. Your call."

Hands up, he shrugged. "Hey, I was just kidding around. Didn't mean anything by it."

She removed the blade. "Get going and don't make me regret not killing you."

Bellowing, he whirled and reached for her throat—then stumbled backward as an ear-splitting blast rocked the ground.

****

As Bronco turned toward the source of the explosion, fire shot out of the roof, and windows blew out—sending glass and metal flying across the tarmac.

A truck parked next to the building flipped over and burst into flames. A series of explosions knocked holes in the sides of the building, and the sounds of rockets mixed with screams. It was as if the fourth of July was being celebrated using every firework in the country.

"It's the munitions storage," his brother yelled over the din. "Keep that fire away from the other buildings." Fists clenched, his body shook, and his head bobbed wildly. "We can't lose my beautiful birds."

The men in black uniforms were gone, running for water pumps, Bronco presumed. He shouted, "Obergruppenführer, your men are working on the fire. Let me take you to safety."

Another explosion rocked the earth and both men stumbled against the jeep.

"We're under attack. This is war. I need to launch the predators." He grabbed Bronco's arm. A puzzled look crossed his face. He shook his head and shouted, "Take me to the birds."

"I'm not the man for the job," Bronco shouted. "I don't know what to do."

An ear-splitting explosion rocked the ground again.

"No time to spare. I'll take care of it. You just get me there." The Obergruppenführer shook his head. "For a moment, you reminded me of my brother."

Bronco held his breath. *Shit. Shit. Shit.*

"Not possible. He's dead." The Obergruppenführer pulled himself into the jeep. "Drive to the building at the end of the tarmac. You can't miss it."

As he climbed into the driver's seat, a flicker of movement in the rearview mirror caught his attention. He turned. Gaucho sat on the backseat. In his mouth was Beautiful's medicine stick.

How had that gotten here? Lucius would never let that thing out of his control unless—Bronco's heart somersaulted. *Dear Lord, was he dead?*

Gaucho shook his head and sent an image of Lucius slumped in a horse stall, hidden behind a blanket.

Thank God.

As he turned the engine over and put the jeep in gear, Emma hopped into the back seat. "Going somewhere without me, darling?" At his wide-eyed glance and significant look at the bobcat, she paled.

"We have to get to the drones," the Obergruppenführer said and tapped the floor with his cane for emphasis. "Move."

"I'll get there as soon as we can get around the corral and past the barn, sir," Bronco said in a rough voice. "Can't go past the fire, could be more explosions."

Jouncing over rocks, mud, and smoking debris thrown from the ammo dump, Bronco headed away from the chaos.

"Stop," Emma shouted. "I need to pee."

"Get out, you stupid woman," the Obergruppenführer snarled.

Bronco hit the brakes, and his brother hit his head on the dashboard. "Sorry, sir."

"You idiot." He backhanded Bronco.

Despite the blood trickling from his nose and ire blossoming in his chest, Bronco bit his tongue.

Grasping the Medicine stick, Emma and Gaucho leaped out of the jeep and headed into the barn. Bronco hit the gas and aimed for every pothole and rock pile he could see on the route to the hangar. Five miles away from the inferno blazing behind them, he slid to a stop in front of a sliding metal door. "We're in front of a hangar." He hopped out and went to the passenger side. "Would you like my assistance getting down?"

"Get out of my way." The Obergruppenführer snapped, "I can get down on my own, you moron."

Hand gripping the side of the Jeep, he stepped down using his cane as a guide. Without hesitation, he stomped over to the door, and felt for the keypad. The SS leader tapped a code into a security panel and the door slid open. He shook his head and entered the cavernous space and Bronco followed.

One dozen identical drones armed with AR15s awaited within, a flying squadron of death.

Raising his hands, the Obergruppenführer exulted, "Behold my beautiful birds."

Tapping his way to the closest one, he stroked his hands along a wing. "My lovely raptors, you swoop down, raining death, destruction, and despair on those who wish to destroy me and anyone who believes in the new world order." He kissed the machine. "My beautiful creation, soon you and your brothers will leave this shelter. Some may not return. Be strong. I am your father, and you are my true children." He stepped aside. "Your time has come."

Bronco's stomach roiled and bile rose in his throat. Jack, his twin brother, the kid who fought to protect him from bullies and even took beatings for his little brother, Brandon, was gone. In his place stood the monster his father had created. While hate, drugs, and torture had destroyed the boy, power and corruption had created the man known as the Obergruppenführer. After playing the criminal role for years, Bronco knew all too well how hard it was to come back from the brink of corruption and evil. But he *had* come back. Perhaps there was a vestige of goodness left in the monster before him. He *had* to try to reach his brother. But how?

"Jack," Bronco said in a soft voice. "You don't want to do this."

Jerking upright from caressing the drone, the Obergruppenführer stared at Bronco with unseeing eyes. "No one calls me that, not even my wives." He frowned. "Who are you?"

"Your brother, Brandon." He took a step closer to Jack. "The news about my death was a cover story."

Jack's face twisted in disbelief. "That can't be. My brother's dead—murdered by the FBI."

Bronco shook his head and went with his gut. "When we were little, we were so close, we slept in the same bed. I called you Jackie. When I wanted to annoy you, I called you Jocko. Remember?"

Eyes fixed on a point over Bronco's head, Jack seemed lost for a moment. He shook his head as if to dispel a cloud of gnats. "Anyone could find that stuff out."

"Before we moved to Idaho, we had a dog. His name was Caesar. Dad told us he jumped out of the car window and ran away, but we knew better." Was that a twitch of indecision on Jack's face? He took a deep breath and pressed on. "But we still had the dog house—and the neighbor's chickens built a nest and laid eggs in it—"

"Mom said if she caught the chicken, she'd wring its neck and make soup," Jack's voice trailed off in a whisper.

"You'd bring frogs into the house in your hand, then open it up under her nose while she was doing dishes—"

Jack's lips quirked. "She jumped so high, I thought she'd hit the ceiling."

"Yes! Remember the day the other neighbor's cow got loose?" A warm flicker of hope crept into Bronco's chest. "And stood in the middle of the road, blocking traffic?"

A small smile creased Jack's face. "Mom walked up to the cow—and a driver rolled his window down and said, 'That's a mad cow! Better get away!'"

Bronco laughed. "Then she took the cow back to the pasture—"

Jack's face went flat, emotionless as a statue. "She's *dead*, my mother is dead. Shot to death."

Jack turned his head away from Bronco. The flame of hope sputtered. The longer he kept him engaged, the more likely he was to change his mind. He had to keep him talking, get him back. He tried another tack. "You're right, Jackie," he said. "She is dead—but from cancer. Not from bullets. She died with your name on her lips. She never forgot you, never forgave herself for leaving you behind." He choked up, barely able to speak. "She wanted me to tell you she loved you."

Jack slammed his fist on the side of the drone. "Bullshit. She left me behind to be beaten, abused, tortured"—his voice broke—"every time I cried for her, he beat me more." He shook his head and tears flew off his face. "What kind of mother leaves her little boy behind? If she *really* loved me, she would have come back for me."

Bronco took another step closer to his twin to seize

the moment. "She had no choice. Our father was an abusive monster. If she had gone back, he would have shot her—in front of you—to teach you a lesson."

"Oh, I got plenty of lessons." Jack snorted. "Ever been water boarded, Brandon? How about being kept awake for days at a time? Starved? Left out in the desert to cook and freeze? Drugged with LSD, psilocybin, cocaine, and whatever other shit he could lay his hands on? What about sex education? Did you get a good one? Because I sure did. Every time he picked up another woman at a bar, he and his buddies raped her and made me watch. The only time he showed me any affection was when I kicked the shit out of other kids. That made him *so* proud." Shoulders hitching with sobs, he said, "How could she leave me with him?"

Heart sinking to his boots, Bronco grabbed Jack in a bear hug. "I'm sorry, I'm so sorry." Gut wrenching sobs burst from Jack. Guilt rolled over Bronco in waves. He'd been safe, loved, cherished by his mother and stepfather. Jack had been dealt a horrifying life in hell. It wasn't fair. No child deserved to be tortured like that, much less his brother, his blood. "I wish I could go back in time, fix things, but I can't."

"I killed him, Brandon. When I was sixteen, I'd had enough. Made his assault rifle turn on him when he went out for target practice. Looked like a suicide. That twisted psychopath had no idea what he unleashed with his 'experiments'. I have powers a man can only dream of." He waved his hands over his face. "I'm blind, but I see with remote viewing. I can't drive, but I can guide machines of death and destruction with telekinesis. No radio waves can jam me, no man made gadget can stop me. I am God. And it's time to unleash my wrath."

Holding his brother in a bear hug, Bronco put his lips next to Jack's ear.

"You can stop this madness, Jack. I love you. Mother still loved you. Please, you have the power to disband this hate group, stop the madness—"

"Stop? No, I'm going to go faster, my dear brother. You will pay." Shoving Bronco away, Jack sneered. "You and all your friends who don't see the *real* world. Did you really think you could *love* someone back to a so-called normal life?"

"Yes, I do. My brother is in there, somewhere. I want him back."

Jack raised his hands and an electromagnetic pulse threw Bronco across the room. His head slammed into the metal wall. He slid to the floor and tried to catch his breath. Head throbbing, vision blurry, his brother's voice came from the end of a dark, echoing well. He rolled to his side just as a drone hummed to life. "Hate rules, love drools, Brandon. Too bad you won't live to see my reign of terror."

Another drone started, then another and another, until all twelve vibrated.

For over two decades, Bronco had clung to his memories of childhood—ones colored and shaped by his love for his mother and brother. Once Jack had been the big brother everyone envied. No one messed with Brandon, or they'd have to deal with Jack. He'd been his best friend, confidant, and retreat from the horrors of his father's tailspin into the cesspool of hate. When he found his brother, he hoped, no prayed, the void in his life left by losing Jack would be filled with the joy of their unexpected reunion. Instead, the hole in his heart was now an abyss of grief and despair. It wasn't bad enough he'd lost his brother once. No, this was worse. Once the man before him had been a little boy full of fun and mischievousness. Now, he was a monster filled with evil.

I must stop him. Bronco slid his hand down his leg to his ankle holster and his Glock 27. A wave of vertigo washed over him, and he closed his eyes.

"I am the God of Hate," Jack shrieked and raised his hands. "And everyone will pay."

As if one hive unit, the drones began to roll toward the open bay door.

"Go, my darlings, wipe out the seat of what passes for government in this state." He clapped his hands and burst into maniacal laughter. "Spread your fire and brimstone, fill the streets with bullets and flames. Rain chaos, death, and destruction on my enemies!"

I have to move. Can't just sit here while he kills people.

Grasping the hand grip, Bronco withdrew the gun from its hiding place and paused. Normally the weapon felt like a part of his hand—but now, it felt as if he was trying to lift a cinderblock with one finger. He dragged the Glock alongside his leg, keeping the weapon hidden. Even though Jack couldn't see him, one of his loyal followers could pop in at any moment. Another wave of dizziness struck and he paused. The madman who had replaced his brother wavered in his vision, becoming two men, then merging back into one. A black aura with long oily tentacles stretched around Jack's body, pulsing, growing larger with each moment.

Focus.

Lifting the weapon with both hands, Bronco

exhaled a deep, slow breath, aimed down the sights of the barrel at the center of the dark mass, squeezed the trigger—and prayed.

Jack flew backward into a drone, then slid down its side onto the concrete floor.

Bronco pulled himself up on a metal work table and using his upper body strength rose from the floor with caution. The room wobbled and his legs shook. *Was Jack dead?* He hadn't aimed to kill.

"No, no, no," he cried, "Jack, please, don't die on me." Staggering across the space, he threaded his way through the idling mechanical birds. A red blossom spread on his twin's chest. Bronco fell to his knees. "No, God, no!" He pressed on the wound, hoping to staunch the bleeding. "Don't leave me, Jack, please don't leave me."

His brother didn't move. Feeling for a pulse, he couldn't believe Jack was gone. He hadn't meant to kill him—just wound him, stop him from doing the unthinkable, attacking the capitol of Montana—and worse. He slid back on the cold concrete floor, covered his face with his hands and sobbed.

A body slam threw him backward ramming his already throbbing head against the concrete floor. Stars swam in his eyes as hands clutched his throat. His brother sat on his chest, choking him. Desperate, about to lose consciousness, he mustered every ounce of strength left, swung his Glock up, and connected with his brother's temple.

Jack clutched his head and stood, lurching between the drones, he cackled and crowed, "Oldest trick in the book, my brother, coyote plays dead. Let's see how *you* like being dead."

Turning in a circle, all twelve drones aimed their AR15s at Bronco and began to fire. Hit in the shoulder, arm, and leg, bleeding badly, the edges of his vision began to turn black. Pain resonated and found a home in his body. He crawled behind a metal workbench for protection. As bullets ricocheted around him, a tunnel with a light at the end opened and Bronco floated up toward it. *No, not yet.* He hovered on the ceiling over Jack's head and shouted, "No, you don't." If Jack could use a pulse to knock him out of a remote viewing session and to knock him across the hangar, then maybe he could do the same. His brother looked up, and Bronco channeled his seething rage into a bolt of fury and struck his twin.

Jack stumbled back into the direct line of fire of the ring of drones.

As the scene below him faded into shadows, Bronco's last thought was how he and Jack had been together at the start of life and now, it was only fitting they be together at the end.

Chapter Nineteen

Following Gaucho's bounding steps, Emma found Lucius sitting on a pile of clean hay behind a horse blanket with the reins of a bridle wrapped around his leg.

Pale, sweaty, mustache drooping, but still alive, thank God.

She touched his cheek, and his eyes fluttered. "Hello stranger. What brings you to this part of town?" He groaned when she touched his thigh. "Mind if I take a look?"

He nodded and hissed when she sliced his pants open.

"Good thinking on the tourniquet."

The cat butted his head against Emma's hand. "And on sending Gaucho out with Beautiful's medicine stick." What could she do now? They were good and truly screwed. Since the explosions, she'd been sending a distress call to Bert on their usual channels—but received nothing in return. Even if he got a sense of her danger, Homeland would be hard pressed to scramble a team to this remote location. The satellite phone had been their back up plan—until that moron Leroy confiscated it. The FBI undercover agent had never revealed himself to them—if he was even alive. For all they knew, that guy had pissed off the lunatic and been executed by a firing squad. Bronco had gone off to the

drone hangar with a madman—*God. Don't go there.*
Focus on Lucius.

Glancing around the barn, she spotted a large, brand new red and white barn first aid kit hanging on the wall. Well, that was unexpected. Someone cared about the animals and the people who tended to them. With the bag on the floor next to Lucius, she opened it and placed the sealed packages around the bag. Quickly scanning the labels, she found what she wanted.

"Lucius, you're a lucky man. The wound goes through and through, that's the good news. No arteries, but a large vein, so we need to get this packed and wrapped until we get you to a hospital."

Eyes closed, he grunted and nodded.

"I'm going to need to clean the wound first, squirt some antibiotics in, and then sprinkle in some blood abatement powder. After that, I'm going to pack the wound and wrap it with this flexible gauze. Okay?"

He nodded again and popped one eye open. "Anything for pain in that bag?"

"The best I have is ibuprofen."

"I'll take it, whatever that is."

She ripped a packet open, stuffed the two pills in his mouth. "Hold those. I'll go look for water." After locating a spigot and a metal bucket, she returned with water. "Sorry, this is all I could find." Cupping her hand, she pulled water up to his mouth. Most ran down her arm, but after three attempts, he swallowed the pills.

As she worked on his leg, he asked, "Where's Bronco?"

"With that crazy brother of his." *Probably getting killed.* She changed the subject. "How did you get here?"

"The night you left. After you went up to your room. Looked out the window. Saw Otterlegs. In the hotel parking area. To impound the CPAs' cars. I thought." He grimaced and sucked in his breath when she began to pack the wound with gauze. "Damn."

"Deep breaths, you know, like you're having a baby."

He closed his eyes. "Tallulah's gonna kill me."

"If one of these crazies doesn't, that's a very good possibility." She lifted his leg to wrap it several times, then pinned the material in place. "Done. Breathe."

Lucius took a deep breath. "He was snooping around your truck. Saw him put something under your bumper."

Emma nodded. "And?"

"I used the Medicine stick. He was taking a leak in the bushes. I climbed into the backseat of Otterlegs' car."

"Too much information."

"You guys left. He followed. GPS tracker on your truck."

"Idiot."

"Yup, he is."

"No, you. Tallulah is going to be so pissed, she'll never talk to me again. If we all get out of here alive, it's going to be a miracle. How did you get shot?"

"Things looked bad. You needed a diversion. I set a fire in the ammo storage unit."

"And got yourself shot."

He frowned. "Worked didn't it?"

"Yes, thank you." She patted his hand. "Bedlam and chaos. Well done."

Smiling, he rested his head back against the blanket

and closed his eyes.

Beneath the background warzone noise of gunfire, explosions, and shouts, a low rumbling sound and the *whup whup whup* of a helicopter gave her heart a jolt of hope.

Couldn't be—could it?

Lucius straightened up. "Did you hear that?"

"Yes, but I can't go out to see if it's really a helicopter to save us or kill us. I wish I could talk to Gaucho the way Bronco does," she sighed. "I'd send him out to see what's going on."

The cat, who'd been lying next to Lucius, sprang to his feet and ran out of the barn—and within minutes flew back into the stall. Boot steps followed. Lots of them.

She handed Lucius the Medicine stick, watched him disappear, and stepped outside the stall with her hands raised. Leroy, the moron with the halitosis and rotten teeth led a team of five men in full SWAT gear, all of whom carried assault weapons.

Shit. She was dead.

"Freeze," Leroy shouted. "FBI. Who the hell are you *really*?"

Emma nearly wet her pants with relief. "Homeland Security. Anomaly Defense Division. Call Bert Blackfeather for confirmation."

"I will." Leroy pulled out her satellite phone and dialed. "Thanks for the phone, by the way, those assholes took mine away the first day I arrived."

Leroy? An undercover FBI agent? Man, he's good.

He shouted into the phone. "We've got a situation here, woman says she's with you." He started to go into detail, then clearly got cut off by the other end. He handed the phone to her. "Your brother wants to hear your voice."

"Bro, it's me, I'm alive."

Bert's sigh of relief was mixed with concern. "What's the real deal? I don't want to hear FBI speak."

"Lucius is wounded—" She peeked around the side of the stall and gave the clearly visible Lucius the thumbs up sign. The bobcat was glued to his side. "—needs medical attention. I don't know where Bronco is, I haven't seen him in over an hour. Okay, good. Love you, too." She handed the phone back to Leroy. "Have you found Bronco?"

The FBI agent ordered one of the SWAT team members to get help for Lucius, then turned to Emma. "I have bad news."

His mouth kept moving, but she couldn't hear what he was saying. Sounds ceased, the room spun, and the world went black.

****

Emma woke up in a helicopter with a medic peeling her eyelids back and shining a light into her eyes. "Stop."

Jerking back in surprise, the EMT pointed to his head set. He reached up and placed a set on her head. He smiled. "Welcome back."

She tried to sit up, but found herself strapped onto a board. "Think you could undo this?"

He shook his head. "You passed out, might have a head injury."

She closed her eyes and counted to ten. "How and where's Bronco? Where are Lucius and my cat, Gaucho?"

He gave her the thumbs up. "The one with the

mustache is fine, thanks to your doctoring. He's holding the cat. But that animal glares at us when we touch the tattooed guy"—he shrugged—"head, arm, and shoulder wounds, a leg wound, no major organs or blood vessels hit, but—"

Alarmed by his tone, she strained against the damn strap. "What's going on with him?"

The medic shook his head.

"I'm his *wife,* dammit, you have to tell me."

He motioned to someone to come over. Leroy, if that was even his name, hovered into view. The EMT moved away to allow the FBI agent to crouch at her side. "He's not responding."

"To what? Voices? Light?"

"Anything." He shook his head. "He's breathing, heart rate and pulse are strong and steady now, thanks to the EMTs, but he's not responding to anyone or anything. We're headed for St. Vic's, it's a Level One Trauma Center. They'll take good care of him." He patted her arm. "Good work back there. You saved a lot of lives."

Puzzled, she shook her throbbing head. "I only saved Otterlegs—if he made it."

"Oh, he made it." Leroy snorted. "Some crazy chick named Stephanie showed up halfway between the compound and the Crow Reservation—along with a couple hundred friends, all in pick-up trucks, all armed to the teeth. Told my guys on the ground her job was to keep an eye on Otterlegs. Spotted him heading out of town. Followed him for an hour, then realized there was only one place he could be going out in the middle of nowhere. She got on what she called her 'Indian telegraph.' Organized a war party. She was coming to save him—and you."

Hot tears leaked down the side of her face as she chuckled. "Stephanie has always been a bit dramatic."

"The local public health department has been notified about the measles outbreak. They're sending in a medical team to treat the kids. Thanks to you, the mothers and children were all isolated in their living quarters, away from the fire and the fight zone. They're all safe—even the Obergruppenführer's wife. Seems he planned to execute her after he launched the drones."

Her weeping turned to choked back tears of joy. No matter her bad choices, Eva had been trapped and making the best of a horrific situation to protect her children. She didn't deserve to die.

"And Immigration and Customs Enforcement, I.C.E., is deploying people to manage the trafficking victims. We freed some slaves, today, Emma Bearkiller—if that is your real name?"

Voice clotted with emotion, she said, "Emma Horserider. And you? Is your name really Leroy?"

He grinned and the rotten brown teeth were gone, replaced by nice even white ones. "Fauntleroy. Can you imagine sticking a kid with that name?" He shook his head. "My mother loved that book, *Little Lord Fauntleroy*. I got the crap kicked out of me every day in elementary school. Changed my name to Leroy in middle school." He stood. "We'll be at St. Vic's soon. Hang in there."

She waved the EMT over. "Just so you know, that cat is my anxiety animal. He stays with me at all times."

The medic stared at her and glanced at the crouching bobcat. "I don't see any—"

"My paperwork's at home. When I get to the hospital, I'll deal with it. That cat and I are inseparable. Is that clear?"

Giving her and the cat a wary look, the medic nodded. "Crystal."

Hours later, the ER doctor declared Emma fit to go home after X-rays, CAT scans, and numerous other tests, but she refused to leave the hospital. With Bronco and Lucius still at St. Vic's, she had no plans to leave anytime soon. Lucius was stable, but in need of surgery, IV antibiotics and a hospital stay, which was good because shortly after their helicopter landed, Tallulah arrived at the ER—in active labor.

Taking the role of delivery coach Lucius had been expected to play, Emma gowned and masked and held her friend's hand as she cursed the pain, the no anesthesia birthing process, and her "ridiculously heroic" husband. After three hours of some very colorful language, including some words Emma didn't know even existed in English, a healthy, eight pound, five ounce, twenty-two inch long redheaded girl arrived in the world.

Emma retrieved Gaucho from the changing room and called her brother with updates on all the patients, and then headed to the ICU and Bronco. She found Stephanie and Tommy Otterlegs outside the unit's doors. Looking forlorn, the little man wore a two sizes too large warm up suit and kept pulling up his pants as he shifted from one foot to the other. "I'm so sorry. I had no idea he was an undercover agent. I thought I was doing the right thing." He shook his head. "Now I've screwed everything up."

Lump in her throat, Emma said, "It's not your

fault. His brother created that monster out there, not you. You're a good investigator, Tommy."

He lifted his head, and his eyes widened. "You really think so?"

She nodded. "I do. You followed the leads, and you did your job. It's not your fault we couldn't bring you into the loop. We wanted to keep you safe."

"You and the horses saved me." He stared at her, and his voice dropped. "How did you do it?"

"Oh, you know me. I'm just a horse whisperer." Tears pricked her eyes. "Where are they now?"

"On your ranch. Hank's taking care of them." He shook his head. "You're out of my league. I get it now."

"Tommy—"

"Go to him, Emma." His voice grew husky. "He needs you."

Stephanie put her arm around his shoulder. "Come on, baby, let's get you home." She waved at Emma. "You heard him. Go to your man."

After stopping by the nurse's station to get directions, Emma paused in the doorway of Bronco's private ICU room and took a deep breath, preparing herself for the worst. Someone inside the room was speaking. Was that Bronco? Was he awake? Heart tripping with joy, Emma shoved the door open, only to be greeted by a smoky haze in the air and the beeping of monitors. Off leash, Gaucho loped into the room, placed his paws on his partner's bed and chirped. She stood alongside the cat and rubbed his head. "Hard to see him like this, isn't it?"

Wires and IV tubes snaked under the blankets, and a graphic monitor displayed his heart and breath rates— both normal. With his head swathed in gauze, a bulky white bandage encasing his shoulder and arm, and his leg covered in a similar manner, he looked like a half-wrapped mummy. Leaning over the railing, she kissed his full, warm lips, with a crazy notion she could awaken her sleeping prince. No response. Hot tears trickled down her cheeks and splashed on his pillow. She smoothed his wild hair back and trailed an index finger down the scar on his cheek. "Poor guy. You don't deserve this. Come back to me. I'll help you forget your past and create your future."

Glancing around the room, she saw a TV—as if a man in a coma would watch it—and found the control. Exhausted, she and Gaucho dozed off watching the late news in the uncomfortable orange vinyl encased folding chair next to Bronco's bed. Every two hours, nurses came in and checked his vital signs, IVs, and monitors, and asked Emma if she needed anything. Gaucho curled in her lap, she pointed at Bronco each time. "Everything I need is right here."

****

The next day, safely tucked in her clear plastic bed and behind the nursery glass, Miriam Beautiful Stewart entertained a throng of teasing cousins, aunties, and uncles—until the baby nurse came to take her to her mother and father. In a wheelchair, with his leg up, Lucius held his baby girl and kissed her head, while thanking Tallulah and telling her how much he loved her over and over. Emma closed the door to Tallulah's room and shooed the family away. "You'll have the rest of Miriam's life to spoil her. Now, go make some toys for her. I have a feeling she's going to like horses."

Turning away from the life affirming scene, she traveled to the other end of the hospital and the opposite end of her emotions. In the ICU, filled with beeping monitors, IVs, and around the clock nursing care, Bronco continued to lie in a coma. Physical brain trauma had been identified with MRIs, but the intensivists would not rule out chemical injury, in addition, given the nature of the compound and the maniac in charge of it. Since only the twins had been present at the time of injury and Jack was dead, no one knew what transpired in that hangar. Sitting at his bedside the day after Miriam's birth, Emma spoke to him, knowing that hearing was the last sense to go.

"Bronco, I know you're in there and you can hear me." She took his hand. "You're my captive audience, so here goes. Thanks to Homeland Security, as far as the rest of the world is concerned, I'm your wife and can be here at your side every day. I love you, and I want to marry you for real, with a big wedding feast, a gala affair. If you accept my proposal, you're going to have to move in with me, because that's my tradition. Meantime, I'll be hanging at your bedside every day of my life until you come back to me. I'm not giving up on you, Brandon, Bronco, whoever you are right now. Never giving up on you, or on us."

Exhausted, Emma dozed off with Gaucho in her lap. In her dream, Gaucho spoke, but she heard Bronco's voice. "I don't deserve to live. I killed my brother. Please let me die."

Wide awake, she screamed, "Don't you dare leave me," as the code alarms went off. The rapid response team stormed the room and pushed her out the door. Slumped against the wall in the hallway, Gaucho climbed on her lap as Emma sobbed and prayed for a miracle.

Chapter Twenty

One month later

The code team had brought Bronco back, but now questions about his care filled her conversations with the St. Vic's financial management office. Right or wrong, he had no living family, and she was for all intents and purposes, his wife. Every day was an argument.

"No, he did not have any advanced directives. He's a young healthy man, why would he file those?"

"No, I don't have written power of attorney or health care proxy. Why are we discussing this? This is a clinical decision, not a financial one."

"He has excellent healthcare coverage. What do you mean 'they're' talking about denying his coverage? He's in a long-term care unit, not the ICU. I want to speak to your supervisor. Now."

At the end of each day, after caring for her home, horses, dogs, and Bronco, her ritual was to join Tallulah and Lucius at the hotel for dinner on her way back to the reservation and get her baby fix. This evening, while Franny and Gaucho frolicked in the high grasses, Emma sat on the wrap around porch and rocked the sleeping infant in her arms. Miriam's personality was like Franny's, sweet and infectiously happy. The child breast fed with gusto, slept through the night, napped four hours a day, and gave her parents nothing but joy.

"I don't know what the holdup is. It's half-past five. Normally, Lucius is back from his three o'clock physical therapy appointment by now." Tallulah placed a tray with a bottle of wine and three poured glasses on a wooden table next to the rocker. "Ho hum, another day in paradise. I never get tired of this sunset."

Emma snuggled with the baby and watched the clouds pile into a quilt of blue, purple, red, and orange overhead. "It is a gift, like your darling girl." A little fussing came from the bundle in her arms. "Oh, she heard her Mama. She wants you now."

Tallulah cooed and placed the infant at her breast. Miriam began to nurse noisily. "This girl loves to eat. Just like her mother."

Emma toyed with the wine glass swishing the contents without drinking. "So, I have an important matter to discuss with you."

"What's that?" Tallulah's gaze snagged Emma's. "About Bronco?"

Emma shrugged. "Yes and no." She took a deep breath, set the glass down, and sighed.

Tallulah gazed at Emma, concern etched on her face. "You can tell me anything, Lucius and I are here for you."

"My friend—such a quaint term—did not come calling this month." Emma held her hand up. "Before you say it's stress or ask me why didn't you use protection, let me tell you, minus the gory details, we used spermicidal condoms." She reached into the back pocket of her jeans. "This is the last of those bad boys. Apparently, Bronco had them in his wallet a long, long time. The expiration date on them is from two years ago."

Tallulah sucked in her breath. "Ohmigod."

"Yes, the love of my life did not update his inventory. And now, thanks to the miracle of at home tests, which are ninety-nine point nine percent accurate, it appears I'm expecting." She gazed at Miriam. "Not that I'm complaining. My biological clock has been ticking and—"

The rocker on the other side of Tallulah began to move of its own accord.

"The absentee ghost has made her long awaited return." Emma pointed at the chair. "Perhaps you'd like to translate?"

Just as Tallulah shifted the baby to the other breast, a white van pulled into the circular driveway. "There he is now. Perfect timing."

The passenger side door opened, and Lucius climbed down with the assistance of a cane. "Thanks for the ride, Marjorie." He closed the door and waved as she sped out of the driveway kicking up dust. Hanging onto the railing and pushing with his cane, he took the stairs one at a time. "That woman can talk the ear off of an elephant. Sorry I'm so late. The therapist had a family emergency. I had to wait an hour to be seen." He kissed Tallulah, grabbed a glass, and headed straight for the rocker next to his wife.

Both women shouted, "Don't sit in that rocker!"

He stopped. "Is Beautiful back?"

Emma nodded, and Tallulah said, "Yup."

"What's the special occasion? We ain't seen hide nor hair of her in a month."

"Pull up another chair," Tallulah said. "You'll want to hear this sitting down."

Eying the women and the manic chair, he complied. "Shoot."

Emma took a deep breath. "I'm pregnant."

The rocker shook so hard it whacked the side of the hotel.

"I see her," Tallulah said. "She's not angry. She's thrilled, excited, and worried."

"This should be good," Lucius said. "What on earth can she be worried about?"

Tallulah squinted and nodded. "The baby's father—she says she's been searching for him for weeks. I guess that's why I haven't seen her around here for a while. Beautiful says, he's not here—with her—and he's not there—with Emma."

"That's one way to describe it," Emma said with a trace of sarcasm. "Neither here nor there."

Lucius' head snapped up from his wine glass. "Neither here nor there—dammit, ladies. He's where I was. He's in limbo."

"If she says I need to tell him I love him, please know I've been sitting at his bedside for the last thirty days saying that and asking him to marry me. The last thing he told me through Gaucho was that he didn't deserve to live because he killed his brother and he wanted to die. That's the day they called a code on him." A tear slid down her cheek. *Hormones. Already.*

Tallulah stared at the wildly moving chair and held her free hand up. "Stop. I need to concentrate." She nodded. "Lucius has been in limbo, you love this man and now are expecting his child. Together you can bring him back."

Emma stared at Lucius. "You're the key. I can't cross into that space, but you can—with Beautiful's medicine stick."

Shaking his head, Lucius said, "I'm kinda beat. Any chance we can do this tomorrow?"

The rocker flipped over and crashed into the railing.

"I'm guessing that's a no," he said. "Okay, okay. Let me grab the Medicine stick and a sandwich for the ride to Billings. Let's see what we can do."

She whistled for Gaucho. He needed to be there when they did this.

A short ride later, they stood in the hallway outside the hospital room with the bobcat in his service jacket on a leash. They pushed the door open and stopped. Gaucho stood stock still, bristled and hissed. His black-clad back to the door, a man stood at Bronco's bedside. The monitors chirped and beeped erratically indicating a declining heart rate. Thinking it was a physician or technician, Emma cleared her throat. He didn't respond. "Excuse me, is he okay?"

The man turned. Emma gasped and staggered back into Lucius. It was Jack, Bronco's twin. "They told us you were dead—"

The Obergruppenführer's features dissolved into a grinning skull, like the insignia on the lapels of his uniform, and then he disappeared in a flash of black, oily smoke.

Shaking like an aspen, she grasped Lucius arm. "This is why Bronco isn't coming back. His brother is haunting him, here at the hospital, feeding his guilt and despair. He felt responsible for leaving his brother behind, but he was just a kid, a baby, really. His mother had no choice."

He patted her hand and thumped his cane. "Never

fear, Lucius Stewart is here."

Pulling the folding chair closer to the bed, he sat down, extracted the buckskin package from his pocket and opened it with care. "I suggest we place Gaucho in bed with him. You hold his hand and tell him your news. He needs to know you need him here, now, in this world not drowning himself in a river of remorse."

The cat required no prompting. He leaped onto the bed, positioned himself alongside his partner, and placed his head on Bronco's chest. Emma grasped his hand, glanced at Lucius, and nodded. At her signal, Lucius gripped the Medicine stick and disappeared.

"Bronco, we're not giving up on you. I just saw your brother's spirit here, he's the reason you haven't come back to me. He's enraged, an evil being without a body, who wants you to suffer. Well, screw him. You and I have a bigger reason than ourselves for you to return to the land of the living. We're going to be parents, Brandon Winchester, and our little boy or little girl or maybe it's twins—they do run in your family after all—our child, our children need two parents, you and me. Come back to me Bronco, come back to the promise of something bigger than us. Please come back to your future."

His index finger, which had been resting in her palm lifted, then wriggled, the first time she'd seen any movement in a month's vigil. She kept talking, her voice growing louder.

"Lucius, Tallulah, Stephanie—we all love you and miss having you with us. Let go. Release the guilt that's been holding you back. Forgive yourself. You were a kid in an unbearable situation. You had no control over your father. There was no way you could have prevented your brother from becoming a monster. Let it go, please, for the sake of your unborn child, *let it go*."

The last words she spoke were practically a shout and as they flew from her mouth, Lucius shimmered back into the chair, dripping sweat. "I saw him. Talked to him, tried to explain. He's stuck, really stuck. It's as if he's padlocked himself to a massive boulder and threw away the key. I'm not sure I can do this alone." His eyes pleading, he said, "Come with me."

Her heart beating like a caged bird, fear mixed with hope. "He wriggled his fingers. First time in a month." Emma licked her dry lips and closed her eyes to give herself a moment to think.

Would going with Lucius cause harm to her unborn child? And, if the evil spirit of Jack could torture Bronco like this, what would he do with to his brother's child? No matter how many arrows she painted in the infant's room, she couldn't be sure they would ward off an evil spirit with this magnitude of malevolence. She couldn't stay awake twenty-four seven and she couldn't post guards on the crib. She needed Bronco at her side to help protect their baby.

At length, she opened her eyes and nodded. "I risked life and limb for him. What's a little thing like limbo?"

She reached over grabbed Lucius's arm. The world shifted sideways, blurred, and grayed. Through the ashen mists, she picked out shapes and shadows, some moving, some sedentary. From a distance a woman keened, the sound winding its way through the murk, her mournful voice rising and falling to the thudding of Emma's heart. Fear gripped her—until she saw Bronco. He stood next to a swirling vortex of colorless leaves—

or were they? He turned his head and smiled. "I see you brought reinforcements, Lucius."

Emma wanted to run to him, pull him close, and kiss his face, but feared he would vanish into the mist if she did. "I'm the big guns."

His sad eyes gazed at her with longing. "I don't deserve you. You're too good for me."

"Have you not heard a single thing I've said to you over the last month? I love you. I want you to come home. And by the way, you're a father."

"You weren't just saying that to get me to return?"

"Have you ever known me to lie to you?"

He shook his head. "No, never. I—I just don't know."

"I know. I have faith enough in you for the two of us. You will be a wonderful father. You are a good man. You saved a city. You saved me from being a childless, unloved old maid." She paused. "Unless you don't love me?"

His eyes widened. "Love you? I worship you. You're the biggest, baddest Amazon goddess I have ever met."

"This badass woman needs her badass man to raise what will probably be a brood of badass children." She extended her hand. "Come home with me, please. I love you. I miss you. I need you at my side, my partner in life and love forever."

He reached out, took her hand, and she gasped.

When she opened her eyes, Bronco was awake and gazing at her in a way she'd never seen before. He licked his dry lips, and his voice emerged in an amazed croak. "Did you say you're pregnant?"

Lucius whooped, Gaucho head butted his partner,

and Emma said through her tears, "Yes, I did. You can thank those old condoms in your wallet."

He waved her over, and she leaned in to give him a kiss. "No, I can thank you. I never thought I'd find a woman I'd want to spend the rest of my life with—much less make me a father."

"Enough to have a real Crow wedding feast with all the cousins, aunts, uncles, and every relative in the tribe?"

"Yes."

"And you'll move in with me?"

"I capitulate to all your demands. In return, I have just one condition."

"Which is?"

"I'd like an Elvis impersonator to officiate. I loved those photos."

"You can have Elvis, Buddy Holly, and the Big Bopper." She laughed. "As long as we do it at the Hotel LaBelle and Beautiful can be there."

"Well, she is family, isn't she?"

She kissed the tip of his nose and bumped his forehead. "Together forever."

And behind them Lucius whispered, "And beyond."

Epilogue

Two Months Later, Hotel LaBelle, Montana

Hand at the base of her back, Emma stood at the open window of the honeymoon suite, rubbed her baby bump, and smiled. The sun glinted off the Yellowstone River in the distance, and a small herd of mule deer waded in for a drink. Half the Crow Nation had arrived, filling the parking pad and surrounding grassy areas with pick-up trucks, four wheel drives, vans, and motorcycles. The dance floor, hammered into shape by Lucius and Bronco, had withstood the weight of a beetle-shaped car to ensure it would last through the night. Stephanie waved her hands, and directed the band to its place on the grass next to the dance floor. Emma doubted she'd be doing the Electric Slide anytime soon, but she would enjoy watching everyone else put on their best dance moves.

Servers circulated with trays of champagne flutes, while Lucius inspected the bars—one at each corner of the party—to ensure everything was in place. Franny trailed close behind Tallulah as she directed a small army of interns from the Montana State University hospitality program, all dressed in white shirts and black slacks. Armed with a pitcher and a napkin folded over her arm, she instructed the team on the proper form for pouring water at the white clothed tables.

Emma was so engrossed in the scene below, she jumped at the rap on the door.

"Bronco, you're not supposed to see me," she called.

"It's just me, come to give you some brotherly advice," Bert answered.

Emma opened the door, leaned down, and hugged the man who would be giving her away. Handsome in his white suit and beaded vest, he wore the halo war bonnet of eagle feathers well.

She ran a hand over the feathers. "Nice hat, bro'."

"I wasn't planning to dress this way." He adjusted the red, white, and blue beaded band on his forehead. "But the Tribal Council insisted."

"Because you *earned* the right to wear it." She shook her head. "Everyone respects you, knows you represent the best of us. You're a role model, young people look up to you. That includes keeping our culture alive."

"Enough about me." He indicated her clothing with a wave of his hand. "What about you and your outfit? Make-up, turquoise jewelry, braided hair, beautiful beaded headband, white elktooth dress—"

"Which will require the jaws of life for me to get out of it," she grumbled.

"Moccasins worth thousands of dollars—"

"Stephanie gave them to me. My feet wouldn't fit into my boots. Too swollen."

"What do you expect? You're carrying twins!" He grinned. "I think you should name them Curtain Boy and Spring Boy."

She snorted. "Not a chance."

"How about Thrown-Behind-the-Curtain and

Thrown-in-Spring?"

"No, a thousand times, no. Those are legendary twins with great powers. The babies are going to be perfectly normal."

He quirked an eyebrow. "You sure about that?"

"How about you shut up and listen to the music?" She pointed out the window. "Everyone's in their places. Time for us to go."

"That's just telling the guests to be seated." He grabbed her hand. "I know I don't say this very often"—he shrugged—"okay, never. I love you Sis. You are one helluva of a Warrior Woman and you are going to be a terrific mother."

Tears blurred her vision. "Don't. Stephanie spent an hour on this damn make-up."

"Bronco is a very lucky guy. I want you both to be as happy as I was when I was with Susan."

Emma's heart stuttered. Susan Foxtail was a rehab nurse who took care of him and helped him get back on track when he lost his legs to the IED. Killed by a drunk driver, Susan's name rarely left his lips after her funeral.

"Without her love and support, I wouldn't be the person I am now. She came into my life when I most needed her. She was a gift from the Great Creator. Someday, if I'm lucky, I'll find a woman like her." He squeezed hard. "You are blessed with a man who adores you. Bronco is your soul mate, a warrior who matches your spirit. Never forget how fleeting life can be. Each moment is precious."

"Look what you've done." Tears splashed on her dress. "Now I'm in big trouble."

He handed her an embroidered handkerchief.

"Tallulah said you should have this. It was her grandmother's." The music grew louder. "Now *that's* our cue."

Emma nodded, took a deep breath, and lifted her simple posy of Montana wild flowers, purple blue lupines, and yellow Echinacea flowers. "Let's do this."

A short time later they arrived at start of the path to her beloved. The guests stood and a palette of vivid colors met her eyes at every step. From tiny infant to the oldest of the elders, everyone had come in their best apparel. It looked like a miniature version of the Crow Fair—minus the Indian relay races. She nodded at Marjorie Longjaw and Jimmy Two-Toes, who gave her a grin and a wave. There was Otterlegs holding hands with Wanda, a petite red-headed deputy who gazed at Tommy like he was a god. Her best friend from high school, Jessica, was in from Pryor with her husband Noah Littlebear.

Emma wondered who was minding her brood of kids. Maybe they were with Noah's mother? A little further up, Eva who had renounced the Neo-Nazis, held her blond boys—Bronco's nephews, soon to be *her* nephews, too—close to her sides and smiled. She had thanked Emma a million times for saving her life and was making amends for her past behavior. When not volunteering at the Indian Health Service clinic, she worked at St.Vic's ED, identifying potential cases of domestic violence for intervention, among other duties. Bert held Emma's hand and squeezed it reassuringly. Up ahead, the Elvis impersonator stood before a white teepee Emma had spent a month preparing, painstakingly painting each horse in her stable on it, along with Powderkeg and Indigo.

Wearing white gloves, an eighties-style purple mid-thigh chiffon creation with huge poufy sleeves and the big hair to match, Stephanie held a small bouquet of bright reddish orange Indian paintbrush in one hand and fanned her face with her other. Emma suppressed a giggle. Her cousin was in her element. Not only was she her maid of honor, Stephanie had been her wedding planner, band coordinator, and Elvis recruiter. The last part had been the easiest since Stephanie and Elvis, whose real name was Rod, were officially an item.

Resplendent in a white rhinestone studded jumpsuit, matching belt with gigantic cowboy buckle, and a flowing yellow scarf, the faux King of Rock and Roll grinned at the crowd. Bert and Emma halted, and Bronco stepped out from behind the teepee, a black bow-tie wearing Gaucho at his side. Cotton-mouthed, she could only stare at her soon-to-be husband. From head to toe, the love of her life wore the contemporary attire of the men in her tribe. From his white cowboy hat, black hair hanging in braids on either side of his face, red shirt with turquoise bolo tie, white vest beaded with floral designs, down to his polished black cowboy boots, her fiancé looked as if he belonged to her tribe. Touched by his efforts to show her how much she meant to him by dressing this way, butterflies swooped in her belly, and her heart felt as if it would burst out of her chest.

Emma clutched Bert's hand.

Elvis drawled, "We are gathered together to celebrate the fact that this couple can't help falling in love, and they've decided it's now or never to pledge their love. If there is anyone who has cause to believe this couple should not be united in marriage—keep it to yourself!" Elvis put his hand over his eyes like a visor and made a show of searching the audience. "Who gives this bride?"

Bert shouted. "I do!"

Stephanie put her hand on her chest as if about to faint.

"Bronco," Bert continued, "I give you my sister's hand, but in truth, she is her own woman. You are dressed as one of our clan and at the end of this ceremony, you will truly be a member of our tribe, with all that entails. Take good care of my sister—or you'll be hearing from me." A ripple of laughter rolled through the crowd. "Okay, Elvis, you're on."

"I unh, unh, want to say you are a handsome couple."

The crowd murmured agreement.

"Today we are gathered together to celebrate this couple's desire to be one. Right now, Bronco is your hunka hunka burning love, and Emma has got you all shook up. You are young and beautiful, have those tender feelings, and a house that has everything. But when your summer kisses turn to winter tears, and time slips away, that's when you'll be sayin', what now, what next, where to? Hey, hey, hey, you gotta say, who are you, who am I? But there is no you, no I, there is only we. And when we surrender to the power of love, then we know these words to be true, I can't stop loving you."

Choking back a laugh at all the Elvis references run together into a wedding ceremony, Emma held her breath, hoping he wouldn't burst into song just yet.

Instead, he said, "Unh hunh, unh hunh, Do you have your vows?'

She nodded. "I, Emma Blackfeather Horserider, take you Brandon, aka Bronco Winchester, to be my partner, lover, spouse, companion, and hero in sickness and health, in good times and bad for today, tomorrow, and forever."

Bronco smiled and looked deep into her eyes, his blue eyes matching the big sky above. "I, Brandon, aka Bronco Winchester, take you Emma Blackfeather Horserider, to be my partner, lover, spouse, companion, and heroine in sickness and health, in good times and bad for today, tomorrow, and forever."

Elvis nodded. "Do you, Bronco, take Emma to be your wife?"

"I do."

"Do you promise to love, honor, cherish, and protect her, forsaking all others and holding only unto her?"

Bronco grinned and said, "I do." Gaucho chirped. "And he does, too," her soon to be husband added.

Stephanie giggled, and Emma bit the inside of her cheek.

Elvis nodded. "Do you, Emma, take Bronco to be your husband?"

"I do."

"Do you promise to love, honor, cherish, and protect him, forsaking all others and holding only unto him?"

"I do."

The King nodded at Bert, who handed a velvet pouch to Bronco.

After extracting the jewelry, Bronco said, "This ring symbolizes your connection to your people and this land." He took her left hand and slid the Black Hills band onto her finger. "It also represents my steadfast love, which has no beginning and no end. I honor you and your tribe and promise to move into your home and be with you forever."

Taking a band into her hand, Emma said, "This ring is from the hills that remind me so much of you. A strong man who will be there for me for eternity. I honor you and your family members, some of whom are no longer with us, but live on in our memories. Their love shaped who you are, and for that I am grateful beyond measure. I give you my heart and soul for now and forever, 'til death do us part—and beyond."

Elvis chortled, "By the power vested in me by the great State of Montana, I now pronounce you husband and wife. You may now kiss your beloved."

A hand landed on Emma's back and pushed her into Bronco, her belly bouncing into his. She laughed and murmured, "I can do this on my own, Beautiful."

Eyes crinkled in mirth, Bronco slanted his lips over hers and gave her a hard passionate kiss. She closed her eyes and the earth fell away. In the distance, the crowd roared, whistled, and stomped their feet. Lucius' voice rose over all the others. "Get a room!"

The babies drummed from within, their kicks connecting with their father.

Astonishment wreathing his face, Bronco pulled back and said, "Soccer players?"

Invisible hands rested on her shoulder and time stood still. In the silence, the hairs on her neck stood on end and a reedy voice whispered Crow words into her ear.

These are special babies. There will be those who

want them for bad medicine. Protect them.

Sound roared back, and she shook her head. "Not sports." She looked up at Bronco. "The babies—they're exceptional. I think they have both our powers—maybe more than we have combined." The responsibility for caring for the twins felt heavy, and her heart filled with foreboding. "The future of the world is in my belly. You and I are going to need every ounce of strength we have to protect them."

He pulled her tight. "Right now, let's enjoy the day. This is our celebration, our party to share our joy with our friends." He stroked her back. "You and I will face whatever comes together—with our family and friends at our side."

In that moment, she surrendered and again sealed their love with a kiss.

Other titles from Sharon Buchbinder from The Wild Rose Press…

Obsession
Some Other Child
Kiss of the Silver Wolf
Kiss of the Virgin Queen
and
The Hotel LaBelle Series:
The Haunting of Hotel LaBelle, Book One

A word about the author…

After working in health care delivery for years, Sharon Buchbinder became an association executive, a health care researcher, and an academic in higher education. She had it all—a terrific, supportive husband, an amazing son, and a wonderful job. But that itch to write (some call it an obsession) kept beckoning her to "come on back" to writing fiction. Thanks to the kindness of family, friends, critique partners, and beta readers she is now published in contemporary, erotic, paranormal, and romantic suspense.

When not attempting to make students, colleagues, and babies laugh, she can be found herding cats, waiting on a large gray dog, fishing, dining with good friends, or writing.

You can find her at www.sharonbuchbinder.com

~*~

Paranormal Romance Guild Winner
Best Mystery/Thriller, 2012

~*~

EPIC's eBook Award Finalist
Romantic Suspense, 2014

~*~

National Excellence in Romance Fiction Award Finalist
Paranormal, Fantasy, or SciFi, 2017